Shadows of a Lost Poet

Also by Ellie Stevenson

The Floozy in the Park (novel)
Shadows of the Lost Child (Shadows in Time: 1, novel)
Ship of Haunts: the other Titanic Story (novel)
Watching Charlotte Bronte Die: and other surreal stories
Writing for Magazines in the UK: how to get paid to write (booklet)

For more information on Ellie Stevenson and her work

https://elliestevenson.com
https://www.facebook.com/Stevensonauthor
https://twitter.com/Stevensonauthor
https://www.instagram.com/elliestevensonauthor
https://www.linkedin.com/in/elliestevensonauthor

Shadows of a Lost Poet

Ellie Stevenson

Rosegate Publications

For Mary, for being there.

About Shadows of a Lost Poet

A house, an inheritance and two women. But is it murder?

Issington Manor doesn't exist – there's only a park where the house used to be.

1910: To inherit the manor Clara must marry. Then she meets Gwilym.

1910: Phoebe used to live in a slum. Then *she* meets Gwilym.

Miranda wants to save the manor – she has to go back. She didn't mean to interfere…

Map: Issington Halt in Edwardian Times

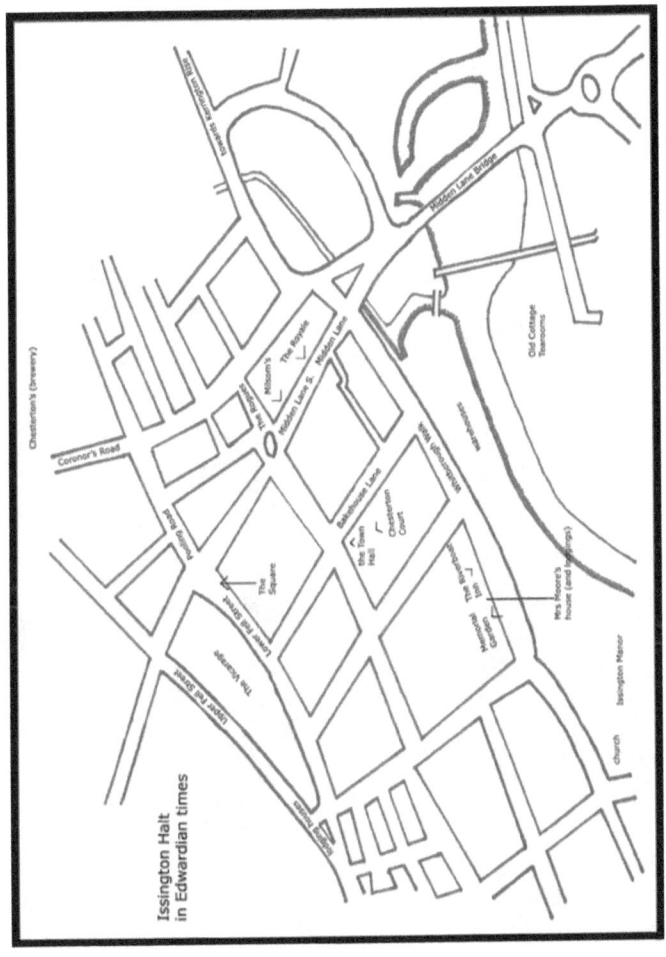

A Short History of Issington Manor

A desirable residence in the market town of Issington Halt, with good access to all major towns. The manor was built for the well-known poet Lucienne Hall in 1852.

A few years later, it was sold and rented out for several years.

From 1858, it was owned and occupied by the Gilchrist family, who had two sons, Jacob and Frederic.

When they grew up, Jacob, the eldest, moved down south, where he built a successful wine business and met his wife, Thirza. They had one daughter, Stephanie Gilchrist.

Frederic Gilchrist, the younger son, lived at the manor until his death in 1910. He too had a daughter, Clara Gilchrist, a talented artist who painted landscapes, and sold them locally. Clara continued to live in the manor after Frederic (and previously Myrtle, his wife) died.

In 1914, the manor was demolished, with a view to the land being used for houses.

Because of the war (1914-1918), the houses were never built, and the land is now a public park overlooking the river.

In warm summers, if you look closely, you can see the manor's outline in the short, stubby grass.

Some say it's a ghost house that wants to return.

The Gilchrist and McKinver Families

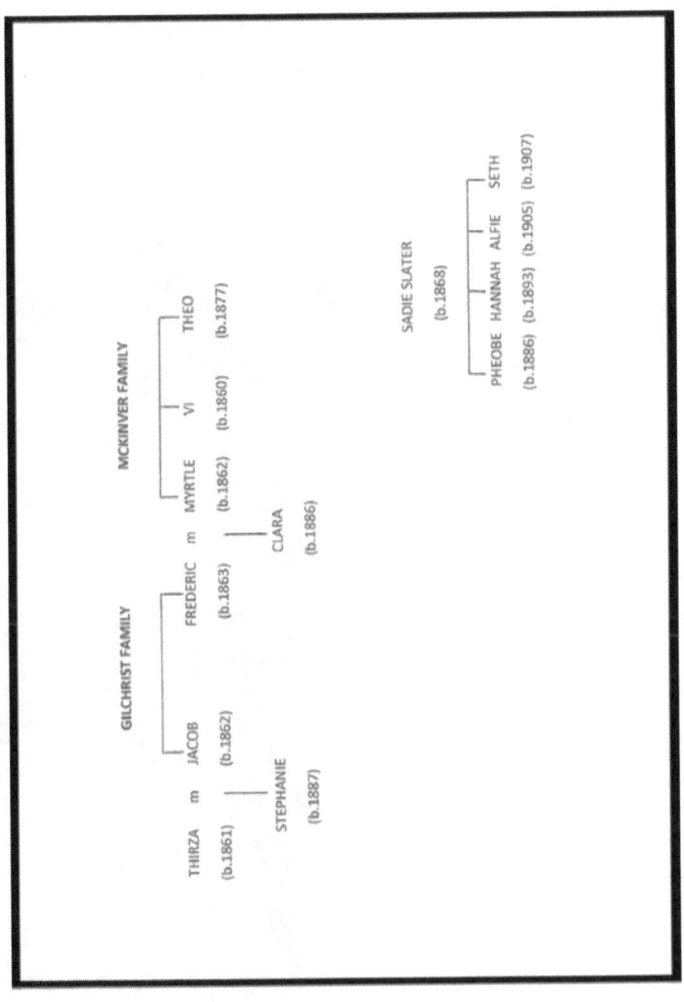

PART ONE

Prologue
1848 – Lucienne Hall

In the early days, before the railways came to town, a coach stopped by the old coaching house and people got out. Lucienne Hall was one of those people. Lucienne carried a carpet bag, with a brass engraved plate. The bag was substantial, as if had once meant something to someone. The bag meant something to Lucienne now. It was all she had. She took a deep breath and looked around. Issington Halt, a fresh start.

It was early spring and rather cool, and Lucienne shivered as she pulled her cloak around her. At least it wasn't as cold as the north, the north *had* been cold, in more ways than one. Eyes alert and taking things in, she stepped out of the yard, she couldn't afford to stay in *that* inn, and walked up the lumpy road to the top. It was two roads really, divided by houses, narrow and thin, and overhanging, and as she staggered up to its peak, she felt the cold blast of the wind hit her, almost sweeping her off her feet. The sky was blue and made of ice. Lucienne sighed and carried on.

As she reached the top of the road, she paused briefly, out of breath. Issington Halt was pretty and lively, with dogs and horses and plenty of people. *Let's hope I like it here.* As she went to cross the road, a man yelled as his cart rolled past and someone pulled her out of his way. She brushed off his arm and shook her head, cross with herself. It wasn't as if she didn't know towns.

Further on, Lucienne reached a wider lane, and decided to take a break in the square, eating the cold meat pie she'd brought with her. There weren't so many people here, but those she saw seemed pleasant enough, and some of them even smiled at her. A few steps further and then she was there, outside the door to the lodging house. It was on Upper Fell Street.

Later that day, after she'd eaten, a wholesome meal of broth and bread, and settled into her room for the night, Lucienne smiled. *Tomorrow, I must search for a home.* It would have to be modest, at least to begin with. But now, tonight, was for something else.

The woman who owned the lodging house had offered to share the parlour with her. 'There's only the two of us here tonight.' But Lucienne shook her head, softly. 'I'm tired,' she said, 'you understand.' It was a lie.

In her room, Lucienne took out a pen and some paper. Paper was precious and not cheap, but to her it meant a lot more than money. Here, in this room, until she found a home of her own, she would sit each night and write her poems. Her first poems about the town, because to her, writing meant everything. Poetry was what Lucienne was, now she'd reinvented herself. And why she was here.

Eventually, she lived at the manor.

Nobody ever saw her leave.

1
Now/1910 – Alice

Alice was standing in the churchyard, peering through the gate in the wall. Dirty wrought iron and flakes of rust. All she could see was rolling grass, not a sign of a house. This wasn't it. Alice sighed. She knew there must be a way in somewhere, and if there was, *she* could find it. But how?

Alice retraced her steps slowly, weaving her way across the graves, and looked up at the tall brick wall. Maybe she had to look *over* the wall, but how to do that? Alice stared.

There, to the left, and next to the wall, was a private grave with just one headstone. It was obviously old, surrounded by its own little wall, more wrought iron and an ancient gate. The gate creaked as Alice went in and onto the grave. She didn't feel guilty, standing on a stranger's bones. Alice was focused. Judy had told her about the manor that morning, and Alice knew it was her job to find it. She knew she could do it.

As she put her hand on a post, on top of the railing, Alice blinked and then she smiled. It was as if a door had been opened for her, a door to the past. Alice was there.

The wall vanished, and up ahead was the house she'd sought. It had huge stone walls and masses of glass, and in front of the house was a small parterre. Alice laughed. She picked her way across the grass to the door to the house, suddenly happy. For although she'd never been there before, she had come home.

2

Now – Miranda

A few hours earlier.
I'm standing outside the door, cursing. I'm late for work, yet again. Damn, double damn.

I stand and wait, knowing I'm meant to be in the kitchen, making the lunch. But I can't go through the lecture room. Not until there's a suitable moment. Inside the room, the tutor is talking. She's called Judy. I tap my foot.

'What we know about Lucienne Hall,' Judy says, 'is actually *nothing*. We know about the poet Hall, her incisive mind, her major works, such as they are. But as for the woman behind the poet, we know very little. We know she stayed at some very small rooms, lodgings in Upper Fell Street when she first came to town. *Before* she moved to Issington Manor. And that was demolished.

'If you have time, later today or after the session, walk through the churchyard and into the park – that's the place where her house used to be. The house where she wrote all those marvellous poems. And now it's all gone.' Somebody speaks.

'But the poems must tell us something, surely?'

'Not a great deal. Hall's poems are quite obscure, all about the natural world. Some people say they're quite spiritual. I wouldn't know, I'm not a poet, or a believer.' Somebody laughs. Someone else speaks.

'She never married?'

'Not that I know. She lived at the manor and wrote her poems, then she vanished, leaving the world rather bewildered. She left us some work, though not a great deal, but as for the woman, *she* left nothing.'

'So, *this* building, the one we're in, isn't where the manor was?' Judy laughs.

'This is just the conference centre, although some of the rooms were modelled on hers. We don't own the parkland, more's the pity. That belongs to the local council.' Judy goes on.

'According to some of the stories I've heard, the manor was meant to be saved for the town, to be turned into Issington Halt's library. A library for poets and students to use, in Hall's memory. That never happened. The manor was demolished, with a view to the land being used for houses. Because of the war that plan failed.'

'Which war was that?' Judy swears.

'Tell her someone. Let's get going.'

I stop listening. This is my chance to get through to the kitchen and do my job, boring though it is. Keeping the delegates fed and watered. I walk in.

Alice didn't return after lunch.

This is a course on business skills, not as you'd think, on English or history. There are only a few delegates on it. And now there's one less.

This is where it all begins, in a long bright room, with a church outside, and an old brick wall leading down to the river. With a ghost of a house behind that wall. And no Alice.

I stand in the kitchen, my usual haunt, catering being one up from the pub, the Keepsake Arms, where I used to live. That was a long time ago, longer than anyone else would believe. I won't go back, so now I'm here, a little bit older, and wanting to be with Judy's students. I want to be different.

Laughter ricochets through the walls, followed by clapping and Carl looks across at me and grins. 'They must be having a bloody good time.' I nod.

Carl's okay, he's sturdy and strong like a cook ought to be, we've worked together on many occasions, catering on the go, that's us. We travel around, cooking for people. He's the boss and I'm Miranda. If only he knew where I was from.

It sounds like fun, seeing inside other people's homes, making the food and pouring the wine, but it's always the same, a rush, a disaster or some kind of crisis. Then, in the end, it usually works. The food's great, the wine's superb and Carl takes home a wodge of cash. I get some. It's always the same, but this time I know it'll be different.

After Judy made her speech, the one I heard waiting outside, one of the delegates left the course and didn't come back. Even though they started late, waited for Alice, she didn't return. Now, Judy's telling the group that Alice has texted and sent her apologies, something about family commitments. It makes me feel cold.

I also feel hopeful. I wanted to be on that course, and now I'm going to take her place. I can do the course *and* the cooking, Carl won't care if the work gets done. Most of the food is cold platters. But inside I'm worried.

I knew Alice from *before*, and when I last saw her, just before lunch, she'd frowned and shocked me with her words.

'I've had it with this world.'

And, knowing Alice as I did, and thinking about the house and Hall, I realised at once what Alice had done.

She'd gone back to the past.

3

Now/1854 – Miranda

I don't live in Issington Halt, and when I'd left for work today, I hadn't expected the extra adventure. Very few people can do what I do, apart from Alice, and when I do, it helps to have the right attire. Today I'm in trousers. I *should* go home and come back tomorrow, in a long dress. I don't bother.

I mean to find Alice, and bring her back here, where she belongs.

Maybe, I think. Alice can be *very* stubborn. Just like me.

I slink furtively out of the building, glide through the gate and weave my way across the churchyard, past all the graves and up to the wall. This, I know, is the way to go – but how do I know? Alice isn't exactly a friend. Making sure no-one's around, I open the gate to a private grave, climb onto the railing, and hoist myself up to the top. It's easy in trousers. Then I peer over the wall. It's just a park.

The bird's eye view is great from here, trees and grass, and a river to the right, a road to the left, a couple of tourists holding hands. But there's no house. *Damn*, I think. I'll have to give up.

Back on the ground, I study the railing surrounding the grave, I don't even know whose grave it is, but Alice *must* have come this way. There's nowhere else. Tired, dejected, I lean on a post, then I gasp, the wall has gone and it's darker, night, and the road to the left seems nearer, wider. *And* there's a house. I stare, in awe. But it's evening now. What should I do?

I edge slowly down the bank, heading towards the road, not the house. *I'll have a quick look around,* I think. Because there's no moon, and because I don't live in Issington Halt,

I'm not quite sure where I am. But I think I've seen this road before, on my way to the centre. Now it's a dirt track, a wide lane for horses and carriages. I step onto the road.

As I walk, I'm suddenly glad I'm wearing trousers, there's no-one about and it feels late. I bundle my hair into my jacket, turn up my collar, hoping I'll look like some kind of boy. As I wander down towards town, I can hear men shouting. There are stables to the left, fading into houses, tall and thin and not very smart and over to the right are sheds, warehouses. I can see a faint flicker of light in the distance, but I can't see the river. That must be where the men are.

I shiver, it's cold, I must have changed season, I can almost smell the bite in the air. And, something else, a different smell, what the hell is it? Then there's a bang, it comes out of nothing, loud, horrendous. I'm thrown backwards.

When I finally get to my feet, shocked but unharmed, I stare in amazement.

Right up ahead, smothered by rubble, with dust falling down, is a broken space where a house used to be. As I look, and the air clears, bits of tile fall from the roof. I stare amazed at a tree uprooted, at piles of brick and broken glass. The smell's still there. The house that's damaged, no, half gone, must have been small. I know this from seeing the house next door which, unbelievably, is still standing. The wall between the two has been damaged. *Underpinning needed there.*

I hurry towards the broken house. I know it's crazy, probably dangerous, but I still have to do it. There would have been a wall here once, a garden gate, now there's just rubble. I step onto the tiny plot. What can I see? A plate, a cup, half a chair, flung onto the cobbles, along with the shredded remains of a throw. The garden behind the cobbles looks grim, a load of bright pots, all of them shattered. This place smells of death. Then I see it, the flat shadow. I stumble towards it.

A bundle of rags is lying next to the still-standing wall. I know it's a woman. *Don't look.*

Come on Miranda, think of all the things you've done, had to do, to get out of your life. Get out of the past. Don't be a wimp. But I don't want to do it.

Yet, I must.

Then I hear the sound of footsteps running this way, to see what has happened. I have to get out.

I step back, onto the street, cross the road and lurk in the shadows, hidden from sight by a couple of sheds. Men stop outside the space. I study their clothes. These and the dirt track confirm my suspicions. This must be an earlier time. I watch, warily.

People huddle in tiny groups, not saying much and one of the women, she looks quite young, tries to get closer, but one of the men, a burly bloke, he seems to know her, pulls her away. 'No, Pat,' he tells the woman, 'you can't go in there. It's not safe.' She clings to his arm. Then a man who must be in charge chases all the women away and most of the men, then gathers a few and does what I did, steps onto the site. And now that awful smell returns, and I know what it is, I must have been mad going in there. I can smell gas! But I still can't leave.

I stand there for what seems like forever as the mist descends and my feet go numb, and my hands hurt, being so cold. Eventually, the men emerge and one of the men carries a woman, a bundle of rags. I stare, silent. I need to know who the woman is, but I can't get near her. I know they won't tell me.

I have a terrible thought.

What if Alice had done what I'd done, and ended up here? What if Alice had been here before me, before the explosion. Then that bundle of rags could be her. If that *was* Alice, then she'd be lost, not just in a different time, but lost as in dead. I take a deep breath. It's all I can do not to scream.

4

Now/1914 – Miranda

After what I'd seen last night, I should have kept away from the past. A woman's body being carried away – but had it been Alice? I didn't know. I knew I hadn't been in the right time, I'd have to go back and look at the house. Alice had been searching for the manor, Lucienne Hall's home. I needed to go there.

So, today, just after dawn, I'm back in the churchyard, feeling like I haven't slept, and I hadn't slept much, what with the worry, and wondering whether I'd get back home. But that had been easy. Now I'm ready to try again. Had it been Alice? Time to find out.

Back in the churchyard, I squeeze into the private grave, and reach for a post, on the right this time. Hoping I'll move forwards from last night – it's just a theory but worth trying. The wall disappears, but what will I see? I smile, success! Now, I'm in daylight.

I stare down the bank at Issington Manor, the house Alice set out to find. Thoughts of Alice make me pause, but I mustn't waver. Issington Manor demands my attention.

I slide down the bank, as fast as I can, rushing towards the house this time instead of the road. I head towards a low balustrade and a small parterre, then down a path that leads to a porch. I stop, stare. The house is impressive. I think briefly of the Keepsake Arms and what my ma and Tom would say, if they could see me, see this house. Then I forget them. The manor is all stone walls and glass, and at the back an orangery, with even more glass and wide stone steps that lead to a door. I admit it, I'm awed.

But, wait, no, something is wrong. The grass looks wild, long and unkempt, and the small parterre is overgrown, and it's *too* quiet, the only sounds I can hear are birds. I think of the park as I know it today, boats going past on the nearby river, calls of laughter rising up and I'm waiting for someone to shout at me, to tell me I'm trespassing. But nobody does. So I walk back up the path to the gate, a five-bar gate that stops at the road, the same road I walked down last night. I see a For Sale sign.

SALE BY AUCTION

The board is huge, anyone walking past could see it, and then when I turn, go back to the grounds, and walk along the other way, I find another, just the same, by the wrought iron gates at the end of the lawn. And then there's a third by the path that takes us into town, that follows the river. *Damn,* I think.

Yesterday, on the road, it was cold. Night, yes, but also freezing, with draughts whipping around the huge warehouses. Cold as in winter.

But, today, it's a different world, now we're in summer, roses in bloom, fading and falling, everything looking so dry in the heat. The seasons have changed along with the years.

I study the manor's For Sale board closely. All the contents are up for sale, including things that relate to outside, garden seats, some tools and a carriage. Even the plants. Wouldn't the plants stay on with the house?

Yesterday, I'd been in the past, what year had it been? Judging by the state of the lane, the mid-1800s. Last night, the manor looked new. Now today, I've come somewhere else, later in time. The For Sale board tells me exactly when. 1914. I frown.

Yesterday evening, I was distracted, now today, I'm much too late. I've missed the story of the manor and now the house is going to be sold. Sold and demolished.

Unless I can stop it.

ISSINGTON MANOR

SIGNIFICANT SALE OF VALUABLE AND SUBSTANTIAL HOUSEHOLD FURNITURE AND ASSOCIATED ITEMS

By order of Mr Gwilym Lawson, on

Thursday and Friday the 9th and 10th

of June 1914

The whole of the Valuable

FURNITURE

AND EFFECTS

BEING THE CONTENTS OF ISSINGTON MANOR

comprising

drawing room, library, dining room, study and hall

furniture

grand pianoforte, kitchen utensils

as well as the contents of

6 bedrooms and 3 dressing rooms

carriage and harness

and various outdoor effects, garden seats, tools and

plants

On View by card only, to be obtained of the Auctioneers on Wednesday 8th from Eleven to Four o'clock, and one hour prior to the sale each day.

SALE BY AUCTION AT TWELVE O'CLOCK

Gabbot and Frears, Printers, Issington Halt

PART TWO

Prologue
1911 – Phoebe

I could have walked to the house by the road. That would have been the obvious choice. I could have stepped off the road, walked through the gate, and followed the short winding path to the house. Stepped into the porch. Why didn't I?

Instead, I chose the long way round, followed the river and walked through the private grounds, through the wrought iron gates. I knew they were only closed at night. Or, when private events were on. We had researched *all* the routines. I swallowed my guilt.

Why did I choose to go this way, go to the Palm House? I didn't know. But I did know that I loved the manor, loved it from that very first moment, stepping across the grass slowly, breathing the air. The air was more pure than I'd been used to when I was younger. I loved walking up the steps that led to the Palm House, led to the hall. But the door to the Palm House was firmly locked. I knocked on the glass, lightly at first, and then a bit louder, knowing eventually someone would come. And I'd be able to see them coming, I'd be able to see *her*.

I'm Stephanie Gilchrist, I said to myself, as I was waiting. And then out loud, just to be sure. 'I'm Stephanie Gilchrist, and I'm your cousin.'

But that was a lie.

1

1908 – Phoebe

I'd never believed I was brave. I had to be *strong*, of course I did, growing up in Chesterton Court. The place was a dump. But Sadie, my ma did the best she could, and I believed I could do better. A damn sight better. But it didn't turn out quite like I'd thought. Life never does.

Ma had brought us up properly.

'You're going to be a lady, Phoebe,' that's what she'd said, and I'd laugh, and say, 'like how?' But Ma would still say it, over and over, and in the end I believed her, me and my brothers, ladies and gents, that's what we'd be. She was talking about manners, of course, being polite, respectable people. But I wanted more than just good manners, I had dreams, enormous dreams and I had to start somewhere. So, I got a job in a shop.

Getting a job in a draper's shop doesn't sound grand, but back where I came from, it was *special*. Most of the girls worked in the brewery, and some in the glassworks on Coroner's Road. But *I* excelled and got a job in Milsom's.

Mr Brown smiled. 'I hope you know how lucky you are?'

I nodded and smiled, of course I knew. I stood a little taller, ramrod straight with *no* stooping. Ma had taught me how to behave. Inside, I was dancing.

'Yes, Sir, I'm know I'm very lucky.' It was my first day.

Ma, surprisingly wasn't that keen. 'Don't get ideas above your station,' she'd said, sharply, when I'd got home. *But that's what you wanted!*

I was too happy to argue with her, so instead, I gave her the buns I'd bought, *fresh* currant buns, such a big change from yesterday's stale ones. That was the normal sort we had. Even now, I can still smell those buns, yeasty-warm mixed with spice, the smell of success. Now that I had a proper job, where I could dress smartly.

'Don't forget, you've still got your chores.' I sighed.

Ma loved to bring us back down to earth, she ploughed a hard furrow. But going to Milsom's changed my life. Because that's where I met Jacob Gilchrist.

I started my life at Milsom's in Haby, Haberdashery to you. All the girls started in Haby, winding the threads and selling lace trimmings, touting the fine stuff posh women liked. But if you were good, you could progress, and I meant to get on, meant to advance. Milsom's was *the* draper's in town, all the best people shopped with us. Or, they sent their servants, for we weren't just smart, we were progressive.

We were all gathered around Miss Scott. She was the actual person in charge. Mr Brown was always out, buying new stock, that's what he did. He liked to experiment, unlike Miss Scott.

'This is our new ready-to-wear range.' Jasamin Scott frowned as she said it. I stared. I couldn't believe it.

Ready-to-wear was a lot more than new, it was indecent. Some of the others came a bit closer.

'Isn't that for the common sort?' Millie Smith said and I almost laughed. Millie was a fine one to talk. Miss Scott frowned. She didn't look happy.

'No, Millie, it's… the future, it saves time.'

Suddenly, I liked Miss Scott more. She obviously hated ready-to-wear, thought it was wrong, clothes off the peg. Just like everyone else's clothes. *It's not what we do.* A large part of me agreed with her. But I could see the profit in it, if you could sell something over and over. With a lot less work.

'Some of the clothes are partially made,' Miss Scott went on, handing a skirt length to one of the girls. 'So the ladies can make them up, or get one of their servants to make them up for them. And, they're in the latest designs.'

I nodded, showing my hand and daring the others to do the same. 'Well I think it's a great idea. I bet we sell loads.'

Jasamin Scott frowned at my words, I knew she didn't trust me yet, but I was right, and once I'd told Mr Brown the same, he took me off Haby, and gave me the chance to prove myself. I'd heard him to talking to Miss Scott once.

'You keep an eye on that girl,' he'd said, watching me work. He'd meant me to hear. 'I'm sure she'll go far.'

I will as well, I told myself. Then I moved to Hats.

Hats for ladies were big business, even my ma wore a hat of sorts, but not the kind we sold in Milsom's. Our hats came with ribbons and lace, even for funerals our hats were special, lilac or black, but still pretty fancy. Hats for weddings, christenings and wakes, you name it, we sold it. Personally, I never wore hats. I told myself they spoilt my hair. Ma told me off.

'It's not proper,' Ma would complain, 'going out without your hat.' *Too bad.*

When I wasn't at the shop, I liked to have fun, going out boating with some young man. I even used to ride a bike, when I could borrow one, racing along, the wind in my hair. Hats were no good for rivers and bikes. I borrowed my bike from a lad down the road, but then I fell off, the hem of my skirt got caught in the chain and I got a fright. I rarely cycled after that. I told the boy whose bike it was that I'd other plans. I mean to ride in a carriage instead.

'Some chance!' Ma said, when I said it to her, but I just laughed.

'You'll see,' I insisted. Ma had done her job too well. *I* knew I'd go far. Then I met Jacob.

2

1848 – Lucienne Hall

When Lucienne saw the tiny house, she knew it was hers. Since she'd moved to Issington Halt, she'd looked at a few, but until that day, none had been right. This one fitted the bill perfectly. She'd never thought they'd send her money, but then they did, and she hadn't thought she'd find a house, yet here it was.

The house stood on Whitborough Walk, not far from the river. It was modest and quaint but elegant too, a suitable house for a poet, she thought, for that was what she'd wanted to be and what she was now, now she'd found a place of her own. The house had tiny leaded panes, and a neat panelled door, with stained glass above. It also had a high brick wall, to keep people out. Lucienne smiled. She'd had her fill of people and towns. But this one was different.

Behind the wall, there'd be a garden, a rather full garden, to judge by the trees spilling over the bricks, *and* there'd be more, as many trees as she could plant. Lucienne loved to write about nature, and in the short time she'd been in this town, she'd written so much. It was a good sign. There'd be more poems *and* trees, once she'd moved in.

Inside, the rooms were fine, if small, there was even a tiny library to work in, although not many books, but that too would change. She had plans for the house and plans for the town – when she was gone, it would remember her name and her work, and maybe even have its own library, larger than this, with grey stone walls, windows and light. Lucienne sighed and looked around. Perhaps this wasn't the house after all. As she stepped back onto the street, she imagined her library, spacious and vast, with high ceilings reaching to heaven, and light flooding in and shelves packed with words. Some of them hers.

She *would* make her dream happen.

3

1909 – Phoebe

It was such a lovely day. Sunny and bright, boats on the river, ice-cream and cake, not that *I* had any of that, it was the start of the week for me, Monday at Milsom's. I'd been there quite a while now and I was getting a little bored. Only a little. I still liked dressing up for work, and trying out the latest stock, the newest scented gloves for one, fashionable scarves, and sometimes the hats, telling myself that I was a lady. Talking nice, and asking Madam if she'd like me to 'call for the boy, to carry your goods.' Millie just laughed.

'To listen to you, you'd think we were a huge store in London, instead of being just being a small town draper's. I want to move on, to somewhere bigger.'

'Me too,' I agreed, grinning, taking the hat off and straightening the ribbon before Jasamin Scott could catch me. But I had bigger plans than a shop. I meant to change my life as well. Then I met Jacob.

He was buying a hat for his wife. *As if she couldn't she buy her own.* I scowled.

'I know what she likes,' Mr Gilchrist said. Almost as if he'd read my mind. 'Besides, it's a present, it's my wife's birthday.' I reddened.

Jacob was much older than me, but unlike the others, he treated me well, more like a friend, rather than a shop girl. He even asked me what I thought. Most of them acted as if I was a servant. That made me mad.

'Goes with the job, Phoebe,' Millie said wisely. 'Just keep smiling.'

Never! I thought, but I smiled at Jacob, showing him one of our very best lines. 'This is one of our newest hats, it comes in grey and blue as well. But I think cream's just the thing.' Jacob nodded. I went on.

'The lace trimming's a little bit extra, but ever so pretty. And we can change it to suit Madam's taste.' I glanced at Jacob.

'I'd normally ask if Madam would like to try the hat but in this case...' I smiled again, and he smiled back, his eyes twinkling. Then his smile faded.

'Have you got any others?' he said. My heart sank. This was where things could get tricky. Maybe he didn't like the hat, or it maybe he thought it cost too much. I couldn't ask, but I had to figure out what was wrong and sell him the right one. I glanced across at his tailored coat and his smart, polished shoes. Not about money. I lifted my chin.

'We also have it in mauve or white, if you prefer.' Sometimes, you see, someone has died and they can't always say. But not in this case.

'No, thank you, the colour is fine.'

I studied his face, as if by staring, I could determine just what he needed. Quite debonair, intelligent-looking, but also tense. *Then*, I got it.

'Perhaps you'd like a simpler style, without the lace?' Yes, I was right, his face relaxed. He was quite handsome when he smiled.

'My wife is quite... conservative.' I understood.

But a man like that needs a woman with spirit. What a waste! Now back to work.

A little while later we'd chosen the hat, made the arrangements, then he looked at me and paused.

'Thirza, my wife, she also likes handkerchiefs, nothing too fancy, perhaps with just some delicate trimming. Do you have some items I can see?'

'We certainly do,' I said, pleased, enjoying myself, now I'd finally made the sale. 'They're downstairs, in Haby, right by the door. Miss Hancock will help you.' The man's face suddenly changed and I realised at once, I'd got it wrong.

'Is there anything *I* can help you with?' I said, softly, and Jacob Gilchrist shook his head. Jasamin Scott was walking towards us.

'No, Miss Slater, not at the moment. But thank you, *for now*.' And then he was gone.

When he'd been back several times, and always to buy more hats for his wife, Millie sidled up to me. 'That man's not here to buy those hats. He's here for you.'

'Rubbish,' I said, polishing the counter for the third time that morning. 'His wife loves hats, he's said so, often.'

'He's buying her off,' Millie said, sagely. 'Because he feels guilty.'

'Guilty for what?' I said, grinning. Then I shrugged. 'What does it matter, so long as I get the sale from him?'

'So long as you're not the next on his list.' I stopped polishing.

'Does he have a list?' Millie shrugged.

'He might do,' she said. 'With looks like that. And he's well-heeled.' I laughed.

'Well if he does, I'll be the last,' I said, firmly, and Millie laughed too. We both thought it was a joke. But six months later, I moved into his house.

4

1909 – Steph

Cross Saddle House

Dear Cousin Clara

I've finally got round to writing to you, I can't imagine what you've heard. I'm Jacob's daughter, Steph, his only heir, and that, Clara, makes me your cousin. How's *your* father, Uncle Frederic? Isn't strange that we've never met? I'm sure you know why.

We've been back here quite some time, and I told Papa I wanted to meet you, even though it's a bit of a journey. You're lucky to live in Issington Halt, it's such a nice place. Papa said no, of course he did, he said we'd have to stay away, at least for a while. It's perfectly stupid.

Papa did very well down south and he did it all to spite Gramps, he made loads of money in wine, which is kind of ironic, given that Gramps hated his drinking. Not that Papa drinks much now, or at least he didn't, not until recently. There's money in wine and we made a small fortune. When we first got here, Papa talked of having a shop in Issington Halt, a wine merchant's. What do you think of that, dear cousin? If Gramps was alive, he'd turn in his grave, and serve him right, that's what I say, for keeping our two fathers apart, for dividing a family.

Everything had been going so well since we'd got back, until Mama found the letters. You can guess what they were.

Papa had kept them, can you believe it, he'd even tied them up with ribbon and hidden them in the back of a drawer. That's where Mama found the things. If he'd asked his daughter what to do, I'd have told him to burn them, but you know how silly men can get over a girl. She's not the first, just the first in a while, and not much more than a slut, I've heard.

Dear Cousin Clara, I can almost feel you shudder.

We've not met, but I've been told that you've got class, so I guess you'll think that I'm being cruel. I know it's not nice and she's not a slut really, she works in a shop, a respectable one, but all the same, she's younger than him, a lot younger, more *my* age, and now she's taking my father away. Mama's gone crazy, screaming and shouting and crying a lot. When, in truth, she's to blame.

'It's only a dalliance Mama,' I said. 'You should ignore it.'

'I should ignore it? Have you gone mad? Your father's flaunting his floozy about, taking her places, showing her off, while I have to face pitying looks. Everyone knows, it's all around the county. I can't bear to go anywhere now. How can I ignore it!'

'It's not as if it's the first time, Mama.'

'And, that makes it alright, does it? When I found out we were coming back home, I wasn't happy. I didn't want to come back here, I liked it better where we were, we'd been there years, but you know your papa, he insisted *and* he said it would be a new start. *No more women*, that's what I thought. I should have known better.'

'She's only a girl, Mama,' I said, meaning that she'd be like the rest, here today but soon gone, once he got bored. *But was she like the rest?* I wondered.

'*You're* just a girl, Stephanie, dear. Wait until it happens to you.'

I sighed. I loved her faith in human nature. Stupidly, I carried on talking.

'It's quite common these days, Mama, in some circles. Everyone knows you just ignore it.' Mama looked cross.

'I tried that before and the time before that. And, as for being common, that's the girl. Younger than me, *and* just a shop girl. How dare he!'

I grinned. *So that's what it was.* Mama's such a dreadful snob, she likes to mix with all the right people. Her pride was hurt, not her heart, and this time was worse, because the girl was so much younger and just a shop girl. Papa had let the side down properly. I waited.

'So, darling,' Mama was speaking. 'I've decided, I'm taking a stand.'

'Oh?' I said. It didn't sound good.

'If he continues seeing this Phoebe, a damn stupid name, if you ask me, I'm throwing your father out of the house. He can find himself another home, and then he can do what he pleases *and* with whom. But *not* while he's living with me.'

I panicked. 'No, Mama, you don't mean that!' Thinking about all the things I loved that Papa provided, dresses and balls, the carriage and the pony. Seeing my life falling apart. 'How would we manage?'

'I have a small allowance,' said Mama, glaring at me. 'One of the maids would have to go, and maybe the cook, or go part-time, but we'd manage, yes we would.' She frowned, distant, as if being poor was quite her style, which it definitely wasn't. I wasn't having it.

'If you think I'm taking up cooking you've clearly gone mad. Remember, you brought me up as a lady. Ladies don't cook, ladies don't sew. *Ladies* have servants.' Mama laughed.

'Well, Steph, I have to say, it's not always obvious you're a lady. But I'm glad that you agree with me. Though being a lady isn't about how many servants you have, it's about how you behave.' I blinked.

'That's not strictly true, is it? And besides, our hands will get rough like the maids', if we don't have servants.' Mama stood up and stared at me.

'Well, Steph, you have a choice. You're a young woman now, although sometimes I wonder. One day, of course, you'll get married. But until you do, if you don't like living here with me, you can always live with your father instead, him and his... floozy. That's if he'll have you.'

'He'll have me,' I said, feeling backed into a corner. Watching her burn the last of his letters.

So, Cousin, in the end, after terrible rows and enough tears to fill a lake, Papa did leave and I went with him, him and his woman. If nothing else I'd make her life tough. I felt guilty, leaving Mama, but I couldn't back down. Mama kept a maid *and* the cook, so it wasn't as if she was actually slumming it. And I'd always been closer to Papa.

We moved into Cross Saddle House, a small country home with plenty of room. It even had stables, although, at the moment, I've just the one pony. The pony's called Buzz. Sometimes we go for a ride in the fields or I take the carriage to Issington Halt, that can be fun. Having a house in the country is great, even though it's all we have, and a bit run down, a gentleman's home in need of repair.

I've heard Issington Manor is lovely with fair-sized grounds and right by the river. It sounds delightful. I can't wait to meet you, Cousin, and to see your home and for us to be friends. We'll have a good time, lots of laughs and maybe meet young men. Perhaps you know of a chaperone? Or perhaps you've got a young man already. Do tell...

I looked up from the letter I was writing. Phoebe stood there. I frowned.

'Phoebe, you're supposed to knock. This is *my* room.' Papa's woman smiled.

'I'm not your servant.'

I got to my feet, pushing the letter under a book. 'True,' I said, 'you're not my servant, but in the circles we move in, we respect privacy. I'm surprised you don't know that.' Then I smiled. 'Or perhaps I'm not.'

Phoebe swore and raised her hands, then she stormed out. I never found out what she'd wanted. I smiled.

Round one to me.

I didn't send the letter to Clara, Papa wouldn't have approved. 'Not the right time,' he'd have told me, as he'd told me before, over and over, whenever I mentioned meeting my cousin. And all because of a family feud. I wanted to meet her, wanted a friend more my own age.

'Let's wait until we're fully up and running, then we can meet them,' Papa had insisted. He'd had to start again up here. On our own terms. On *his* terms was what he meant, it made me pause. I'd thought he'd bought Cross Saddle House to impress Phoebe, or even for me, but all of a sudden, I wasn't so sure. Maybe he'd bought it to impress *them*.

'Leaving your wife won't impress Frederic,' Mama had said, when he'd walked out. I'd finally realised what she'd meant.

Papa and Uncle had never got on, both brothers wanting to be favourite, but Uncle Frederic always won, despite being the youngest. He was the artistic one, just like Gramps. That was why Papa had left. And, even though many decades had passed and Gramps was dead, the feud continued. But, now my father was back in the running, wealthy, successful and still good looking. I frowned.

Papa had ignored Mama's last comment, much as he'd ignored the others. Sometimes he had a heart of steel. But he didn't ignore Phoebe, *ever*, she could get what she wanted. First a chaise longue, then a new carriage, and now we're having the library done. 'What's the point?' I said to Buzz, not that Buzz could answer back, 'we've got plenty of books already.' I'd have liked another horse. But Papa said no.

'You've already got a horse, Steph.' I sighed.

'But two would be nice, then the other could have a rest, when I went out.' Papa was meant to smile at that, my little joke. Instead he looked angry.

'I don't like it, when you're greedy.' Now, *I* was frowning.

It's Phoebe who's greedy. Not that I said it, it would only give her more ammunition. Perhaps he'd heard about our spat.

'We're going out, for a drive and some tea. You'll be alright?'

Of course I would, I wasn't a child. 'Yes, Papa,' I said, nodding, 'and if it rains, I'll play the piano.' Papa gave me a sharp look, he knew I hated playing the piano.

'I wish you'd learn to be nice, like Phoebe.'

I nearly choked. 'I'll do my best. Now, go, please, or Phoebe will think you've forgotten her already.' More steely glares. He knew it was a dig.

After they'd gone, I rang for tea and climbed the stairs to my room, slowly. Maybe I'd write to my cousin again.

One day I might send the letter.

5

1850 – Lucienne Hall

She'd never imagined that with the poems, might come a man. There had been so many poems, even she'd been amazed at how much she'd written in such a short time. In her tiny house close to the river, Number One, Whitborough Walk. The modest house with the high brick wall.

A couple of years had passed since she'd moved here and quite a few people knew of her work, she'd had her poems bound into pamphlets, and surprisingly, people had bought them. *No, not surprisingly*, her work was good. What was surprising was how much she'd made. And she had a little left over, from before. Lucienne had been thinking.

It might be nice to have a new house, nearer the river. A beautiful house, just for her. She could afford it. A house that had its own poetry and its own light, and much more garden than she had now. A place where she could walk, alone.

So when a boy, just for a lark, threw his ball over her wall, and smashed one of the yellow glass panels over the door, it seemed like a sign. Then she bought the hoped for land, next to the river. It seemed like a miracle.

'It's prone to flooding,' someone had said. But she didn't care.

'Some land's not a house,' someone else told her, someone she knew.

'But, it's a start,' Lucienne said. Thinking then, that years before, she'd had nothing, only the one small bag and some money. She smiled, then. 'The house will come, I know it will, I just need a plan. And an architect.'

'I know someone,' the man had told her. 'Though he doesn't come cheap.' Lucienne shook her head, dismissive.

'I have enough,' she'd said, modestly. In fact, she had plenty and poetry was the thing these days, or so it seemed, and money had followed. She intended to spend it.

'I'll invite you to tea, then you can meet him.'

So Lucienne met the architect, although he wasn't much more than a boy, she thought, and she doubted he would be the one.

'I'm old enough,' he said, firmly, reading her thoughts. 'I'm trained, and experienced, and we're closer in age than you'd think.' Then he made his crucial point.

'I've got vision. That's what you need.'

'That's what she needs,' said her friend, sagely.

'You'll need to take me around the site and tell me your plans. Then I'll make them real for you.'

She smiled at the man. *Arrogant boy.*

'Assuming of course, you can afford me.'

'I can afford you,' Lucienne said. She'd taken his challenge. They went for a walk, just her and the boy, and although the sky was a beautiful blue, the day was like ice, it had put people off. There was hardly anyone else by the river.

'It's the perfect site,' the young man said, after they'd walked the length of her land, and come to the end, right by the church. 'I'll build you a beautiful home, it will do you proud.' Lucienne smiled but said nothing. She rather thought he was beautiful too.

'Then, when you've talked me through your thoughts about your house,' he leant across and pressed his finger to her lips, 'then you'll be mine.'

Lucienne gasped. This was unexpected. She wasn't displeased, but still she said nothing. Augustin looked stern.

'I thought you wanted a vision, not a house?'

'I do,' she said, 'I'm a poet not a seamstress.'

'Then, Lucienne, there must be passion. If I can feel the beat of your heart and hear your soul speak, then I can build the perfect house, where your poems will spill out of its walls. To have that knowledge, I must have you.'

Lucienne felt a little flushed. 'You're very plain-speaking.' Augustin laughed.

'It's a fair exchange. I can build your house of dreams, but in return I need your heart.' The young man smiled.

'You don't need to worry. I only need it for the day, it's not forever.' The poet relaxed.

She took his hand in one of her own and gently placed it on her breast. 'This is my heart,' she said, softly. 'But it's only on loan.'

And so, Lucienne's house was dreamt, and also built. And afterwards, they stood outside, on Whitborough Walk and admired the view. 'It's marvellous,' she said and Augustin smiled.

'I agree, it is. Although at one point I thought I'd built *my* vision, instead of yours. Happily, I think it suits us both.' He kissed her firmly on the lips. 'I'll send you a bill in the post soon. But, just one thing.'

'Oh? What's that?'

'A house like this needs something to ground it, some sort of legend. Yes, I have it!' His face sparkled. 'This must be your first house in Issington Halt. Where you became inspired to write.' Lucienne laughed.

'Augustin, that's crazy. Everyone knows where I lived before.' She gestured back down Whitborough Walk. The architect nodded.

'That's true, Lucienne, they do, *now*. But, what we're building isn't for now, it's for the future. A future that will last longer than you. That little house, the one back there, it may not last. But this one will.' He smiled broadly at Issington

Manor. '*And* your work will live on, because it's so good. Just like my house.'

'*My* house?' Lucienne stared.

'So,' said Augustin, smiling at her. 'Issington Manor, the first, the only home of the poet, Lucienne Hall, in Issington Halt. What do you say?'

'Yes,' she said, and kissed him again.

6

1909 – Clara

Clara was writing to her aunt Vi.

Issington Manor

Dear Aunt Vi

I hope this letter finds you well.

I'm a little downhearted, as I'm sure you've guessed. Father has been ill again and mithering on about the past. Such as what's going to happen when he's not here. I keep telling him he'll be fine but he doesn't believe my words anymore and neither do I.

He's not even fifty, but as you know he hasn't been well, and he's not getting better. The doctor says it's probably his heart, but shouldn't a doctor ought to know? The man's a quack.

The treatment calms Father's nerves, so when it's warm he sits outside, or in the Palm House, looking through books, all the books I should look at, if I could face them. I'm too restless.

Most of them we've had for years, gathering dust, some on the shelves, some in that horrible room downstairs. Father says he'll sort them out, but, of course, he doesn't, he hasn't got the strength right now and I'm starting to think he never will. There, I've said it.

He wants to do it all himself, but he does very little, being so tired, most of the books are still in that room.

It's nearly the time when we hold our Lucienne Hall event – remember last year, when we were so busy? People came from miles away to hear about our famous poet? It was *so* much work.

'This was her home,' Father insisted when I got angry at all the things I had to do. 'The home where she wrote all her marvellous poems.'

So what, I'd thought sourly, *who the hell cares,* but father cares and that's what matters. Nobody knows what happened to Hall, she just vanished, and that was several decades ago, but she was a great poet and we live in her house. I run the Lucienne Hall event for Father's sake, like I do most things.

Because I'm an artist, Father thinks I should care about Hall. As you know, I mostly do scenes, but I painted a picture of Hall once, it was a challenge. No-one seems to know what she looked like. She could still be alive, but given her age I'd say it's unlikely. Father didn't like my portrait. When I showed him the painting, all he said was, 'who's that then?' I won't be painting *her* again.

As you know, I'm better at landscapes. I've just completed one of the grounds, it's one of my best, all colours and light, showing off all the trees by the river. Not that Father was impressed, he'd rather hear a dead woman's poems than look at my work. So, now I'm reading poems to him, *hers* of course and other books too, all the time, or so it seems. That's down to you, sending him even more to read!

I hope you'll come here for the Hall event and stay for a while, dear Aunt Vi, I'd love to see you. Also, I could do with the help, now that Father's so much weaker. It's only a reading or two with tea and Flora's going to make some cakes. I'll write out all the well-known poems, to give to people. Maybe you could help with the teas.

I know I shouldn't grumble so much, it's only one day and if *I* was Hall, I'd expect a lot more, considering how successful she was. I do it for Father, it matters to him.

I've kept the juiciest news to last. Uncle Jacob's back in the county, or so I've heard, and for good this time, he's got a new house up at Kerrington Rise. Cross Saddle House. That's a few miles from here, which is just as well, I'd hate to bump into him in town. Not that I'd know him if I did. I've even more news, but for that you'll have to wait till I see you, that's my way of getting you here. I haven't mentioned my uncle to Father, he'd have a fit.

I owe this latest gossip to Burns, he's such a good butler! Now that I know my uncle's back, I'm wondering if I should write to my cousin, invite her for tea? I haven't much family, apart from you and Uncle Theo, who, for all he's your brother and works down the road, I never see. What do you think about Stephanie, Aunt? Should I invite her?

7

1909 – Phoebe

Life had changed such a lot in a few short months. I'd left Milsom's. Ma wasn't happy.

'I hope you won't regret it, girl,' she'd said, angry, while I said nothing. I hoped so too. It had been hard, leaving the shop, but Jacob had insisted.

'You don't have to work there now,' he'd said, smiling at me and patting my arm.

But I like it, I'd thought. What you mean, is *you don't like being seen with a shop girl.* But I did want to please Jacob, he'd given me a home of my own. And, what a home! Cross Saddle House was just amazing, I loved every bit of it. Shame about the daughter, Steph.

'Only my friends call me Steph!' That's what she'd said when I'd tried to be friendly. The meaning was clear, I wasn't her friend. And, of course, how could I be, being with her father? She was loyal to her mother, naturally, and that was right. But Steph and I were close in age. I'd have liked a friend.

'You're just one of a line!' she'd said. Another cruel comment to add to the rest. But I didn't care, Millie at Milsom's had said much the same. I'd laughed in her face.

I *knew* I'd be Jacob's last. I couldn't give up Cross Saddle House, the place was incredible. It's odd how you can be wrong.

Jacob was a lovely man, a pity his daughter was such a child, and Jacob so old. *No, I didn't mean that.* I gave him a hug.

'Your brother lives in Issington Halt, and you've not been to see him yet?' Jacob looked grim.

'I don't want to see him. Frederic was always the favourite, not me. But I was the eldest and the heir, I should have lived at the manor, not him. Damn him to hell!' I frowned.

'So *that's* why you chose a house out here, so you wouldn't meet Frederic.' Jacob nodded.

'Damn right. I thought out here was far enough.' I smiled.

'You're being rather harsh. He might have changed.' Jacob sighed.

'Frederic wasn't the problem, really, it was my father. He didn't like me, so he let Frederic have the manor. Now go away, Phoebe, please, I'm busy.' I sighed. That was a lie.

Jacob had made his money in wine, was wealthy, successful. Rich, I thought. That's how we could afford Cross Saddle, could have it refurbished.

'What would you like, Phoebe?' he'd ask, over and over. It was like a dream come true. I didn't stint.

Curtains and carpets *and* a new carriage. Huge rooms to dance in, drink in, make love in. Not that *it* was exactly love. Everything beautiful, perfect and clean. A bright home for my mother and brothers, Alfie and Seth. Little and cute and living in poverty. I hadn't quite managed the last part yet.

But being back here wasn't making Jacob happy. Things were going downhill, fast.

'Papa never works now,' Steph often said, glaring at me. 'And, that's *your* fault. You took him away from mama!'

Maybe the last part was true, I thought, but as for the rest, no, she was wrong. The problem with Jacob ran deeper than me, was rooted in the past with Frederic and their father.

And I was right.

8

1909 – Clara

Issington Manor

Dear Aunt Vi

Father's taken a turn for the worse, that's why I'm writing. It doesn't seem long since you were here, but oh, how I miss you. We had such a lot of things to catch up on, not least Uncle Jacob's scandal, back from the south, leaving his wife, *and* for a floozy. Father was outraged at that, he said he'd brought the family down. I thought Uncle had done that already.

The doctor says whatever it is that Father's got has spread to his lungs. You know that I think the man's a quack, but Father *is* weak, and there's no-one else to ask for advice. I feel so alone. When Father tries to talk it's awful, he gets so distressed, he can't talk and breathe as well, it's too much of a struggle, and that upsets me *and* the servants. We're all in a state.

Father keeps talking about the library, naturally, Hall's library, that was the plan, Grandpa's I mean, to turn the manor into a library, a place for the future.

'But we've got a library already,' I'd said to him gently, the first time he said it, wondering if his mind was going. But no, it was me, *I'd* forgotten about the plan. He meant the whole house, not just a room, a place where students and scholars could go. Apparently, that's what grandfather wanted, and Father won't stop talking about it, it's driving me mad.

You're right about my cousin, Aunt, I can't have her here, not when Father's like he is *and* given her father's *arrangement*.

Father took the news badly, he'd been hoping things would change, that he and his brother could build a few bridges, but now he knows that won't happen.

Why did Uncle leave his wife? Though, technically, *she* threw him out and all because of a woman from Milsom's. I won't shop there anymore and it's a damn nuisance, they're the best in town. Sorry, Aunt, I know I shouldn't swear.

None of this is Stephanie's fault, yet all the same, I still can't invite her, she and I are the ones who are suffering and I'm *so* vexed.

Now, Aunt Vi, I'll have to go, if I'm to post this letter today. Write soon, please, and I'll send news of Father daily.

9

1910 – Phoebe

I dropped the fork and ran like hell, racing towards Cross Saddle House. As much as I could with these stupid skirts. Herbert followed close behind, he was the gardener. He'd been teaching me about plants. I'd discovered, apart from the house, I loved gardening, shrubs and flowers were new to me, they didn't exist in Chesterton Court. There was barely room for a washing line.

Not that Herbert would let me do much, Cross Saddle's garden was *his* kingdom and he was in charge. Not having enough to do all day was driving me mad, I liked to be busy. Sometimes, Jacob drove me mad. *No, I didn't mean that.*

'Madam, Miss Phoebe, you'd better come now.' This had been Cissie, one of the maids. Jacob was ill and gasping for breath, propped up against his study door, on the first floor. That's what she'd said.

As I raced towards the house, with Herbert in tow, I couldn't help wondering what I'd see. Jacob drunk, that's what I saw. It was only eleven in the morning.

With Herbert's help, I dragged Jacob into the study then closed the door firmly behind us, barely giving a nod to Herbert. I eased Jacob into a chair.

'Now, Jacob, what's the matter?'

'Frederic's dead,' Jacob gasped. 'Ah,' I said. I sat down.

Of course I'd heard his brother was ill, news travels fast, especially the bad stuff, but not *that* ill, Jacob rarely spoke of him. Steph said more, and about cousin Clara.

'I want to meet her!'

'You'll have to talk to your father, Steph, you know he feels.'

'Damn him to hell and damn you too, it's none of your business!' And then she'd stormed out, slamming the door for the third time this week. I was tired of her tantrums, and her father's drinking. If only I'd known he was like that when I met him… And as for Steph, my age was a problem. If I'd been older, had a bit more authority, if I'd been married to her father – no – *did I want that?*

I shook my head. And now, today, we had another crisis. Frederic was dead. Jacob was ranting.

'It was his heart, or so people say, or maybe his lungs, I've no idea. Nobody's told me anything directly, I had to hear the news from a friend. Can you believe it, my own brother?'

You were the one who didn't want to see him.

Jacob slugged back more whisky, as if the stuff was going out of fashion. I touched his arm.

'What happens now? What about the funeral? I can't go, I know that. But you and Steph will have to go. And Thirza too?'

'No!' he yelled, jumping up and throwing his glass into the fire. The glass exploded and I leapt back, only just in time. Jacob was livid, he'd lost his chance to talk to Frederic, have his say and change the past. It was too late. He turned to me, his gaze fierce.

'Not one person from this house, or Thirza either, is going to that funeral. Do you understand?'

'Yes,' I said, knowing I was helpless here. But Steph would go mad. 'How did you hear about Frederic's death?'

'From a man I used to do business with, back in the old days.'

Probably someone dodgy then. I'd heard about his youth before.

Jacob's father, not that I'd met him, he was long gone, hadn't much liked his eldest son when he had been young. Jacob had been lazy back then and a little bit wild, he'd hung around with a rakish crowd who liked to drink. He hadn't worked as hard as he should have. So when eventually Jacob's father gave up on his son, Frederic got to stay at the manor and Jacob had gone south to work. To prove himself.

'It's such a beautiful house,' Jacob said softly, drinking more whisky, out of the bottle. 'Issington Manor was meant to be mine.'

Can't you forget the house for once? Frederic's dead! I'd never been to the manor, but I loved Cross Saddle with all my heart, I couldn't imagine anywhere better. A house can take your very soul.

'Cross Saddle is quite impressive,' I ventured. Not a good move.

'Cross Saddle is nothing,' he yelled, 'it's just a few bricks and a lump of land, the manor is special. The manor was meant to be mine, Phoebe, *my* inheritance, I'm the eldest, and then my father, damn him to hell, said Frederic could live there, and even when I'd proved myself, even *now* when Frederic's dead, it's still not mine.' He swung his arm back.

'No!' I yelled, 'Jacob, no!' I leapt forward and grabbed his arm, finally wresting the bottle from him, and quickly dropping it onto the floor. Briefly imagining what would have happened if the bottle had followed the glass. Whisky trickled into the carpet.

'Oh, Phoebe, I'm so sorry.' Jacob reached across to me, meaning to pull me into his arms. Instead, he collapsed, stumbled and fell, dragging us both onto the floor. Then he started crying, and banging his fists. 'That house was meant to be mine, Phoebe. It's so unfair.'

Life's unfair, I thought, bitterly. I tried again.

'Now that Frederic's no longer... with us, what's to stop you visiting the manor and getting to know your niece, Clara? Making a place for yourself at the house. Steph would like to meet her cousin, you could go there with her. Now Frederic's no longer with us, things could be different.'

'No they couldn't,' Jacob yelled, shoving me away. I must have looked blank.

'When Father made his will,' Jacob said, 'he cut us both out and gave the manor to the next generation. He'd always hoped that we'd have sons but instead we had daughters. Serve the man right! '

Now I understood. 'So which of the girls inherits?' I said. Jacob scowled.

'The one who nets a husband first gets the manor or, rather, her husband does and their descendants. The other girl gets nothing at all, although she can live there if she wishes, until she gets married. Over my dead body!' Jacob said, sourly. Then he went on.

'There's not much difference in age between them, Clara's the eldest, but only by a year, but she's bound to marry first, she's there, in situ, and besides, Steph's…'

Stupid, I think but I don't say it. Things were bad enough already. But Steph *was* pretty. 'Does Steph know about the will?' I asked. Jacob looked grim.

'Of course she does, and now all the unsuitable men will come to our door, just for the manor, and all because my father disliked me.' I shook my head.

'You've proved your worth. Look at all this.' But Jacob wouldn't listen.

'My father was a professional man, he wasn't in business, what I achieved meant nothing to him. He was just the same as Frederic, all he cared about was books. Someone told me, just last week, that Frederic means to turn the manor into a library for poets and scholars, can you believe it?' Jacob raised his hands. Then he sighed. 'Meant, I mean. My brother was crazy!'

Someone was crazy, I wasn't sure who. 'Cross Saddle House is a fine old home,' I repeated, lost for words. 'I like it, anyway.' Jacob sighed.

'Cross Saddle House is just a house, Issington Manor is grander, has class. It should have been mine as the eldest son. Now my father *and* brother are dead, my only hope of getting that house is if my daughter marries some scoundrel, before her cousin. Is that right?'

'No, of course it's not right.' *But is it right that we're sitting here, while Ma and my brothers are struggling to cope at Chesterton Court, in a dark, dank house? And you won't help?* I hardened my heart.

'What if Frederic's made a will?' I said, thinking. 'That might have changed things.'

'Yes, but he didn't,' Jacob insisted. 'I've already checked. Issington Halt is so small, they've only got the one solicitor. The man gets all his wine from me, and at a discount, in return for favours. Frederic didn't make a will. And Clara will do what her father wanted and turn the manor into a library. And all because of a dead poet. It's outrageous!'

A dead poet? The dead poet was news to me.

'Lucienne Hall, she was the poet, she owned the house years before, before my father bought it. Hall was well known and must have had money to live in the manor, but then she vanished. Frederic wanted to revive her memory and turn the manor into a library, and all because our father wanted it. God knows why. I hate poetry.' I smiled.

'I've heard Steph's cousin Clara is a painter.' Jacob nodded.

'Apparently so. I've been told she's not bad. People actually *buy* her paintings.'

'Wouldn't you like to meet your niece?' Jacob frowned.

'No,' he said, 'I damn well wouldn't. It's hard enough managing Steph, and Steph won't be meeting her cousin either, and I keep reminding her every day, in case she forgets.'

So the feud goes on. I smiled. 'She'll be far too busy looking for a husband.'

'Unless Clara finds one first.' We locked eyes, in agreement.

'That won't happen,' I insisted. 'I'll make sure of it.'

10

1910 – Clara

Her father was dead and she was alone. Apart from Burns who kept the house running, and Mabel and Flora, her loyal maids. Flora brought her tiny treats, beautiful cakes and scones with cream but none of it worked. Even though it was now summer. Clara usually loved the summer. She got to her feet.

It was late, almost dark, and on nights like these she loved to sit on the tiny porch and study the trees, the shapes they made. She would glance across the garden to the churchyard, or left to the old church spire in the distance. But tonight had been too cold for that.

Instead, Clara was in the library, she could still look out at the garden from here, look at her land for as long as she had it. Clara sighed. It was three months since her father's death, and still no sight of a man or her cousin.

'You can't invite that woman here.' This had been Vi.

'But Aunt, really, it's not as if I've *that* much family.' Vi had been stern.

'Remember what your father said.'

Clara frowned. Yes, she remembered. She recalled her father grabbing her wrist, surprisingly strong, despite him being weak. She remembered what he'd said to her.

Clara, get married, as fast as you can. And, never, ever make friends with your cousin.

But now she was thinking he'd been wrong, that maybe meeting her cousin was right. She needed a friend. Clara gasped.

A woman was stepping through the French windows into the room, pushing the cream muslin away. Was it her cousin?

'Are you Stephanie?'

The stranger didn't answer. Instead she paused and unwound the scarf from around her head, folding it carefully in her hand. *Nice taste,* Clara thought. The scarf was beautiful. The woman was fair and as pretty as a picture.

'Sorry to disturb you. My name's Alice.'

Not my cousin. Clara frowned. Who was this woman? 'It's a bit late to be calling now. What do you want?'

Alice laughed. 'Yes, right, sorry about that. I've lost track of time. And when I saw you sitting there, it made more sense to come this way. I always manage to upset people somehow.' Clara stared, then made a decision.

'Would you like some tea?'

'Isn't rather late for tea?' Clara laughed.

'Touché, Alice. Well, I have got wine, or I could ask Burns to bring us some sherry. There's some left over from Aunt Vi's visit.' Alice frowned.

'Sherry? No, I think I'll pass. I'm sorry, now I see I shouldn't have come here, not this late. I'll come back in the morning if I may? I've only just got here. I've been... travelling.'

'No, wait!' Clara said, sharply, as Alice turned round towards the French windows. *Damn*, she thought. *The first person I've talked to in ages apart from the servants, and now I've alarmed her, frightened her away.* She couldn't let the woman leave. *Why was she here?* It had to mean something.

Clara knew she was clutching at straws, desperately lonely, missing her father. Now there was Alice. She took a deep breath.

'You'll need somewhere to stay in town, as you're not local. Are you staying for long?'

Alice shrugged. 'That depends. You're right, I need to find a place.'

'I know of some lodgings, they're perfect for ladies and just down the road, on Upper Fell Street. I could take you there tomorrow morning.' Clara paused. Have you booked somewhere to stay tonight? Alice shook her head.

'I didn't expect to arrive so late.'

'You can stay here. I'll get Burns to make up a room.' Alice looked shocked.

'But you don't know me.' Clara shrugged.

'And, you don't know me. I promise you we're all quite friendly.'

Alice seemed wary. 'Yes, if you like, if it's no trouble. That's very kind.'

'Have you come far?'

'No, not really, but before that, Curdizan. You've probably never heard of it.'

'No, sorry.'

'And... other places, in between.'

'Really? How... interesting.'

'You'd be surprised.'

The next morning, Clara showed Alice around the manor.

'The trouble is, I want to paint. That's what I do, paint gardens and landscapes, anything natural. I *live* for my work. But I can't, now.'

'Hardly surprising, given what's happened.'

'Yes, I know, father's death. But that's not it.' Clara gripped the banister tightly. 'The night before my father died, he told me two things, that I had to marry to save the manor, so my cousin couldn't have it, but also, more importantly, to remember the poet Lucienne Hall, by creating a library out of this house.' She looked around. 'Not yet of course, I'm still here. Have you heard of Hall?'

'Yes,' said Alice, sounding amused. 'So, how's the whole husband thing going?'

'Not very well. I've met a few men, chaperoned by my aunt, of course, but most of them live miles away, and worse than that, they're old and dull. And even worse, not one has proposed.'

Alice grinned. 'Were you very disappointed?'

'No, not really, I don't want to get married, not just yet. Which is rather inconvenient.'

'So, what about Hall's library then? Was all this in your father's will?'

'No, in my grandfather's. I don't even like Hall's poetry, or any poetry, if I'm honest. But Father did and he believed that people have a right to books, and a place to read them, or that's what he told me grandfather said.' Clara trailed off. 'I owe it to my Father, as much as for Hall, she's probably dead.' She glanced at Alice.

'Every summer we hold this event in honour of Hall, it's nearly time to hold it now.' She raised her hands. 'And I've done nothing.'

Alice stepped out into the garden and strolled towards a very old tree.

'So what do you do, usually?' Clara shrugged.

'Not very much, until the last minute.'

'And yet you expect people to come?' Clara felt hot.

'I couldn't care less. But I have to care, because of my father.'

'Yes, I can see that. It could be a problem.'

'Are you making fun of me?'

Alice smiled. 'Perhaps I am.' She glanced across the lawn to the river. 'Where do you hold it?'

'Here, where you're standing. We have a few chairs, some banners and flags and Flora makes her marvellous cakes, they go down a treat. We've done it for years, and people *do* come, a few people...'

'And the point of it is?'

'To raise funds for the new library.' She paused, looked grim. 'If it happened in my lifetime I'd be homeless. But Father said that's what Grandfather wanted and that's what I promised him. But it seems unachievable.'

'You needn't worry,' Alice said softly. 'It won't happen.'

'What?' said Clara.

'The library thing. It's not going to happen.'

'How do you know?'

Alice looked smug. 'Trust me, I know.' Clara felt a sudden rage.

'How dare you,' she said. 'You turn up here, far too late, you drink my wine and eat my food and now you think you can mock my plans. You'd better go.'

Alice grinned. 'That's better, now you're angry.' She stepped closer to Clara. 'I haven't mocked your plans, Miss Gilchrist and that's because you haven't any plans, all you have is a fairy tale. A dream this big needs loads of work. Not one event every year.' Alice went on.

'You *could* make the library happen, but you'd have to put the work in first. Get angry, get busy, get others on board. Get Issington Halt involved in the project and spend some money promoting the event, find other writers and poets to support it. Have several events, not just the one. Do you have others?'

'No,' said Clara, feeling embarrassed. 'We have a small fete for the church workers once a year, but that's different.' Alice nodded.

'So lots of things would have to change. Don't just invite the people you know, instead, invite strangers and tell them some stories, compare Hall to other poets.'

'I don't know much about the woman. Only that she vanished.'

'So? You can learn. There must be something in her poems, stuff about her and who she was. Make it a story and grander than it is. You're thinking too small.' Alice went on.

'And once you've put some passion behind it, some kind of magic and built up momentum, a man might appear when you least expect him. By then,' she grinned, 'you won't even care.'

'But what about the manor?' said Clara. 'If I don't marry soon, I'll lose my home.'

'I wouldn't worry,' Alice told her. 'Concentrate on Hall's library.'

After lunch, Alice seemed pensive. 'I ought to go, I need to find more permanent lodgings.' Clara nodded.

'I'll walk you through the grounds into town. I'm sure you'll be happy in Issington Halt, though very little happens here.'

'You'd be surprised,' Alice said softly. But Clara wasn't listening. Instead, she was staring at Alice.

'You can't wear that scarf, it's... far too bright. I'll lend you a hat.' She went upstairs and brought one down.

'How lovely,' said Alice. The hat was old and quite severe.

'I'm afraid it's the only spare I've got.' Alice sighed.

'I *am* grateful, honestly I am. It's just that I'm not great in hats.' She put it on and smiled at Clara. 'I'm sorry I wasn't Stephanie.'

'I'm not sure I'm ready to meet her.' Clara smiled and took Alice's arm.

'You can be my cousin instead.'

Later that evening, when it was dark, Alice stood in the grounds of the manor. She was alone. She watched the ducks and geese mooring, settling down for the night. This river was different from the one she knew in the twenty-first century, it was narrower, quiet. It was also different from the river in Curdizan, cleaner and clearer. Alice rather liked it here.

I could stay, she thought, *just for a while.*

She glanced down to the wrought iron gates, they divided the manor from public land. Burns closed them every night, so Clara had said, just as he locked the five-bar gate down by the road. Alice saw that the gates were closed. As she stared, an older man, attractive, well-dressed, but rather dishevelled, appeared at the gates and rattled them, hard.

Alice watched him turn the handle, but the lock was strong and the gate held firm. The man glared and kicked the gate, a waste of time, which made him swear. Then he peered through them, but Alice knew she was safe from his eyes. She wondered who the man was and whether she ought to do something. She waited to see.

The man swung his arm back and hurled a bottle over the gate, as hard as he could. It fell on the path and smashed into pieces, a few splinters landing not far from Alice. The shards glinted and a dark pale liquid frothed on the gravel. Alice stared.

'Go away,' she said, under her breath, and then a bit louder, knowing that the man couldn't see her or hear her. 'Go away, *now.*'

The man turned and went.

11

1910 – Steph

It was summer and I was bored.

Not that this was anything odd, I spent most of my life bored. We'd been here, at Cross Saddle House, for over a year. It seemed like forever.

When we'd first moved, I was excited, my first, my very own country house, more than a cottage, although the cottage was fine back then. Mama had always made it so. Cross Saddle House was a hundred times better, it might have been Papa's but it would be mine. Eventually. I would inherit, once Papa was bored with Phoebe. He wasn't bored yet.

'It's only a dalliance Mama,' I'd said. But now, a year later, *she* was still here, and Papa, it seemed was still very smitten. *And*, he was drinking. More than before.

The house itself looked fabulous, it had all been refurbished, thanks to Phoebe, and I had to admit, her taste was spot on. She didn't look that bad herself with all her new dresses and trinkets to match. By which I meant jewels. But, sadly, there were no dresses for me.

'We *all* have to tighten our belts,' Papa had said, after he'd spent thousands on her. I didn't dare think *exactly* how much. It rankled, I admit it, him spending so much on a shop girl, while Mama and I had to struggle.

Not that I felt sorry for Mama, she'd made the choice to throw him out. And I was glad we had Cross Saddle House, but money was tight. Really tight.

Uncle Frederic's death didn't help. I wasn't allowed to go to the funeral. In the end, none of us went.

'But, Papa, he's your only brother!'

'What does that matter? We were estranged.'

'Only because you chose to be.'

Papa looked so angry at that I thought he might hit me. But that's not his style. Instead he stormed off into his study, slamming the door hard behind him. I tiptoed up and listened at the door and I could hear the clink of crystal, the sound of liquid being poured from a bottle. Whisky probably. Oh, dear.

'It's mine, damn it,' Papa had said, talking about Issington Manor, over and over, usually when he'd had something to drink. 'I was the eldest son, not him. It should have been mine.'

But because Gramps had made that will and neither son was allowed to inherit, he'd lost all his rights. I used to think it didn't matter, yes he'd been lazy when he was young, but now he'd come back wealthy and sober. Even after Phoebe turned up, we still had Cross Saddle and money to burn. But not anymore.

Now, a year later, all our funds were falling away, the wine shop he'd dreamt of didn't exist and Cross Saddle House was swallowing cash. It was all Phoebe's fault.

'I didn't need a new chaise longue,' Phoebe had protested, 'or a new carriage. I quite liked the old one.' But I, for one, didn't believe her.

And now Papa was drinking again after years of being sober, stopping the gambling, getting his head straight. It was Phoebe's fault.

Sometimes Papa would talk to me privately. He couldn't talk to her.

'Even though Frederic's dead, I still can't get inside those grounds. That house, the manor, should've been ours.' His eyes became greedy, dark and piercing. 'The manor still could be, if you marry before your cousin.' I stared.

I wouldn't mind getting married, I thought, *if I could find a suitable man.* But where could I find one? We weren't exactly the country set. And, who could be my chaperone? Phoebe would hardly be up to the job. And as for Mama... I thought quickly.

'I could cosy up to Clara, get to know her *and* her friends. Then, if she had a suitable man friend, I could steal him.'

Papa laughed, a rare moment. 'That's my girl, I'm sure you could. But, I can't have you going to the manor just yet, not while we've got a cash flow problem. I want you to visit in style.' I sighed.

I was beginning to doubt that would ever happen.

Papa patted me on the shoulder as he wandered off down the passage to his study.

'I'm going to check my accounts,' he said. By which he meant, *have another drink*. It wasn't even twelve o'clock. I frowned. The days were turning out all the same.

I took the carriage to town.

Issington Halt was looking good. It was high summer, but rather surprisingly not too busy. Not many girls had the freedom I had. I knew I was lucky.

What to do next? I thought about wandering up to Milsom's, updating the girls on Phoebe's life, but I couldn't be bothered. Instead, I decided to walk by the river, wave at the men working the barges. They always waved back. Taking the path that led to the manor. I couldn't resist. But today was different, I could hear music.

As I drew closer, I could see the streamers and flags in the distance. Mostly, people stayed out of the grounds, even though the gates were open during the day. They knew it was private.

I'd been to the gates previously, hoping to see Clara. I never had. I'd never been *inside* the grounds, but today I saw some people going in.

'Are *you* going in?' someone just behind me asked, and I jumped and turned around.

A young man was staring at me. He looked amused.

'Maybe,' I said, and smiled right back. I didn't meet many men these days. 'What about you?'

'I might,' he said, 'if you do too. They're having a poetry day today. For the well-known poet, Lucienne Hall.'

'Really?' I said, smiling at him. 'Not *that* well known. I've never heard of her.' The young man laughed.

'Don't you like poetry?'

'Not very much,' I said, restless, turning away and peering further into the grounds. There were too many trees. The man coughed.

'I was going to take a look. I'm an artist, you see.'

'Are you?' I said. 'Well, don't let me stop you.'

'I said, I *was*,' he said, lightly, putting his hand on my arm, 'until I met this lovely young lady. That's you, in case you hadn't guessed.' I smiled at him.

'I had,' I said. 'I'm used to the charms of fickle young men. So what are you thinking of doing instead?' The young man grinned. He was rather good-looking.

'I'm thinking we might have some tea, with cake of course, just over there.' He gestured across the river to a café. 'What do you say?'

'Maybe,' I said, taking his arm. 'But only because I'm fond of tea, though I don't eat cake. It spoils my figure.' The young man grinned.

'I very much doubt that. Maybe I can change your mind.' We headed back towards the bridge.

Issington Manor could wait for now.

12

1910 – Clara

Clara glanced around the grounds. She smiled at Alice. 'We did it,' she said.

'We certainly did, and here's to us.' Alice raised a glass.

'No, here's to you,' Clara insisted, as the champagne bubbled and tickled her nose. 'I couldn't have done all this without you.' The flags fluttered in the breeze. Alice said nothing.

It was *the* most glorious day. Warm and sunny and out on the river the boats sailed past, weaving past the ducks and swans. Birds soared. Clara sighed.

It was paradise. But so far there was just her and Alice.

They'd planned today to the very last detail, with poetry readings, punch and prizes, sweets for the children and, later on, tea and cakes, made by Flora.

'I haven't seen this type before,' Clara said, picking up the tea and studying the label.

'I bought it when I was travelling,' said Alice, taking the tea out of her hand. Clara smiled. It was all perfect.

Except that there was nobody there.

'I'd hoped to sell some paintings,' said Clara, staring across the lawn at the tree where all of her landscapes were lined up in a row.

'It'll be fine, you have to be patient. Have more champagne.' An hour went by.

A few people came, they wandered in, some she knew, they'd come up from the town, and then a few more came down from the church, but Clara was starting to lose all hope. They'd never had so few people before, even when her father was weary and couldn't be bothered. Perhaps now her father was dead nobody cared. She leant against the porch and sighed. 'We might as well give up,' she said. 'I'm going in.'

'I wouldn't if I was you,' said Alice.

Clara glanced across the lawn towards the gates, and saw a few people walking towards them. More than some, two dozen or more, the men in top hats and stripy shirts. Led by a woman, stout but well-dressed. Clara gasped.

'That's Marie Corelli! What on earth is she doing here?' Alice looked smug.

'I told her it was her duty to come. Given that she's a well-known novelist. "Though not as successful as Hall," I said.' Clara laughed and stared at Alice.

'Did you really? Don't you know she's quite famous? Look, my hands are almost shaking.' Then she frowned. 'Damn you, Alice, for keeping it quiet, for letting me think no-one would come.'

'But all the better now, I think. I suggest you put some music on, our guests have arrived.' She stretched out a hand. 'Oh dear, it's starting to spit.'

'Nothing can spoil today,' said Clara, raising her eyes up to the sky. 'I can't thank you enough, Alice, really. Thank God you turned up. Where did you say you used to live?'

'Far away,' said Alice, softly. 'You wouldn't want to go there.'

Later that day, when the guests had gone, and even Alice had finally left, Clara sat on the steps by the Palm House. Today had been wonderful, the kind of event her father had dreamed of. Pity he hadn't been here to see it.

She glanced around her lovely grounds, thought of the home she wanted to keep and her father's dream, a dream which burnt brighter after today. A library for poets, in memory of Hall. Today they'd raised a lot in donations.

Alice had made the dream seem real.

For once, rarely, Clara was alone, the servants were out, the visitors gone, that freedom from people was marvellous, special. She took off her shoes and danced on the grass, the music blaring louder than ever. Later on, when day turned to dusk and the rain came down, heavier now, Clara still danced, drunk on success. The rain soaked through her dress to the skin but Clara didn't care. Eventually, when it was dark, she picked up her throw and discarded shoes, and carefully climbed the steps to the Palm House. Not looking back at the open gates. Burns would lock them when he got back.

She didn't see the young man standing by the gates, just outside.

But he saw her and the young man smiled.

The dark silhouette of Clara's future.

13

1910 – Steph

I'm not supposed to take tea with strangers, and certainly not with strange young men. *Mama would have a fit if she knew.* I was having a glorious time.

Not that the man with me was strange, though his name was odd.

'My name's Gwilym, Gwilym Lawson. Pleased to meet you.' He took my hand.

'Your name is quite... unusual.'

'Odd, you mean.' Gwilym laughed and we sat down in the riverside tea room, across from the manor. He offered me scones, fruit or plain, but I took both. I'm hopeless at choosing, or so Mama says.

Then Gwilym sat back and stared at me.

'I only went to the manor by chance. I was hoping to get an artist's commission, I'm a painter by trade. Then I found you, which was much better luck. And pretty as a picture.' I frowned.

'Flattery doesn't work on me.'

'Even if it's true? I *am* an artist, I know what looks good.'

'What do you paint? Walls and ceilings?' Gwilym laughed.

'Ha ha, no of course I don't. Do I look the sort? I paint portraits, ladies and children, even the family dog if they want and sometimes their home. I'll even paint a seascape or two, I like to keep my hand in. Then they pay me, if I'm lucky. If they don't, I just starve.' I laughed at that.

'You don't look as if you're starving to me.' I glanced at his shirt, top of the range, and then at his shoes, fancy with buckles. 'I think you do well.'

'I do,' said Gwilym, 'and early next year I'm back down to Dorset to paint some more portraits, but I'd like to be more than just an artist, painting can be unreliable. I'd like a more secure income.'

'Such as?' I said, pouring more tea, we were both very thirsty. Gwilym laughed and picked up his cup.

'Well, Miss Gilchrist there's the rub. The only thing I can do is paint. And, charm the birds from the trees, of course.'

'Maybe,' I said. But inside I was smiling.

So, that, dear Cousin, is how I met Gwilym, and all thanks to you. I didn't go up to your house in the end, though judging by the hoards leaving later, it must have gone well. I watched them walking back into town, laughing and talking and I felt a tiny twinge of envy. Who would have thought that poetry, words, could make people happy? You'll have to explain it to me when we meet.

I know you'll want to meet Gwilym, and I expect he'll want to paint your portrait, he's already asked if I'll sit for him. Something about my bone structure. I know it's all charm, but it's still rather fun, especially as we shouldn't be alone, without a chaperone. Please don't tell.

A few days later I took Gwilym to meet Mama, but it didn't go well. Mama didn't like him, not that she said so, I could just tell. But she's not that fond of men right now. I can't think why.

'You shouldn't be on your own with him. It's not proper.'

'The maid was with me, Mama,' I lied. Mama, of course, knew I was lying. She knows me too well.

'Don't you have any standards now? Now you're living with your father and *her*.'

'How dare you!' I snapped. 'Of course I've got standards. We didn't do anything wrong, Mama. We went out for tea!'

'Nothing wrong, *yet*.' She was thinking of Phoebe.

'I'm not in the least like her, Mama. I don't even like her.'
Mama looked sour.

'It's still not right, not in *our* world. And being an artist's
not proper work.' I laughed at that.

'Maybe it isn't, but it's much more interesting. And
Gwilym makes money.'

'Oh, well, that makes it alright, then!'

I swore, under my breath. Our conversation was going
nowhere, so I left soon after. Gwilym had gone hours before.

Things were going downhill fast. Mama always seems
disgruntled and Papa does too and even Phoebe looks fed up.
She's run out of things to change in the house, so now she's
started working in the garden. Herbert's not pleased, but she
doesn't care.

I know now I was wrong about Phoebe, she's not like
Papa's other women, she's far too sharp. If she'd been
wealthy, I'd have quite liked her, we could have got into
scrapes together. But as she's with Papa, and only a shop girl,
I have to be distant. Not that it seems to bother her much.

So, dear Clara

Gwilym tells me you're a painter just like him, only
landscapes, not portraits. But how did *he* know? He'd just
shrugged.

'I think I saw her name somewhere, in that small gallery
near The Royale.' Then he grinned. 'You're not jealous, are
you Steph? I swear, darling, you've no need to be.' I snapped.

'I'm not your darling and only my friends call me Steph.'
We were walking back to Cross Saddle House, strolling along
the country lane. It had been perfect.

Unlike the day he'd met Papa, which had been worse than
when he'd met Mama. Especially as he couldn't ride.

I'd offered him Papa's brand new horse. Papa had finally
agreed to a second one. Gwilym went white.

'I'm afraid I don't ride,' he'd said, sadly and Papa looked smug. I was embarrassed. He'd have to learn, eventually, when we got...

No, Cousin, I won't say it, I don't want to put a jinx on things. Besides, I shouldn't, I know you have to marry first, to keep the manor. And I'm happy here.

So, there we were a few weeks later, strolling along the lane and squabbling, beating off flies in the late summer sun when Phoebe emerged from within the house, all in a state. She ran right past us up the path, the one that leads to Herbert's shed. We followed. I've never seen Phoebe run like that, something must be badly wrong. When I got near I saw what it was. Smoke was billowing from the shed and I could see flames. I screamed.

Using a rag on the hot metal handle, Phoebe pulled the door open, and vanished inside but I couldn't move. A few seconds later, she re-appeared, coughing and dragging something behind her. It was Papa. I found my legs and rushed towards him, yelling his name, as Phoebe dumped him on the grass. Then she leant over, ripped open his shirt. I gasped. Thank God he was breathing. Phoebe was coughing, bent almost double.

Gwilym shoved the shed door shut, wincing with the rising heat.

'Go and get Herbert, and the men from the cottages,' I yelled and Gwilym ran off.

I was kneeling next to Papa, not sure what to do. Now he was coughing, at least that was something, but his eyes were unfocused, Papa was drunk. I went and got some water from the house, but Papa didn't want it, he pushed it away. I stood there, helpless. Gwilym came back.

'You need to fetch the doctor, Steph. That's what *I'd* do. Do it, *now*.' I nodded and made my way to the road, trying and failing to walk a bit faster.

When I got back, several men from the village were there, and the danger was over. The shed was sodden and smelt of smoke. One of the men was talking to Phoebe.

'Don't you worry, he'll be fine, as right as rain, once the lads get him into the house. You'll see.' He smiled at her and I could have spat.

One of Phoebe's sleeves was torn, her hair was loose and her face was smudged and covered in soot. She looked a mess.

At least that's something, I thought, sourly, glancing at Gwilym. Wondering what we ought to do next.

But Gwilym, I saw, was staring at her.

14

1910 – Phoebe

I used to live in Chesterton Court. Which sounds, I thought, like one of those places posh people live, with old weathered stone and huge windows, and a turning circle. I asked Jacob if we could have one here, at Cross Saddle House. Jacob just laughed.

'The house isn't big enough for that, sweetheart.' But I disagreed.

'It's large enough for me,' I said. I glanced around our drawing room, which thanks to me had been fully refurbished. Beautifully done, if I say it myself. A long way from Chesterton Court. My mother still lived there.

It rankled a bit, that although I lived in a virtual palace, my mother and brothers lived in a slum, a poky cottage with just three rooms. And, down a narrow, grimy alley, off Bakehouse Lane. I wanted my family to live with us. But Jacob said no.

'No, sweetheart, it wouldn't be right. Not with Steph in the house.'

But Steph's behaviour wasn't right, going around with that strange young man, and no chaperone. But I said nothing. Jacob could be very old-fashioned *and* inflexible. He'd formed his views when he was young and he wasn't going to change his mind now, not for anyone, not even Steph. I'd given up trying.

Steph, being her father's child, tried a bit harder, so he'd play her along, just for amusement, then he'd say no. I thought it was cruel. She didn't get her own carriage, though she did get a horse, but only because he wanted one too. If

Jacob didn't want her to have it, whatever *it* was, Steph wouldn't get it. As I didn't get Ma to stay.

'Not our sort of people, sadly.' I'd heard him say this to one of his friends, talking about my ma and brothers.

Fine, I thought, *so that's what you think*. Damn him to hell.

When we first moved to Cross Saddle House and had it refurbished, Steph's eyes flashed, they were green with envy. *She* thought it was all for me. I thought it was all for Frederic, about proving himself to his long-lost brother. But we were *both* wrong.

As time went on and Jacob continued his feud with his brother, I realised that the house was for Thirza. She'd forced him out but Jacob still loved her. The thought made me ill.

I'd admired the woman for sticking to her guns and throwing him out. *I* wouldn't have waited so long. *No man makes a fool of me,* that's what I'd thought. But now Jacob had.

When Steph and her beau, the tousled young man with the thick black hair, came home that day, and found me literally fighting fire, dragging Jacob from the shed, I realised then that I had to take stock. Jacob was gradually falling apart, he was working less and drinking more, and spending too much. We were running out of money.

Jacob was shocked at the change to his life, now he wasn't married to Thirza. Cross Saddle House was a fine old place and beautifully done, thanks to me, but country life was lost to him, nobody called or wanted to see him. Along with his wife, he'd lost his life, and now his business was crumbling too, due to neglect. None of us were happy here, even the cook was looking for a place.

The only good thing about Jacob's drinking was that I didn't need to be careful now, when I whisked things away. He didn't even notice.

I bent my head under the eaves and stepped into Chesterton Court. The courtyard felt cold, as it always did, even in summer. Now, in winter, it was freezing. Ma was hanging the washing out. I swear to you her lips were blue.

'So Lady Muck's finally come round.'

'Come on please, Ma, don't be like that.' I leant across to kiss her cheek, but she moved away, out of my reach. It was a game we played. We went back indoors, which wasn't much warmer, me following, carrying the basket. I had to stoop at the door to go in. 'I've brought you some things.'

I opened my bag and her eyes lit up, I'd brought some curtains which would do for upstairs, once Ma had cut them to size. I'd also brought some wood for the fire. It was cold in here and I was worried about Seth's cough. He was only three. I wondered if I could sneak him along to Dr Lewis. It wouldn't be easy.

Ma held the curtains up, sniffed and sighed, then put them down. 'They'll need a bit of work to fit. I suppose they'll do.' But I knew she was pleased. 'You'll be wanting some tea?'

'Of course,' I said. 'Nobody makes a brew like you.' Ma frowned. She didn't like flattery.

I gave her some bread made just this morning and a couple of coins I'd found in the dresser, taking money was harder than things, and Ma smiled, more warmly this time. I knew I'd finally won her round, but every time I started from scratch. 'I see you've been busy.'

'Just for a change.' Ma leant in towards me.

'What's that mark under your eye? Has he been hitting you?' I laughed.

'What? Jacob? You've got to be joking. The door to the garden shed swung closed and the handle hit me in the face.' *When I was dragging him out of the shed.* 'I've told you before.' Ma frowned.

'That was several months ago. A simple bruise should have healed by now.'

I shrugged. 'So, it's left a mark. Leave it, Ma.'

'Your da may have gone, but *he* never hit me, or you kids.'

'And neither does Jacob,' I said, angry. 'Do you think I'd stay with him, if he did? And, Da didn't go. Remember, he died.' Ma sniffed.

'Dead or not, he's still not here, he left me on my own to struggle.' *Just like you.* I said nothing. Ma paused, then she went on.

'You do get some benefits, living as you do.' Studying the curtains with some longing. It was always the same.

'You know I bring you what I can. You don't need to worry about Jacob, Ma. He likes his drink, that's all it is, and the time this happened,' I touched my face, 'he set fire to the shed and that's where I found him. I had to drag him out from the flames.' Ma grunted.

'I've told you before, I don't hold with men drinking. Your da never did and I've got no patience with men who do.' She handed me a mug of tea. It was so much better in a mug. Or maybe it was just the tea.

'How's the princess?' She meant Steph.

'Bearing up,' I said, smiling. 'Despite being hard-done-to. And guess what, she's got a young man, he's paints portraits for a living.'

'That could be handy,' said Ma, grinning, it didn't take much to cheer her up. 'Perhaps I can have my portrait done, when he's got time? Or maybe he'd like to paint the back bedroom.'

I laughed and poured us more tea, then topped up the pot with a few more leaves. 'I'll ask him when I see him. He's started coming to the house a lot. When Jacob's *doing the accounts*, mostly.'

Ma stared. 'He might be a better catch for you, than the one you've got. For a start he's young.'

'Oh, Ma,' I laughed, 'I'm happy with Jacob. Honest I am. Besides, the man has great curtains.' Ma smiled and then her face changed.

'Could you get me another blanket, and maybe some pans? My own are so old.' I sighed.

'I'll do my best. I'll get you the blanket, that's not a problem, but pans are a no-no, the kitchen's the cook's, I'd rather buy the things myself than risk her wrath.' *If I had any money.*

If Jacob continues to drink, I thought, *and I keeping taking stuff for Ma, Cross Saddle House will soon be empty.* I didn't want to live like this anymore. Ma sniffed.

'Alice came round last week,' she said. I stared.

'Who's Alice?'

'She works for the mayor, or rather, she works for Theo McKinver, the bloke who's in the mayor's office. I've told you about Alice before.' I frowned. I was sure she hadn't.

'So, Ma. What did she want?' *Whoever she is.*

'She brought me some soup, for the boys you know.' As if to say, *that's meant to be your job*, as if my curtains didn't count. 'She's a strange one, Alice, a bit like you.'

'Rubbish,' I said. 'I'm a one-off.'

'So's Alice. She's younger than you, and she talks all proper, but she seems to know what it's like around here. And how to live better. She told me about evening classes, in history and drawing. She said I should go, they'd cheer me up. And then, she said,' Ma paused and stared at me, 'I could make some money, taking in sewing.'

I jumped up. 'No!' I said, 'you're not doing that! It's dark in here and you know sewing's bad for your eyes. And, as for classes, I bet they cost money, and who would look after Alfie and Seth?' Knowing as I said it, I'd dropped myself in it.

'Some women have daughters, Phoebe.' I sighed.

'Cross Saddle House is miles away and Jacob likes me home at night. I'll bring you more money, when I can get it.' Ma lifted her chin.

'I'd rather not take handouts from you.'

We both knew she had no life, my brothers were only five and three, too young for work, even for jobs like sweeping people's steps. Suddenly, I couldn't wait to leave.

'Things will improve, soon, you'll see.' Hating myself, I knew it was a lie. I reached for my hat and coat. Ma got up.

'Look Phoebe, I know it's not easy where you are, with that girl. But when you moved there, I thought, I hoped that eventually we'd move there too, be a family again. But it's been over a year.'

'But things have got better, you've got new curtains, bread and money *and* I'll be back, with a nice thick blanket.'

Ma laughed and turned away, but her laugh was strangled, not sincere. *They're not a family.* I left.

She wanted us to be together and I did too, but Jacob would never agree to that. One of us had to be strong for the rest. That person was me. I knew I couldn't tell her the truth.

As I emerged onto the street, I saw it was dark, colder and bleak. I shivered. I couldn't stay with Jacob much longer, things were getting worse by the day. But where could I go? I needed the things Cross Saddle provided for Ma and the boys, and I couldn't go back to living at home. I thought again, as I'd thought before, about trying to get my job back at Milsom's, but too much time had passed since then and now I was marked by what I had done. No-one would touch me. The only option for me was the factory and I couldn't face that. What could I do?

I thought then of Clara Gilchrist, Steph's cousin, she had a big house, a huge manor all to herself. A poet's house. I could write poetry, if I lived there.

A man emerged out of the shadows, and I shrank back. The man laughed. It was Gwilym, Steph's friend.

'All alone, my dear Miss Slater?'

'Yes,' I said. 'I was just thinking...'

'About Lucienne Hall.'

I gasped. 'How did you know...' I stopped, annoyed and my voice trailed off. *Damn his stupid party trick.* 'Maybe I was,' I said, thoughtful. Gwilym smiled.

'I'm so glad I've seen you. I need your advice. Let's go for a walk.'

He took my arm and led me down the street to the river. I didn't resist. In the dark, the gas lamps flickered.

Somehow it felt like I had no choice.

15

1910 – Phoebe

I wasn't sure I trusted Gwilym.

We stood in the mist right by the river, the boats moored up. There was hardly anyone else around. I shivered.

'Here, Phoebs, have my coat.' I glared at him.

'My name's Phoebe.'

'Sure, Phoebs, whatever you say.' I sighed.

'What do you want?'

'I've just been to Issington Manor.'

So what? 'Have you?' I said.

'I've been talking to Steph's cousin.'

Now I was shocked, but interested too. 'Is she like Steph?' Gwilym laughed.

'Not one bit, she's sharp *and* restrained. I hadn't a clue what she was thinking. I'd guess she'd be ruthless if she was crossed.' I smiled.

'What were you doing there?'

'Asking her about poetry readings. Yes, I know... it sounds unlikely, but I had to say something. We're both artists, so we had that in common. She did go on about Hall a lot *and* about her father's dream.' Gwilym yawned. 'She's going to do more events next year, or so she says.' Then he grinned. 'Clara thinks we met by chance.'

'But you didn't,' I said. Gwilym nodded.

'I wanted to get to know the woman, it's part of my plan. It seems to be going well, so far. We've been for several walks by the river.'

But you've only just met her. Apparently not.

'What about Steph?' *I knew I couldn't trust him.*

'Hey, Phoebs, you don't need to worry. Steph wants to meet her cousin and I'd like to make it happen. But at the moment I'm keeping it quiet in case Clara says no.' I frowned.

'You'd better not be too nice to Clara. You might give her... expectations.' Gwilym just grinned.

'That'd soon change, when Steph turned up. And that, Phoebe, is where you come in.' *Ah ha.*

'*You* can smooth the ground with Jacob, make him see sense. And, I was wondering...'

'What?' I said, suddenly wary.

'Clara doesn't know her cousin. Perhaps you could talk to her, persuade her to meet Steph.' I stared.

'She's not going to listen to me. I'm living with her Uncle Jacob. The family's black sheep. Besides, I don't trust you.' *There, I'd said it.* Gwilym laughed.

'You don't need to trust me. Think about how it's been, lately. Steph's father is falling apart and I'm going back to Dorset soon, just after Christmas. Steph will need someone while I'm away. We know it won't be you. But it *could* be Clara, if they met.' Gwilym grinned.

'As for you, you'll need a home, when it all falls apart, which it will. Unless you'd like to go back there.' He gestured back towards Chesterton Court.

'How dare you!' I said.

But I knew he was right.

16

1911 – Phoebe

I knew I'd made a bad decision, choosing Jacob. Today, he went to see Thirza.

I'd been flattered by his attention, I'd liked him a lot *and* I wanted the life he offered, I also knew he had money to burn. Jacob was wealthy *and* he'd been fun, he took risks and made money, and he showed me a life that was different from mine. Music, good food and we laughed a lot. Not anymore.

I stood outside the drawing room at Cross Saddle House and listened to Steph playing the piano. *Playing* wasn't exactly it, her notes were all off, and the music she chose was far too modern, even for me. Worst of all, the girl never practised, she had no focus. Neither had I, not today.

How did I know he'd been to see Thirza? Jacob hadn't mentioned it. But when a man who normally drinks *doesn't* have a drink and wears his best suit, then leaves the house without saying goodbye, it has to mean something, something important. I knew it wasn't business, he was far too smart. And if he'd just been going to the bank, he would have said. Then there was the final clue, red roses in the back of the carriage. I could have screamed. Instead I said nothing. An hour later, he was back.

Thirza must have turned him down. Steph and I stared as he charged through the door and raced up the stairs. He pushed right past us without even speaking. I could feel his rage simmering. He strode into his study and slammed the door hard. Steph raised her hands and went to her room. I couldn't move. Then I walked upstairs to the study, slowly. I listened for the sound of the bottle being poured. I could almost see his hand shaking, as he knocked back whisky, glass after glass. Then I jumped as the glass smashed, crystal breaking on the tiles. It had happened before, four times this month. I couldn't help thinking of the cost.

I didn't go in. When Thirza had finally thrown him out, I'd told myself he cared for me, but now he'd gone back and I know he'd have pleaded and she'd still said no. Where was my pride?

I grabbed a bag and left the house, taking the public coach into Issington. It took forever but I didn't care. I couldn't take the carriage this time.

It was cold in the coach, all of us huddled together for warmth. I wrapped a blanket around my knees. I wouldn't be doing this journey much longer.

After the coach dropped me in town, in Midden Lane South, right by The Royale, I hurried through the streets to my Ma's. She'd been grumpy the last time I'd seen her, the weather was eating into their bones. I walked down Chesterton Court's alley, ready to weave my way round the washing, then I stopped abruptly. *Who the hell's that?*

A woman was coming out of Ma's house. She was tall and fair, too big for the space. Then Ma spoke.

'Thanks, Alice, I'm ever so grateful.' My heart hardened.

Alice, the soup bringer, the one who worked for Theo McKinver, who, apparently, according to Gwilym, was Clara's uncle, despite being of a similar age. Gwilym said they didn't speak. I didn't understand it. How could you live in a place so small and not talk to one of your family? I watched Alice, suddenly angry. How dare she tell my ma to find work! They were still talking.

'Phoebe's meant to be coming to see me, not that she always does, of course.'

Damn cheek! I nearly showed myself right then but I managed to hold back.

'And she's taken up with the painter,' startling me.

What? I thought.

'Has she?' said Alice, not looking pleased.

'She never mentions Jacob now, it's always the new one.'

That's a lie! Ma was a stirrer, she liked to tell tales. But telling them to *Alice?* I was furious. Ma was still talking.

'Honestly, Alice, I never know what that girl will do next. It's such a worry. It's just as well that I've got you.' I nearly choked.

I stared at Alice. Why was she hanging around my ma? And how did her hair look so good? Even when I used the iron my natural curl spoilt it all, especially in the mist. My eyes narrowed.

Alice looked perfect. I knew she wasn't.

'Look Mrs Slater, can I say something?'

'Anything, dear.' Ma, concerned, folded her arms.

'The painter, Gwilym, who's friends with your daughter... you should tell her to keep away from him.'

'And what business is it of yours?' Ma's voice had an edge.

'I've heard he likes to play the field.' Ma laughed.

'You needn't worry about that, dear. Phoebe can look after herself.' But Alice wasn't finished.

'I'm a friend of Clara's uncle. Clara Gilchrist, who lives at the manor.'

'So?' said Ma.

'Gwilym's taken an interest in Clara. And she's taken an interest in him.'

Has she? I thought. *Well, I did warn him.*

'Clara's on her own, Sadie, unlike your Phoebe. She needs Gwilym more.'

Ma didn't answer, I knew she was vexed. Then she sniffed. 'I don't tell my daughter who to see. And as for Miss Gilchrist, I don't know her.'

Alice touched her arm, lightly. 'Do you believe in second sight?' Ma shrugged and Alice went on.

'I used to live a long way from here. And I had... gifts. I know something about the future. No good will come of knowing the painter. Tell Phoebe to leave him alone.'

Ma's not often lost for words but she was right then. I was afraid that Alice might see me so I edged along the passage slowly, back onto the street and holed up in a nearby doorway. Could it be true? Did Alice have second sight? She was certainly strange. Seconds later, I watched her emerge from Chesterton Court and hurry off towards the Town Hall, acting as if she'd been on a mission. Perhaps she had. I swore then because I knew she spoke the truth.

I was becoming fond of Gwilym.

And I wouldn't be taking her advice.

17

1911 – Steph

I'd hoped to be gone before they got back, but no such luck. Lately, Papa had found a pub, *The Flying Fish* and when he wasn't *doing his accounts,* he liked to spend his time in there. And that's where he went after Phoebe left. I was worried.

So long as we'd had some sort of income, I was able to put up with Papa's sad ways. But now we were short and that's no wonder, he never worked. I assumed he had managers but I never saw them. Or any money. *What must Gwilym think?*

Your father might be dead, Cousin, but at least you know he cared for you. And he wasn't a drunk. We need each other, Clara. I stopped.

One day, I *would* send a letter, or go round to the house and knock on the door. *And, why not?* I sighed.

I left a scribbled note for my father, picked up my bags and walked down the stairs. The door opened. Phoebe came in.

'Oh,' I said, and dropped the bags. Phoebe paused.

'Going somewhere, Steph?' she said and glanced at my bags.

'Mama's,' I said. 'Just for a while.'

'Is it all getting too much for you?' Phoebe was smiling. I sighed.

'Yes, if you like. I'm fed up with Papa drinking and not working.' *And it's all your fault.*

Phoebe took off her gloves slowly, slinging her pretty bag onto the table. 'Don't stay away too long, Steph. Just in case *Papa* forgets you.'

'In your dreams.' Phoebe said nothing.

Phoebe was the one with the power, she had Papa's heart and ear. *But did she?* I wondered. Something was wrong. Phoebe looked weary.

'Is there anything we can do?' I said to her, in a rare rush of candour.

'Like giving him your support, you mean? Instead of running around with Gwilym.' I stared.

'Damn you,' I said. 'Papa needs me to marry, soon. To save *your* lifestyle.' I strode out of the door, quickly, slamming it shut. The door opened. I turned around.

'You forgot these.' Phoebe dropped the bags on the ground and went back in, shutting the door. I stared.

Why did I let that woman rile me? God only knew.

I did go to see Mama, taking the horse instead of the carriage, but the visit was brief.

Mama stared, amazed at me.

'You want to come back, like your father?'

'What?' I said.

'Your father wants to come back home. He told me so this morning.'

Damn him, I thought. 'What did you say?'

'I said no.'

'I don't believe it!'

Mama laughed and folded her arms. 'I don't want him back.'

So that's why Papa was so angry. 'Why ever not?' Mama ignored me.

'So why do *you* want to come home?'

'Papa's drinking all the time, neglecting the business.'

'Like he did when he was young. Proves I made the right decision.' Mama sighed.

'When he was young he had all the vices, cards and drink and women as well. I thought when we married that that would all stop, but of course it didn't. But when we moved away from here, he *did* stop drinking and did very well.'

'We should have stayed down south,' I said. Mama nodded.

'Your father was desperate to come back home. But I was worried it might mean trouble and I was right. But I would have left him anyway even if we'd never come back. I'd had enough.'

'But what about me?' Mama just laughed.

'Stephanie, dear, you're a young woman, and the way things are going you'll be married soon. So I'll tell you what I told your father, you're not coming back. This is *my* home. *You* chose to move in with your father.' Then she smiled. 'Why don't we talk of pleasanter things? How's Mr Lawson? You know you could do *much* better. And you really should have a chaperone.

I'd asked Gwilym to call at Mama's, knowing I'd be bored, but he didn't show. As the evening turned into night, I knew he wasn't coming. *Just like a man!* I went to bed earlier than normal, feeling let down, by him *and* Mama. Everything was going wrong. I dozed off. Then I woke up. Mama was banging on my door.

'Steph, get up. Please, there's a fire!'

I leapt out of bed, flung on a wrap and ran downstairs. It all seemed fine. I stared at Mama. 'Where's the fire?'

'It's not here, it's over at your father's house. Herbert's sent the carriage for us. We've got to go now. Go and get dressed! Quick, Steph!'

Mama bundled me into the carriage and we both sat back.

'How bad is the fire?'

'I don't know, but it can't be good if they've asked for us. When I think of what I said, and only this morning...' Mama put her head in her hands.

I touched her lightly on the arm. 'Don't worry, it'll be fine.' Mama said nothing.

It wasn't fine, the house was ablaze.

Dragging myself out of the carriage, I hurried towards my lovely home. Flames flickered at most of the windows. Strangely, it looked quite magnificent. I stared, transfixed, I couldn't believe it. When I'd left earlier, it had been fine.

Martha, the cook was sitting on the lawn, sobbing her heart out. I could barely hear her words.

'I did my best, I swear I did. I opened the windows, to let the smoke out.'

'You did what? That would've made the fire much worse. You *stupid* cow!'

I stared in disgust at Martha's tears. Then I walked off.

There were men all over the place, including some who'd helped before when the shed caught fire. *The shed, God! What was I thinking? Where was Papa?* Then a pane of glass exploded. I shrieked and dropped to the ground, quickly. We were all caught in a ghastly glow as light poured out from several rooms but not from the gas lamps.

'Where's Papa?' I ran back to Mama.

She was still shouting at Martha, who by now was a wreck. 'Where's Papa?' I repeated, yelling more loudly. Mama paused.

'I don't know, nobody does. He drank too much then lit the grates…'

I didn't know what she was talking about.

'He said he was cold,' Martha said, gulping, blowing her nose. 'He told me I was to the light all the fires, even though there were only the two of them in. I never thought to question him… You were right, it was my fault, for opening the windows, just like you said.' She stared at Mama. Then she started to cry again. Mama frowned and pulled me away.

'According to what I've been told just now, your father went to his dressing room, took out some shirts and set them on fire. He flung them all in the middle of the room, then piled on some more stuff, clothes, throws, whatever he could find. Then he went next door and did the same, and in the next room, and the next, burning everything he could find. Which, thanks to Martha, was more than enough.' She stared at the house. 'As you can see.'

'So where is he now?' She had to know *something*.

'I've already said, I don't know! They can't find your father, or Phoebe.'

Oh God. 'Maybe they went out,' I said. Mama looked grim.

'The pubs are all shut and we've got the carriage. Jacob's other horse is here. It's very unlikely they went out.'

'Where the hell's my father, then?' I said, panicking, turning on Mama.

'Stephanie, please,' Mama whispered, grabbing my hand. 'Everyone's doing all they can.' I snatched it away.

'No they're not!' I yelled at her. 'You're doing nothing, just like normal. I'm going to find Papa.'

'Stephanie, no!' Her voice faded as I flew across the lawn towards the house, almost tripping with my skirts. I stopped suddenly. The house roared and crackled with flames and the door was ajar. If only I hadn't gone to Mama's.

The fire hadn't reached the hall but the air was hot and thick with smoke. I stepped inside. Where should I look? I glanced towards to the drawing room, but I could see flickers under the door. I headed upstairs. Papa would probably be in his study, collapsed in a chair. If I could drag him out from there...

When I got to the top of the stairs, I realised it was worse up here. Much worse. Most of the doors off the passage were open and the noise and heat knocked me back.

Wrapping my shawl around my face, I hurried ahead, sticking my head around each door as I went. Those at the back of the house were better, most of the rooms at the front were ablaze. I pulled the nearest door closed to hold back the flames and shrieked with pain, the handle was hot. I quickly tore a piece off my shawl and wrapped it around my injured hand then carried on looking. I checked Papa's study but he wasn't there. By now I was nearing the end of the passage. The lamps were all dead and the light from the fire in the east had faded, thanks to my efforts. But I could barely see. At last, I reached Phoebe's bedroom.

'Papa, where are you?' I heard a croak.

I rushed inside and found Papa lying on the floor, near to the window. He was barely conscious. It was just like when he'd been in the shed, except that now I was alone. There was no Phoebe to help us. Where the hell was she?

I wondered if I could drag him to the window and somehow ease him onto the sill and down to the terrace. Even if I could contain his weight, it was quite a drop. I looked down at the solid stone paving and decided against it. Instead I tried a different plan. I grabbed hold of his arms.

Getting him round the bed wasn't easy, he weighed a bit more than he used to do. But at last I managed it. The smoke was really thick by now. I couldn't even see if Papa was still breathing. Struggling with each gasping breath, I dragged my father towards the door. Then I heard a crack.

The door to the dressing room shuddered and collapsed, bringing some debris and the door frame with it. My coughing got worse. We had to get out of here and fast. The door frame was burning. I pulled and tugged at Papa some more, but the door had fallen across his leg and I couldn't move it. It was too hot. Somehow, I had lost my shawl. I ripped my skirt in a desperate bid to grab the wood, but the skirt was silk and just shrivelled. What could I do?

I glanced up again and saw flames, closing in on the tragic room. I had to get out.

After one last attempt to save Papa, I whispered goodbye and clambered out, over the debris, and into the passage. Which way was out? I couldn't breathe. I looked back the way

I'd come, but somehow the flames had escaped my chains. The fire was worse. There was no way out.

I turned left, away from the flames, and stumbled along, trying not to touch the walls. Then I remembered – the servants' stairs. They were stone and wouldn't burn. I hadn't got long.

As I made my way downstairs, I heard the sounds of the house burning. Cross Saddle House, raw with pain, creaking and heaving, a terrible sound. My hands hurt and my chest hurt and I felt as if I was going to choke. But I had to keep going.

When I finally got downstairs, no help was in sight. The kitchen was ablaze and the door to outside refused to budge. I banged and screamed but no-one would hear me. Nobody even knew I was there. The door to outside might burn in time, but the kitchen's flames would get me first. I knew then I was going to die. I sank to the cold stone floor, despairing. *Please God, let it be quick.*

It was then I heard her voice.

18

1911 – Phoebe

It was cold in the cellar, freezing cold and dark as well, but I knew I'd be safe. Safe from the fire. I could hear the chaos upstairs, glass breaking, timber creaking, soon the house I knew would be gone. How had that happened? Then I heard someone scream.

I paused, listened, then I heard it again. God, it was Steph! I had to go up.

I climbed up the rickety ladder, propped against the cellar wall, and pushed on the trapdoor. I knew it was risky. The ladder was long and the cellar was deep, meant for wine, climbing down here had tested my nerves. Climbing back up was even worse, what would I find? Assuming I could get the door open. But I'd heard Steph. I had no choice.

I pushed on the trapdoor and it opened easily. *Thank God for that.* Then I peered out.

At first, all I could see was smoke. Flickers of flame and toasted wood. How would they find me, all but buried under the rubble? I nearly climbed out, I'd rather be dead than buried alive. Then I saw Steph.

Steph, bless her, looked a fright, her skirt was torn and her hair was down and she was floundering, hysterical, screaming. Screaming and shouting, but I could shout louder. Ma and I had had some scraps. 'Steph!' I yelled. 'Stephanie, here. I'm over here!'

At last she heard me, which was just as well, as the fire drew closer. She clambered towards me. We clasped each other's hands.

'Now, Steph, you've got to be brave and climb down here.'

'What? No.' She whimpered and stared, streaked and pale. 'I can't do that. I hate cellars, rats and things.'

Can't or won't? 'Do you want to die?'

Steph moaned. 'You're on the ladder, I'll fall off.'

'No,' I said, squeezing her hand. 'It's a long way down, but you'll be fine. I'll go first.' Steph squeaked.

'No, Phoebe I can't, really, I'm frightened of heights.'

'I'll hold the ladder. Make it stay steady. Then you'll be safe.' But Steph was still shaking her head. I was starting to get annoyed.

'If you don't do it soon, we'll *both* die. Can't you see how close the fire is?'

Steph glanced back and screamed in fright. The girl was a wreck. I had to take charge. I grabbed her wrist.

'Listen to me. We're both going down this ladder and I'll go first to keep it steady. Wait until I call your name, then step on. Don't look down, just keep going. You can do it.' Steph whimpered. I swore, under my breath.

The girl was alive in a burning building and she was afraid to use a ladder. Just my luck.

'Don't be a fool,' I yelled at her. 'I'm going down.' I backed down the ladder, carefully.

I knew time was tight. Once she was down, I had to climb back up again and close off the trapdoor. Assuming I could.

But now Steph had made her decision she wasn't prepared to wait for me. I was halfway down when she took her first step, causing the ladder to judder and shake. I tried not to shriek.

I made my way to the bottom quickly. I thought we'd be fine.

The ladder was old, not fixed to the wall, and the cellar was deep but for all Steph was such a princess, she had been plucky. I hadn't allowed for what she'd been through.

It was dark in the cellar and all I could see was her shape up above as we both hurried down. The ladder was shaking far too much, then I heard Steph's skirt rip. Maybe it got caught or something. Steph screamed, a piercing scream and, at that point, I thought it best to jump. As I dragged myself up I saw her fall, I couldn't save her. Then I heard an awful crack. Stone floor, head, bone.

Oh, God.

I knew then, there was no way back.

Nevertheless, I had to go back, climb the ladder and close the trapdoor, keeping the flames and smoke at bay. Keeping us safe. But I knew I was alone.

19

1911 – Phoebe

I sat in the cellar for what seemed like hours, waiting for the nightmare to end. I smelt the smoke and felt the heat, even though the cellar was cold. Every so often I stretched out a hand, and touched Steph's face, but she was cold too, colder than me. The fire had claimed her. It might yet claim me.

Occasionally, I'd hear a crash, and in my fear I'd hunker down, although I was safe. Nothing could touch me in this space. It was much more likely I'd be trapped, buried alive under the debris, left alone to die with Steph. I tried not to think about it. There were times that night I wished I was her. I also wished I'd left the trapdoor open.

Eventually, the grid in the wall showed a dim grey light and I knew, finally, dawn was close. *At last this awful night is done.* The house seemed to have settled down, so wearily I climbed back to the top. What if I couldn't open the trapdoor? The wood was too hot so I went back down and tore off a piece of Steph's sleeve and wrapped the cloth around my hands. I knew she wouldn't be needing it.

I managed to get the trapdoor up and somehow, incredibly, pulled myself out. I blinked in the light.

The stone floor was strewn with debris, rubble and dust but the house was still standing. Even the door to outside was intact. I hurried towards it eagerly, but heavy and old, charred and still smoking, the door wouldn't budge. So I walked towards the kitchen. It was a shell. I staggered across the hazy room, clambered onto a bench and eased myself out of the kitchen window. I dropped to the ground, hungry for air.

It promised to be a lovely day. The wind was cold and I was shivering, but the sky was bright and a piercing blue. Sunshine would come. Dazed and exhausted, I stumbled across the scarred lawn, getting as far as I could from the house and sank down by a tree. A spiral of smoke rose from the building, then a tile fell off and I shuddered. I was alone. I couldn't see any flames from here, perhaps the fire had burnt itself out. I wondered then, as I had before, where Jacob was. *Probably still inside*, I thought. If only I hadn't been so angry...

Someone, a man, was walking towards me, I could see his feet. I glanced up and it was Gwilym. I was amazed, he seemed like a ghost. I think he felt much the same. He lifted me up, light as a feather.

'Phoebe,' he said, pulling me close, stroking my hair. 'Thank God, you're alive.' But I had to tell him.

'Steph,' I said, 'I'm afraid she didn't... make it. She's in the cellar, she fell off a ladder.' We stared at each other.

'God,' said Gwilym, 'what have you been through?' We sat together, silent, for a while. I didn't want to talk. And then Gwilym spoke.

'We'd better get her out, I think, if it's not too hard. Perhaps you can show me where she is.'

'Where's everyone else?' I asked him.

'At the Flying Fish, all except Thirza, she went home, and Martha too, once Dr Lewis had stopped her screaming. He gave her quite a dose of brandy. Christ, what a noise!'

I smiled, in spite of it all. 'Thirza went home and left Steph here?' Gwilym nodded.

'Yeah, I know. A bit of a cold one, if you ask me.'

'What about Jacob?'

Gwilym shrugged and shook his head. 'The cellar,' he said.

It wasn't easy getting her out, she was taller than me and her clothes were much thicker, those that were left, layers of froth. Gwilym buried his face in her hair, then in her neck, kissing it lightly and I turned away, feeling defeated. I'd failed

Jacob's daughter. Then Gwilym picked her up and hoisting her carefully onto his shoulder he climbed back up the ladder to the light, one rung at a time. He made it look easy.

Once we were back outside, Gwilym laid Steph down on the grass and we knelt down beside her. I covered the gash on her head with hair and made her look tidy. Apart from her clothes, which were ripped and shrivelled, she could have been asleep. Then I slipped on her shoes. Despite everything, she still looked like a princess. I thought about how we could have been friends if we'd trusted each other. Gwilym went to hitch up the cart.

Once we'd got Steph on board, I clambered up and sat next to Gwilym, thinking about how unreal this was, as the horse moved slowly down the lane. Gwilym and I, up early and alone, on a bright fresh morning with nowhere to go. I knew in my heart, Jacob was dead.

'Clara won't ever meet Steph now.' Gwilym said, softly. *And you won't marry her.*

Gwilym had wanted the cousins to meet, but Alice had said that Clara liked Gwilym. Which cousin had Gwilym preferred? Now it didn't matter.

'Yes, right.' I paused, went on. 'You like Clara Gilchrist.' Wondering what he'd say to that.

'Yes, I do,' he said, 'surprisingly, although I'd planned to like Stephanie more.'

So that was the plan. A cousin for Steph but for Gwilym, the gain was much greater, a wife and a house. The magnificent manor. I laughed then, it was probably hysteria, but I was young and still alive, and Jacob, well, he'd made me feel old. *Unsuitable.*

Nothing like fire for a fresh start.

I glanced across at the man sitting next to me and put my hand on his arm. We were still trotting down the lane. The horse stopped.

'Your plan could still happen,' I said, softly. 'Or, part of it could.'

'What do you mean?'

'I know Steph's… gone for good, but only you and I know that. It could be our secret. Given that Clara hasn't met Steph. Yet…' I said. Gwilym frowned.

'You're assuming Jacob's dead.'

My hand went to a drawstring purse I kept for change and handkerchiefs. Slowly, I pulled out Jacob's pocket watch, I'd found the watch near Steph's body. She must have been holding it. I showed it to Gwilym.

'Of course there's Thirza,' I said, thinking.

'Clara's never met her,' Gwilym said quickly. 'And Issington Manor is miles away.' He smiled at me, a sly smile which made me feel guilty. I stared back. Neither of us said anything more.

I realised then, that the morning, though bright and full of promise, was edged in ice.

20

1852 – Lucienne Hall

Augustin went away to work, that was expected, he had commissions. But he always came back.

'I miss the place,' he'd say to Lucienne. 'It's a great little town.'

'Only the town?' She'd smile at him.

'And, the house, of course. The finest house in all the land. Issington Manor.'

'You'd better not build any finer,' she'd say, and he would laugh and promise he wouldn't.

But Lucienne knew he came back for her. Even though they were just good friends.

The best of friends, Augustin insisted, bringing her flowers and stories of buildings, while she read out the poems she'd written, often for him, though she never said.

The poems she'd written in Issington Manor, the home of the poet.

Augustin had brought success to her door.

When he returned after being away, she never asked if he had lovers anywhere else, or if he'd built houses for some of those women, she didn't want to know. She wouldn't break the spell they had. She knew he was here on *his* terms. Lucienne had poetry and success and that was enough. Mostly.

But one long week, when he was away, the poems dried up. There was no more magic, it had all gone, and Lucienne felt bereft, despair. Lucienne *never* felt like this. There were always words, if raw, unhoned, she could polish them up and make them shine, like the precious stones they were to her. She tried *everything*.

She took herself away for a week and that didn't help.

She invited people to stay and hated it, every minute, and that didn't help.

She took to drinking, then she tried smoking, coughed a lot and gave it up. Gave up tea, gave up wine, gave up almost everything, she couldn't even sleep, her mind was too active, restless, unhappy, but still, nothing helped. Then Augustin returned.

'Thank God you're back!' She burst into tears and fell into his arms.

They went to bed, almost at once, and there they stayed for three long days and even more nights, or so it seemed to Lucienne. It was better, even, than in the beginning.

But then, one morning, early on, when all of the rest of the world was asleep, he stroked her cheek and said to her, 'I have to go.'

Lucienne, shocked, sat up at once. 'What? Now? It's the middle of the night!'

'Yes,' he said, his smile fading. 'I only stayed this long for you. But I'll come back.'

'You'd better,' she yelled, angry and wishing he'd warned her of this, and suddenly afraid, as she always was when he went away. Then she was quiet, much later, after he'd left, after she'd watched his carriage leave.

But the magic worked, because after he'd gone, Lucienne got to work again, she pinned back her hair and wrote more poems. The best poems she'd written for a long time. She vowed then, that when he returned, she'd get him to stay for longer this time.

21

1911 – Phoebe

We buried her body in the river. I can't believe the two of us did that, it felt as if I'd actually killed her, which, of course, in a way I had. I'd killed her story.

We took her down to the river at night, went under the bridge. 'We have to be careful,' I told Gwilym, 'the lads sleep in the boats in the summer, they do it for a dare.'

'Well, it's not summer now,' Gwilym said sharply and I knew he was angry. Angry with Steph because she was dead, but also with me, for what we were doing. But we still did it.

We put her in a rowing boat, moored up by the bank. We could have used a working boat but I knew such boats would be missed and searched for. So, instead we chose something insubstantial. Getting her in the boat was hard.

'The damn thing's moving about too much!' Gwilym swore as he eased her in. I was trying to hold the boat steady.

'Shush!' I said, and glared at him. We'd both gone down to the river disguised. I was wearing gardening clothes and had my hair tied back. I looked like a boy.

We sweated and tugged and then she was in, the boat bobbing about on the river. We were both half-soaked. Thankfully, there wasn't much moon that night. We threw in rocks to weigh the boat down, Gwilym had drilled a couple of holes, just to make sure. As the boat begin to fill, he cut the mooring rope with a knife and waded further into the water, giving the thing a vicious shove. Off it floated into the night. Gwilym grabbed my hand.

'Bye, Steph,' I whispered.

'Bye, Phoebe.' Gwilym turned to me and grinned. 'You're Steph now.'

Yes, I was.

Having lived with Steph at Cross Saddle House, I knew quite a bit about her, and what I didn't know, Gwilym did. I was Stephanie Gilchrist now, Steph to my friends, and Phoebe, well, she died in the fire. Or drowned in the river, if the body turned up.

'She couldn't cope with losing Jacob,' Gwilym said, sadly, '*and* the girl was a little deranged. Only a shop girl, after all.'

'Ha!' I said, and slapped him, hard. 'Phoebe was special.'

'I think Steph's pretty special,' Gwilym grinned, then we left the river and went to a hostelry miles away where nobody knew us, and we got drunk. We raised a toast to absent friends.

'To Steph!' said Gwilym.

'To Steph,' I said. Then I paused and frowned. 'Imagine what it's like for Thirza, not even knowing what happened to Steph. Always assuming she died in the fire.' I could feel my heart race. 'What if Thirza turns up at the manor?' Gwilym looked doubtful.

'Thirza's house is miles away and if *your* daughter died in a fire, would you want to meet her cousin, the one who lived and got the house?'

'No,' I said, but I was still worried. Gwilym rubbed my arm, roughly.

'*If* she turns up, we'll make sure it's all fine, once we're established.'

'You'll be hundreds of miles away, working in Dorset. I'll be alone.'

'It'll be better you being on your own. That way, you can get to know Clara. Trust me, Phoebs, it'll be fine. Clara's not a bit like Steph. She's a real pussy cat.'

'Cats have claws,' I said, sharply, *I* was the one who was having doubts now. Thanks to my ma.

She'd been furious.

'So I'm meant to disown you, am I?'

'No,' I said. 'Calm down Ma. Now things will be better for us, I'll be much better off. I've got a new name and hopefully soon a brand new home. You'll get more blankets now,' I said, '*and* they'll be nicer.' Ma sniffed.

'That's not funny.' Then she went on.

'What do I say to everyone then? When they ask what happened to you?'

'Tell them she died... in the fire probably. Nobody's sure.'

Ma looked grim. 'And what do I do if the boat turns up?'

'That won't happen. But if it does, you pretend it's me and cry a lot. Honestly, Ma, you don't need to worry. Steph won't even look like Steph after a while *and* we dressed her in some of my clothes.' Ma frowned.

'Alice was right. No good's come of knowing that man.'

'Nonsense, Ma, it was my idea. And I did try to save Steph, truly I did. It wasn't my fault she fell off the ladder. She should have waited.' Ma frowned.

'I don't like it, Phoebe, not one bit. Alfie and Seth thinking you're dead and Steph's ma Thirza, she's still alive. What about her?' I sighed.

'Trust me Ma, it'll be fine. I'll tell the boys when they get older, when I can be sure they won't tell anyone and as for Thirza...' I trailed off. She was the one who bothered me.

'It's just not right. And Alice said...'

'Damn Alice,' I said, sharply. I hated Alice, the interfering cow. 'I hope you haven't told her anything.' Ma shook her head.

But then I remembered something else. Alice was friendly with Steph's cousin Clara. *What if she turns up at the manor?*

Alice hadn't known Steph, not by sight, nor me either, as far as I knew. But all the same...

'What?' said Ma, looking at me.

'Promise me you won't say anything, about Steph *or* me, especially to Alice.' I glared at her.

'Remember, I'm dead.'

22

1911 – Clara

Issington Manor

Dear Aunt Vi

Gwilym has gone away to work, somewhere in Dorset. Don't ask me where.

Of course, I know he has to work, he's got a commission, and that's because his portraits are good, *and* he promised to write, every week, but men never do. Grandfather used to work away and he never wrote. Or, so Father said.

Gwilym's coming back in the summer but that seems an age.

Things are starting to wake up here, at the manor, despite the cold weather. The garden is showing some signs of life. I'll have to get my easel out. *But, wait, what's that?*

Clara got to her feet slowly, it was Mabel's day off. She padded her way across to the hall, thinking about her letter to her aunt. She wanted it finished and sent today. She could hear knocking on the door to the Palm House. Clara turned and hurried back the way she'd come. She walked through the Palm House and opened the door. A woman stood there.

'There's no need to bang on the glass. The door's round the corner. What do you want?'

'Are you Clara Gilchrist?'

Clara studied the shorter woman, who was plainly dressed with wavy hair. The woman looked a little harassed. 'What if I am? And you're...?'

'Stephanie.'

'Stephanie who?' Clara said sharply, her heart racing. *It couldn't be her.*

'Stephanie Gilchrist, the woman said, smiling and her face lit up. I'm Stephanie Gilchrist and I'm your cousin.'

Well, Aunt, what can I say?

I can't believe you haven't met Steph, but given the trouble my uncle was in and how the two brothers fell out, it's hardly surprising. I'm sad to say it shames me still, poor Uncle Jacob. Steph told me about that night, how Uncle's drinking led to the fire and how she went inside to save him, tried and failed. But she found his watch, it's all she has. And now the poor girl's lost her mother, mother and daughter barely speak.

'But why not?' I'd said to Steph. 'You'll need her more than ever now, after what's happened.' Steph bit her lip.

'Yes, I know, but I can't forgive her. Papa realised he'd been wrong and he begged Mama to take him back, but she said no. If she'd said yes, he'd still be alive.'

'You don't know that.'

'Of course I do! She was the one who threw him out and look what happened. Now he's dead!'

Honestly Aunt, I could have cried.

'What happened to... *her*?' I said, meaning Phoebe, the real cause of all the trouble. Stephanie shrugged.

'Who cares? Can't we talk about something else?' I nodded.

'This must be your home,' I said, 'like Grandfather wanted.' I took off my shawl. 'Turn around.'

'Why?' she said, sounding suspicious.

'Never mind why. Just do it.' Then I covered her eyes with the shawl and tied it. She couldn't see.

'What are you doing?' she said, panicking.

'You're going to have a guided tour, but I want you to sense the manor, not see it. Then you'll really get to know it. As you know, I'm an artist.'

'Yes,' said Steph, sounding hollow. She put her hand to her eyes.

Thinking back, I must have been crazy, putting a blindfold over her eyes, after the fire. But Steph was plucky. She didn't take the blindfold off.

After we'd finished the rooms downstairs we stopped in the hall.

Now for the first floor.

'No,' said Steph. 'I've had enough.'

'Nonsense,' I said, 'here, take my arm.' I guided my cousin up the stairs and into one of the first floor rooms, a wonderful room with a view of the church.

'Are we done?'

'Nearly,' I said, leading her next to a spare bedroom, one that looked across the park. I took off the blindfold.

'Oh!' she said, and blinked in the light. 'What a lovely room.' It was large and bright.

'This can be yours,' I said to Steph. 'This is your home now.'

'Oh, I don't know.' Steph looked uneasy.

'Can you live at Cross Saddle House?' Steph looked sad and shook her head.

'Well, that's your answer.'

'But you don't know me... '

'You're my cousin, that's enough.'

Steph suddenly looked as if she might faint. I smiled.

'Why don't we go down to the kitchen? Mabel's out but I can make tea. She always makes it far too weak.' I felt reborn.

'Then,' I said, 'after the tea, we'll go for a walk around the garden. There's plenty to see despite the cold. You won't need the blindfold.'

Steph laughed, a shaky laugh. 'Thank you,' she said. But her face was still pale.

23

1911 – Phoebe

It was a glorious, bright morning. Not unlike that previous time when Gwilym and I had driven away. Warmer of course, now it was spring. We stood outside Cross Saddle House.

'Oh, God,' said Clara. 'Steph, it's terrible.' I nodded.

'Yes,' I said, 'it's terrible to look at,' and it damn well was. Much of the house was a burnt out shell, the rooms where we'd spent most of our time and those where the servants had lived and slept, up in the attic. The kitchen downstairs was dark and hollow, its guts ripped out. I could still smell the smoke. Clara walked across the lawn which was also burnt with bits of green, and picked up some wood. It was probably from a window sill. Why had we come here? Clara looked up.

'It seems worse, now that we're here. '

Yes, it did.

The rest of the house was also damaged but more together and as we stared, a curtain fluttered in the breeze. It was Steph's room. I knew I'd never go in there again.

I stared hard, as if I might see her, standing at the window, watching, some kind of ghost, but all I saw were her flowery curtains, ripped, in shreds, but still too bright and far too fussy for my plain taste. I felt a pang. Stephanie Gilchrist, just a girl, she hadn't even lived but I would live, in her place. I'd knew I'd make a better Steph.

'What will happen to the house now?'

'It'll all go to Thirza,' I said, without thinking.

'Don't you want to see your mother? As she lives so near to here.' I shook my head.

'No,' I said, firmly. *What would Thirza say if she saw me?*

'Do you want to go round the back?' I nodded.

I knew it would be worse, seeing my beautiful, charred garden and seeing the door that led to inside, led to the cellar.

'It'll be better after a while,' Clara assured me, walking me round the house to the back and she was right. It was hard to look but Cross Saddle House was still my home. I'd loved this house with all my heart, Chesterton Court couldn't compare. But I hadn't known how much I'd cared until it was gone. A damn sight more than I'd ever cared for Jacob. I turned away, abruptly. Now, there was Issington Manor.

And Gwilym.

As we walked towards the carriage, I glanced across at Clara's horse. Wondering what became of Buzz. At least he'd survived.

'In time you'll forgive her,' Clara said, softly, talking of Thirza, and I felt a sudden twinge of guilt, for missing a house more than my lover. And for what I'd done to Thirza, who'd never know what had happened to her daughter. Not that knowing would bring Steph back. I hardened my heart.

At least I'd tried to save Steph. We passed the old shed, which, ironically, was still standing, despite both fires. If only I hadn't dragged Jacob out...

Clara and I climbed into the carriage and we set off slowly down the road. But as we turned into the lane, I realised I'd left my shawl behind. 'Stop!' I yelled. It was only a shawl but it mattered to me. It had been Steph's.

Once the carriage had drawn to a halt, I clambered out and walked back to the house. I stopped, shocked.

There was a carriage where ours had been. It was black, more sombre, more formal and it looked expensive. As I stared, a woman got out, hatted and gloved, and made her way towards Cross Saddle House. I knew it was Thirza.

I'd not come across Thirza much, but from the distance she seemed much smaller and a lot more fragile. It can't have been easy, losing her daughter *and* her husband, known she'd thrown her husband out. Even though the fault wasn't hers. I suddenly wanted to run after her and shout, loudly. 'I tried to save Steph. I'm *so* sorry.' Of course I didn't.

I stood and watched her do what I'd done, stare at the house then go round the back, where I couldn't follow. I wondered if she'd find my shawl and know it was Steph's. I hoped she wouldn't.

If I hadn't taken up with Jacob, he and Steph would still be alive. I'd be at Milsom's and Thirza wouldn't have lost her family. All because I'd wanted the status. It was my fault.

I turned away and hurried back towards our carriage, as fast as I could in my brand new clothes. Clothes Clara had bought from Milsom's. I hated them all.

When I got back to the carriage I was crying.

Clara, being Clara, didn't ask why.

It wasn't the first time I'd been back.

Three days after the fire, I drove to the house once the sun was up. I hoped I wouldn't be seen that early. I hadn't been willing to go back at night.

I walked round to the back and managed to get in by the back door. I breathed in the scorched smell of fire. The flames had taken my life away.

You were already thinking of leaving. Yes, I was.

I climbed the servants' heavy stone steps. I knew they'd be safe. When I reached the first floor landing, I couldn't help gasp, it was worse than I thought. A door had opened into the passage but the door was now damaged. Most of the passage was still as it was, but where the gallery crossed the hall, where we could look down to the floor below, most the railings were damaged or gone.

Jacob's room was on my right, I couldn't go in. What was I doing here? I wanted to get to Steph's room but that was further along the passage, past the gallery. I couldn't do it.

I walked along the corridor slowly, tiptoed really, step after step. I didn't know if the floor would hold. I'd run along here so many times, mostly after Jacob, but now it was bleak and charred, a ruin. Then I reached the dangerous part. Just a few feet without any railings, then I'd be fine. I was numb with fear. A wall to my right and a drop to my left. What if I slipped, stumbled and fell? That horrible night came flooding back.

When I finally made it to Steph's room, I believed I'd faced the worst. But I was wrong. I stared at what remained of her desk, where she'd written her letters to Clara. She'd never sent them, but I'd read them all, after she'd thrown them into the bin. I somehow imagined they were still there. Each letter I'd read had made me sad, apart from one where she'd called me a slut. That made me laugh.

I realised then that Steph had been lonely and I could have filled that space with fun, had I been kinder, had we been friends. It never happened.

I got on with the job.

Clambering carefully over debris, walking through dust, I made my way into Steph's dressing room. Flakes of paint clung to my coat and some of the wood I touched was still warm. I stared at her clothes. Many of them were ruined or damaged, by heat or by water thrown by the men, but some could be saved. I was good with a needle. Ma had taught me all she knew. I hated sewing, which was why I didn't want Ma to do it, but now it would be just a job, something to keep the wolf from the door.

As well as her clothes, I also took shoes, they would be loose, as Steph had been tall and broader than me, but I could pad them out to fit. I picked up some jewellery, three rings and a necklace, they were all I could find. I didn't feel guilty. I couldn't see Thirza coming up here and when, months later, I saw her that morning at Cross Saddle House, with her carriage and veil, I still couldn't see it. I needed Steph's things.

Not for the money, though that would be useful, but mostly because I *was* Steph now. Her possessions were my possessions, and Clara her cousin, was *my* cousin.

As Issington Manor would be mine too.

PART THREE

1

1911 – Phoebe

Summer was running towards us fast and Clara was worried. Clara was obsessed with poetry. We were getting ready for this year's events. All in honour of Lucienne Hall.

Frederic, her father, had plans for the manor, he wanted to turn it into a library, a centre for scholars. People would come from far and wide just to learn about Lucienne Hall. I'd already heard some of this from Jacob.

I tried not to laugh.

Clara frowned, she knew I wasn't convinced by the story. I sobered up.

Not that I was against poetry, far from it, although Steph wasn't keen and neither is Clara. It's her father's dream that matters to her. All the same, she was constantly busy, planning all the special events.

Alice told me I had to work harder if I wanted to achieve his dream.

I scowled. *Alice again.*

I watched Clara walk upstairs to her room at the front with its view of the church. Thinking about how it could be a room in Hall's library, *if* she succeeded. It seemed a long way off. What could I do?

I'd have to start with reading some poems. It wasn't as if I didn't like books.

Jacob had said he liked that about me, that I was different and 'not like the rest.' By which he meant the rest of his tarts. He'd meant to be kind but his words made me angry and that night I'd gone back home and read Marie Corelli's new novel.

I hadn't moved into Cross Saddle then. *I'll show him,* I thought. But now I needed to read Hall's poems.

I went down to the basement, taking a notebook and something to write with. It was hard going down there, the steps were stone like at Cross Saddle House, though quite a bit wider. At the bottom was a stairwell. I focused purely on getting to the study, the Lucienne Hall room, as Clara liked to call it. Frankly, I thought that was a mouthful. I opened the door.

The room was a mess. Three of the walls were piled high with papers, some of them loose, some in brown folders. Most of the papers were sitting on shelves, wooden and rickety. The sort Herbert might have made. I couldn't see Sproat, Clara's gardener, making shelves. There were books as well, by various authors. They all looked so boring. Frederic bless him (I couldn't think of the man as my uncle) had wanted Hall's library to be about books, not just about Hall. I had to agree.

How much poetry does one need? And all by the same poet? I was going to change that.

Light streamed into the room. The window looked towards the road, not that I could see that much, being down in the basement. But when I heaved the window open, after climbing on the desk, I could smell the cut grass. The fresh smell of spring. Horses passed by. I smiled.

Five minutes later, breathing in dust as well as fresh air, I pulled up a chair and started to read. If I was going to write my own poems, I'd better read some of Hall's work first. How hard could it be to write poetry?

Harder than I thought.

I read a few poems, then a few more, and then I read some by other poets. Then I had a go. It was *rubbish.* I had another try. Still rubbish.

Several hours later, I was fed up. Writing poetry wasn't that easy, even if the verse seemed simple. Then Clara called to come for lunch.

I put my books down, I was glad to stop. Thinking that now I respected Hall more, I walked upstairs to my room to change. Looking at Steph's old clothes in the closet, sewing didn't seem so bad.

The food at Issington Manor was fine. When I first moved into Cross Saddle House I loved not having to cook each day. But Jacob had traditional tastes and the meals were dull and I preferred exotic food. Clara, I thought, had quite a lot in common with her uncle. But as I felt more at home at Issington manor, I charmed Flora, Clara's cook and got her to be a bit more daring. Clara looked pained.

'I suppose *this* is down to you. Poor Flora wouldn't dare.' She toyed with some rice. I smiled and Clara went on.

'Well, Steph, you are adventurous.'

More than you know. Clara's thoughts turned to Hall.

'How have you been getting on?'

'Slowly,' I said, 'there's so much to look at. Have you looked through everything?' Clara laughed.

'What do you think? That room was Father's, I couldn't go in there after he died. I just couldn't bear it. And now, well, it's so cluttered, I almost lose the will to live. I stick to the familiar works, the ones people know. They seem to work well. Most of the older stuff is just jottings.' I nodded.

I wasn't sure I agreed with her and I'd had an idea, so I changed the subject. 'What shall we do this afternoon?'

'Don't you want to do more work?' I frowned and Clara laughed and patted my arm.

'Poor Steph, I'm only joking. Let's go for a walk. It's a lovely day.'

'Let's do some gardening.' Clara looked shocked.

'Have you gone mad? That's Sproat's job. He'd never forgive me interfering. I like to keep my staff, Steph. Who'd do the hedge trimming if he left?'

'I would,' I said, but she wasn't having it.

'I know what we'll do, we'll go on the river. I've got a boat.'

'No!' I said quickly, rather too sharply. 'Let's go for a walk, like you just said. I'm not that fond of going on the river.'

Not anymore.

2

1911 – Phoebe

I was back in the poetry room. That's what *I* called it. Such a funny old space.

I often worked downstairs in the evenings, sometimes until late. It was May so the days were long and warm and long but even after it became dark, I could still see. We had electric lights! It was so modern.

We'd had gas lamps at Cross Saddle House, Jacob being traditional. At Chesterton Court, Ma used candles, she would have loved electric lights.

'Candles are dangerous,' I told her, repeatedly.

'But I need to see. And, if I'm going to take in sewing...'

'You're not,' I said, changing the subject.

I liked being in the poetry room. Clara was kind, but frankly, dull, and I was bored being Stephanie Gilchrist. Because I'd known her, it wasn't hard, but sometimes I just wanted to be me. So apart from going to the poetry room, I'd slip out at night, occasionally. To visit my ma.

Chesterton Court hadn't changed that much, it was still pretty grim and Ma looked tired and even more careworn. I wanted her to live at the manor along with my brothers.

Being at the manor wasn't that different from Cross Saddle House, I still had to put on a front and be grateful. But the pickings were better, much better and Clara rarely stinted on anything. We were at lunch.

'What do you do in the Lucienne Hall room every night?' Clara asked, stirring her tea. It wasn't as strong as the tea back home.

'Sort out the papers,' I said mildly. 'It's a long job.' Clara frowned.

'No-one's looked at those papers for years. When he got ill, Father left the room to me and I never bothered. I only need her later work. Maybe I should take a look.' I panicked.

'No, Clara, there's really no need. Not when I can do all that, it makes me feel useful. And,' I hesitated, 'I've written some poems.'

'Really?' said Clara. 'I'd like to hear them. Let's take tea in the library today. Then you can read to me.' She jumped up.

'No, wait, they're not very good...'

Clara ignored me so, wishing I'd never mentioned the poems, I followed her slowly into the hall. Clara could be stubborn, just like Steph. She turned round.

'What does it matter if they're not great? Hall wasn't born a poet, nobody is. She practised, perfected and *then* she got better. Why shouldn't you?'

Ha! I thought, perversely annoyed that she'd believed me. *They're not that bad.*

So, nervously, I read one out, then another, then a third. I was getting into my stride. Clara said nothing. I felt deflated.

'It was just a little bit of fun,' I said. 'I know I'm not a poet like Hall.'

'No,' said Clara, 'maybe not. But there's something there.' She frowned, silent, and then she smiled. 'I know what it is! It's as if Lucienne Hall has been giving you lessons.'

Later on, we sat on the lawn. It was another warm, sunny day and I knew I'd never tire of the manor, of gardens and freedom, being able to write, instead of having to work for a living. I'd thought I'd loved Jacob, I'd liked him a lot when I first met him, but maybe I'd just liked the life. The sun disappeared.

Clara glanced across at me. 'I felt so alone before, until you arrived. Now you're here, I've got a cousin and a friend. Thank God you turned up.'

I nodded and smiled at her, but I was thinking about my poems and how I'd improve them. The weather was changing rapidly. It started to spit.

'We ought to go in,' I said to Clara, reaching for my brand new shawl which had replaced Steph's old one.

'No, wait! Don't get up yet. I remember dancing in the rain after we'd had our best event ever. I was so happy.'

'I'm not doing that,' I insisted. 'Of course you were happy, you'd achieved what your father wanted, a bigger and better poetry event.'

'Pity it took so long,' said Clara.

'Maybe,' I said, 'but this year there'll be no stopping us.'

Clara laughed. Then she grabbed my arm and made me wait as the rain poured down. Steph would have pulled her arm away and run inside but I resisted and felt the needles pound my face, sharp but still warm. I almost enjoyed it.

Clara was right, now she wasn't alone anymore and I was a better cousin to her than Steph would have been. There were just the two of us, but one day there'd be someone else.

Someone called Gwilym.

3

1911 – Phoebe

Clara was right, Lucienne Hall *had* been giving me lessons, lessons in editing.

Working through the overcrowded room, I'd uncovered piles of junk, jottings and ramblings. It wasn't all rubbish. Amongst the papers and folders I'd found, I'd discovered a cache of Hall's poems. I was sure there was more.

I needed somewhere safe to keep them. So I asked Sproat to fix the lock on the old desk's drawer. He did a good job. Now Hall's work would be safe from Clara.

When I'd read my poems to her, I'd been testing out my style, but also her knowledge of Lucienne's work. Did she know who I was quoting, who I was editing? No, she didn't.

I'd taken a couple of Lucienne's poems, early work which nobody knew and made them my own, a tweak or two here, a word or two there and soon they were mine. They weren't of course, but others would think so and if Clara didn't realise what she'd heard, she can't have read the original work.

It was hardly surprising.

There was so much stuff in that room and every time I moved some of it, I disturbed even more. I shuddered, thinking of Cross Saddle's cellar, so much worse than being in here, but all the same... I pushed my restless thoughts away. If I could be Steph and fool Clara, then why shouldn't I be a poet? I smiled to myself. But now for the present. We had plans.

Tomorrow was our open day and Clara had it all arranged, but I was nervous. What would I do if Alice turned up? I couldn't take the chance. So I'd asked Ma to come to the event and let me know if she saw Alice. I didn't want her there. Clara was going to read some of Hall's poems. then I'd be reading one of my own. Supposedly.

The one I'd picked and tweaked a bit was one of Hall's poems about the manor. Her only home in Issington Halt. Clara had told me all about it.

'Hall vanished and nobody knows what happened to her. Nobody even saw her leave. As far as I'm concerned that adds to the mystery. Several years later, Grandfather moved in.'

'Did he know Hall?'

'Apparently so, or so he told Father, though not very well. He was often away on commissions, like Gwilym.' Clara smiled. I swallowed.

'Coffee?' I said.

The day went well, the weather held out and loads of people turned up to hear us, many taking poems away that Mabel had copied out. Most importantly, we'd made money.

Alice hadn't put in an appearance.'

'What a waste of time,' Ma said, grumbling, later on.

'Don't be daft, of course it wasn't. Didn't you like the poem I read? Later on, when it's quiet, I'll grab some fizz and come round to your house and we can have our own party. I'll bring two bottles, we've loads of champagne.'

'*Real* champagne?' Ma perked up. She likes her fizz.

'Real, and old, it's from Burns' cellars. And, look, Ma, I *am* grateful, I didn't want to risk bumping into Alice. She knows too much.'

'Now who's being daft? Alice doesn't even know what you look like.'

'Maybe,' I said, but I didn't trust the woman. Alice was fey.

That evening, as day turned into night, the lights Sproat had rigged up came on, along with the music. People were dancing, their shoes kicked off, glasses in their hands. I grinned. Despite the champagne I'd taken to Ma's, I was glad to get back, to the gardens, the poems. I felt as proud as a queen. As proud as if I *was* Steph Gilchrist, no, wrong, proud of me, Pheobe Slater, an ordinary girl who now had this *and* was a poet. A sort-of poet.

Clara rushed up to me.

'Steph, at last! There's someone here I'd like you meet.'

'Marie Corelli?' I said, hopeful, but I knew it wasn't her, she'd cried off this year. Clara laughed and slapped my arm.

'No, Steph! This is someone much more important.' I was intrigued.

Then I saw him.

He looked much the same as when we'd last met. Maybe a little more tanned. *Well, it is summer.* Gwilym looked amused. I wasn't.

You were meant to write to me. To let me know when you'd be back. He'd written to Clara, obviously, but she'd never said. *Damn you, Gwilym.* A small seed of jealousy sprouted.

Clara pulled him towards me.

'Gwilym, this is my cousin, Steph. She's a poet like Lucienne Hall, or trying to be.' I smiled. Gwilym gave me one of his stares.

'Pleased to meet you, Steph,' he said, taking my hand. I stared back.

'Lovely to meet you, *again*,' I mouthed, knowing Clara wouldn't be able to hear my words, over the music. 'I'm just going to choose the next dance.'

'No, wait!' Clara insisted, grabbing my arm and pulling me round. 'Now you're here and Gwilym's back, I've something to tell you.'

'Yes?' I waited, knowing the something wouldn't be good. Was I going to lose my home?

'You've been such a friend, as well as my cousin, since you've been here.' Clara smiled at me. 'And now you'll have another friend too, or rather, a cousin.' She paused for effect.

'Because, dear Steph, Gwilym and I are going to be married.'

4

1853 – Lucienne Hall

Lucienne stared out into the garden and grounds. The day had been cold despite it being summer and rain was slamming against the window. Lucienne sighed. She was in her room, the one upstairs with the view of the church, it made a change from the library downstairs. Augustin still wasn't here.

He'd been due to arrive at the manor at eight.

She'd planned a special meal for him, ordered the food and bought that special wine he liked, it hadn't been easy. Issington didn't have a wine merchant. But Lucienne had managed it.

The weather had cast its spell on her and as the clock dragged on to nine and then to ten, and still her lover hadn't arrived, she became downcast. Downcast and angry. The meal was dry and overcooked. Lucienne sent the servants home.

Then when she thought she'd go to bed, there he was.

'You're late,' she said. Augustin shrugged.

'The coach was delayed.'

'By *three* hours?'

'Yes,' he said. 'Why would I lie? It's quite a long way, as you know. And I'm tired.' He smiled, softly.

'Well I'm hungry. And *I've* been waiting.' She flounced away.

He didn't want the food she'd cooked, he said he'd eaten on the way, besides the meal was pretty much ruined. He wanted to go straight to bed and normally that would be what *she'd* have wanted, but this time, she'd decided no. He had to make it up to her. It took a while.

Which made it worse to be woken up, at what felt like the middle of the night, even though the sun was up. He was dressed and standing by her bed. Lucienne sat up.

'What's going on?'

'I've got to go, I told you last night. I've been offered another commission. It's very important.'

'They're all important, according to you. And you didn't say that it was today. You've only just got here!' Augustin shrugged.

'I didn't have to come to see you, it took me hours. I came because I wanted to. And as for telling you it was today, well it was late...'

'You didn't have the guts,' she spat.

'You *were* a little cross last night.' Augustin grinned.

'I was *angry* because you were late and the meal was ruined.'

'The coach was late, I couldn't help that. And the food didn't matter, it was you I came to see. I'll be back, in the spring, and for longer this time.'

'In the spring!' she said. 'But it's not even autumn, and now you're going and you've only just got here. You'd have been better not coming at all, for a few wretched hours.'

'I didn't think they were all that wretched.' Augustin smiled. That did it.

She jumped up, got out of the bed and pushed Augustin out of the room. He raised his hands to counter her.

'Hey, wait a minute!'

'No, you're going and you're going right now!' She almost shoved him down the stairs. 'Get out of my house!'

'So it's your house now? My coat's in the porch.'

'Fine, so get it.' She moved to one side to let him pass. 'You'd better run, you wouldn't want to miss that coach.' Lucienne felt cheated. They usually said goodbye in the Palm

House, that was their place. Now it seemed he didn't care. Well, damn him to hell!

She followed him out onto the step. He flung his rucksack over his shoulder.

'That doesn't look very big,' she said, 'for a few months' stay.'

'They're sending my things on, from the last place.' Augustin was sulky.

Then he leant in towards her, angling for a kiss as he always did, but she stepped back up into the porch. And glared at him coldly.

'I'm not putting up with this again. You turn up late, reject my food and don't even bother to stay the day. You'd better not do this anymore.' Augustin grinned.

'I won't have to. After this one, I've got some time off. I could stay for the week, if you like?' He paused, went on. 'Unless you'd rather I didn't come back.'

Lucienne thought. God, she was angry. Could she say no? No, she couldn't. She folded her arms.

'Well, I guess that's up to you, Augustin. As it always is.'

Then she went back in and closed the door and sank to the ground. Then the tears started.

5

1911 – Phoebe

When the guests had finally gone and Clara had gone upstairs to bed, we met in the Palm House. I was on fire.

'You were supposed to write to me!' Gwilym just shrugged.

'Writing's not my strong point, Phoebs. Unlike you, now you're a poet.' Reaching across to pull me to him. I moved away.

'Not on your life! You should have told me about your engagement!' Gwilym looked smug.

'How could I have told you, Phoebs? It's only just happened.' I almost hit him.

'That's such a lie! Clara's just told me, she agreed to marry you before you left, but you insisted she say nothing.' Gwilym laughed.

'So, Phoebs, my story's been rumbled. What does it matter? You don't need to worry. My plans include you like they always have.' He paused, grinned. 'You haven't fallen for me, now? Wasn't I meant to marry your cousin?'

'She's not my cousin and no I haven't. But we were meant to be friends, Gwilym, and you went behind my back.' I stopped, cold. 'You haven't told her I'm not Steph?'

'No, of course I haven't, and I'm not going to. Now you're being silly. Come over here and give me a kiss.' I stepped back.

'In your dreams, you're engaged.' Gwilym grinned.

'What does that matter?'

I scowled. *Damn Gwilym, he'd let me down.* 'Everything was just fine, the way things were.'

'Ah, now I see. You *are* jealous, but of me, not of her. You've been lording it over the manor all this time and now I'm back she'll listen to me and not to you. You're only the cousin.' Gwilym winked.

'Rubbish!' I said, knowing he was right. I liked having the run of the manor and when they got married that would all change. I frowned.

'I wouldn't be too sure of Clara.' Gwilym looked up.

'What do you mean?'

'She keeps a lot to herself does Clara. I don't always know what she's thinking.' Gwilym yawned.

'I can charm *any* woman.' I laughed.

'Yeah, right, apart from me. And I want to be kept informed, we were supposed to be working together.'

'Sure,' said Gwilym. Lazily running his eyes over me. I smiled.

'According to Clara, my poetry's improving. She thinks Hall's been teaching me.'

Gwilym smirked. 'Isn't Hall dead? I'm an artist and I make money and people travel for miles to see me, and buy my work. Unlike you.'

'*Yet*,' I said and glared at him. 'You're impossible.'

'Takes one to know one,' Gwilym said and I threw up my hands.

When Gwilym finally left, I went downstairs to the poetry room, too restless to sleep. It was true, he was good at his work *and* he made money. People would always need portraits of their families. Clara's landscapes sold too, if only locally. I wanted some of what they had. Once in the room I locked the door. Why had I done that?

I realised then the room was mine, I didn't want Gwilym rooting around, especially once he'd married Clara. Or her either.

I thought about the poems I'd 'written', borrowed off Hall. They hadn't made money but they had made friends. This year we'd had even more visitors and some of them had liked my work. Clara had sent some poems to an editor, someone in London her father had known. What would he say?

The other day, when I'd been in here, searching for poems, I'd come across a scrap of verse, at the bottom of a pile.

Cracked glass on an ice-blue day
Breaks apart my house of dreams
dreams and words
But if it could talk, the yellow stained glass
would tell the truth, now reshaped.

For I'll re-build my house of words
Put pen to paper again, and more
So I find in the shards, some small comfort
The truth may be lies, but the lies *will* last.

I stared at the words. What did they mean? And, what had happened to Lucienne Hall? Where had she gone? I sighed, frustrated. I didn't even know these words were hers. But they did mention a house of dreams, so it must be the manor. But although I searched the whole house, later and even asked Clara, in desperation, I couldn't find any yellow stained glass. Then I dismissed it, how could I know Lucienne's mind? But the style was like her early work.

Clara knew the acclaimed pieces, the work she and her father had shared, but she was an artist, not a poet. I had the advantage there. I knew this room.

So that night and into the morning, I sat at my desk in the poetry room and copied out the scrap of verse, all the words and made them mine. Embroidered, embossed them.

I was a natural. I could take Lucienne's thoughts, sharpen and hone them and make them my own. Which is just what I did, over and over and no-one guessed what I was doing. Even my cousin.

So when I put pen to paper again and re-build my house
A house of words
The words may be lies, but the house *will* last
And the words will build more, a library, a dream
Something which will stand in time, which *will* be true
And in the meantime, I'll find a hearth and a home.

I took a deep breath. I hoped I was right.

6

1911 – Phoebe

I was back at Chesterton Court, updating my ma.

'Clara's been talking about the will. Her grandfather's will that caused all the trouble.' Ma frowned.

'At least her grandfather had a will. Yours didn't make one, he had nothing to leave. Nor did your da.'

I sighed. Ma was in a testy mood. Monday was washday.

'Come on Ma, listen to me, this is important. The will took away Jacob's home, he ought to have had had the manor, not Frederic, he was the eldest.' Ma frowned.

'Why do I have to remember all this? I'd wish you'd help me with these sheets. Or take the boys from under my feet, like other girls do.' I swore.

'You know I'm not like other girls, Ma and I help you out in other ways.' Thinking of the steak I'd brought, I'd told the servants Sproat's dog had eaten it.

I didn't want to help with the washing. I remembered too well what life had been like before I'd met Jacob. Dragging damp clothes across the yard, cooking the tea. Begging at shops for stale bread and biscuits. It had been grim.

No, I thought, *I'm not going back.*

But that didn't mean I didn't feel guilty, Ma was still here and so were my brothers. I wanted them all at the manor with me. I was working on Clara, I knew I could do it, then Gwilym turned up. He was a problem.

All he ever talked about now was marrying Clara and owning the house. But it wasn't his house, it was *mine*. Ma's voice broke into my thoughts.

'I'm getting too old for this.' She dropped the sheets and fell into a chair. 'When I'm gone, you'll have to do them.' Glaring at me.

I laughed and scooped them all up. *When I'm gone?* 'You're tough, you'll last forever.' Ma sniffed and watched me work. I poured out the tea. It was nice and strong and worth coming back for. Ma spoke.

'So tell me then about this will. If Frederic and Jacob are both dead, who gets the manor?'

I sighed. 'I've explained all this. Because Jacob blotted his copybook when he was young, Issington Manor was given to Frederic, though just for his lifetime.'

'Which annoyed Jacob,' Ma said, stirring her tea. She liked four sugars.

'It ruined his life. He got into wine, made plenty of money, but he never forgave his brother or his father. He thought the manor should have been his. Then he came back.'

'More fool him.'

'Yeah, right. It ate him up, losing the manor, even after buying Cross Saddle House.'

'*A lovely house*, or so I've been told.' Ma sniffed. She'd never been there.

'Yes, it was, once, and more than enough house for me, but it wasn't a patch on Issington Manor. It wasn't as big, or half as grand and we didn't have the river and the access into town. But even after Frederic died, the manor wasn't Jacob's. Clara got the house not him. Steph could have lived there, that was in the will, the cousins could share it, but Jacob didn't get it, and he wouldn't have Steph going there, not even for a visit. His pride killed him in the end.'

'The whisky, you mean,' Ma said, sharply.

'Maybe,' I said. 'His life fell apart and Thirza wouldn't take him back. In the last few weeks even Steph wanted out. It was such a shame, on all counts.' I got up and put the cups in the sink.

'He was the eldest son,' said Ma. 'He couldn't back down.'

'And, look where it got him!'

We were silent for a while. Ma spoke first.

'So the house belongs to Clara and Steph.' She stared at me.

'Until Clara marries. Then the house belongs to Gwilym, not her. But as Clara's cousin, and while I'm not married, I can live there, and he can't sell. That's because of the library thing.' Ma looked sharp.

'But what if Steph married first?'

'Then I'd get the manor, or my husband would.' I grinned at Ma.

'Do you like this Gwilym?'

'You were the one who warned me against him. Thanks to Alice.'

'Never mind Alice,' said Ma, sharply. 'We're talking about your future here. Do you like the painter?'

'Maybe,' I said. 'I like him more than I liked Jacob. He was too old. Not that I thought that at the time.' I glanced at Ma. 'Gwilym's a bit of a handful, though.' Ma hooted.

'Gwilym's a man, of course he's a handful.' Her eyes narrowed. 'I reckon Gwilym likes *you* best. You and he have a lot more in common.' Ma grinned.

'So there's your plan *and* your chance. It's the only one you're likely to get, given your history. Give up the poems and marry the painter. Unless you want to be out on your ear.'

'There's only one drawback, I'm not Steph.' Ma stared.

'Since when has that mattered? You put that poor girl's body in the river and both of your brothers think you're dead. But now, when you need to stand up for yourself, you're wimping out. If you don't do something fast, you'll lose Gwilym *and* the house. I know what I'd do.' But Ma wasn't finished.

'You started this thing, you've got to be strong. Who knows you're not Steph, apart from us and the painter man? And I won't tell.'

'Gwilym won't either, it's not in his interest.'

'Well,' said Ma. 'That's your answer.'

7

1911 – Clara

It was a few weeks later. Clara sat in the library alone. Steph and Gwilym had gone for a walk. She hadn't asked where.

Gwilym had asked if she'd come with them, but she'd said no. Clara needed some time on her own.

Once they'd finally left the house Clara felt relieved. She opened up the French windows, releasing the muslin into the breeze. Now she had peace, was alone at last. She set her easel up by the mirror.

Since Gwilym had returned, she hadn't been painting. She loved having her fiancé here and being engaged, but all the same...

Something about those two troubled her. Steph was pretty and such good fun *and,* surprisingly, a good poet. But now Gwilym was back from Dorset and visiting them, Steph was different, watchful, quieter. Maybe they didn't like each other. Yet now they'd gone for a walk together. *Should I be jealous?*

Clara sighed and snapped herself out of it. *Stupid girl, you're wasting time.* She glanced in the mirror. Time to draw.

A little while later she sat back, pleased. *The sketch,* she thought, *was almost right.* Not that bad for a self-portrait, drawn in the mirror. Now the lines were ready for colour, muted blues with a touch of brown. Showing off her hair. Clara smiled and broke for lunch.

When it got dark the others returned. Steph was tousled and almost radiant. She rushed straight to the fire. 'It's freezing outside!' she told Clara, rubbing her hands. Clara agreed.

'I asked Burns to light the fire. It was cold in here.'

'I'm starving. Let's have crumpets.' Steph went over to ring for Mabel, then she stopped. 'What's that? Oh, it's a portrait.'

'Self-portrait.' Clara smiled. 'And not a bad likeness, if I might say so. Though it's not finished.'

'No, but you're right, it's damned good...' Steph stopped. 'Sorry, Clara. I know I shouldn't swear.' Clara shrugged.

'It doesn't bother me. And after everything you've been through... I wonder what happened to that dreadful woman?' Steph paled.

'What? You mean Phoebe? I don't know. But she wasn't *that* dreadful.'

'Really?' said Clara, wiping her brushes. 'That's not what you used to say.' Steph shrugged.

'I'm going upstairs to change,' she said. 'It's still cold.'

'Isn't it just? 'Clara stared at the portrait with an expert eye, she rather thought she'd improved herself, made herself kinder, more ideal. Gwilym came in and she looked up.

'How was your walk?'

'It was alright. Steph's a laugh.' He stared at the portrait. 'Did *you* paint this?'

'Of course I did. I am an artist, after all.'

'You usually paint landscapes. Now I'm looking at it more closely,' he peered at the painting, 'I can see it's very good. We must find a place to hang it.'

'*We*, Gwilym? You're not in charge of the manor just yet. It's still *my* house.' Gwilym paled.

'It'll always be yours. I'm only saying that the painting's good. Very good in fact.'

'So you said.' Clara smiled. 'I'm glad you approve. I think I'll put it in the hall. When it's finished.'

'Fine,' drawled Gwilym. 'I've come to tempt you in to tea. Burns has brought it in and Steph's starving.'

'Then we'd better not keep her waiting, had we?'

Clara stepped away from the painting and watched as Gwilym's face went white. Now he could see the whole portrait, including her hand.

With its enormous diamond ring.

8

1911 – Phoebe

Gwilym and I went out in his car. It was such fun.

'You never told me you had a car,' I said to him as we strolled along Whitborough Walk. The road was quiet, but not for long.

'I bought it when I was down in Dorset. Getting down there by coach is hell.' Gwilym stopped and waved his arm. 'What do you think?'

It was amazing.

'Fancy a spin in my steed, Phoebs?'

'Shh!' I said, glancing back towards the manor. 'Clara will hear.'

'Don't be silly, of course she won't. No-one can hear me and Clara's probably sitting in the Palm House, painting her portrait. Or maybe one of her daft landscapes.'

'Don't be cruel. She's a good painter, better than you.'

'Ha!' said Gwilym. 'That's not possible.' He patted the bonnet of the car. 'What do you say?'

'We'll freeze to death without the hood.'

'Tough,' said Gwilym, 'it's part of the fun, that and the speed. Did you bring your scarf?'

'Yes,' I said, reluctantly. I wanted a ride in Gwilym's car, but I didn't want to wear a damned headscarf. Too much like my dear old ma. But I didn't dare go through town without it. I climbed in carefully and after Gwilym had cranked the engine we set off.

'You should have asked Clara,' I told Gwilym, pulling my coat around myself. It was freezing.

'I did,' said Gwilym, 'but she said no. Total wimp.'

'Ha,' I said, annoyed that Gwilym had asked her first. 'Well, more fool her.' We picked up speed as we crossed the bridge and left Issington. *Damn Gwilym.*

Later, we had tea and scones, up at the café next to the river. I knew it was risky, but I didn't care. I showed Gwilym a few of my poems. He nodded.

'They're not bad. We could make money from these *and* the teas. And I think we should charge for entry.' He sat back. 'You're a poet, I'm amazed.' I felt hot.

'Sort of poet,' I said, shamed. 'Clara won't charge for admission, I'm afraid. She says it would make it too commercial.'

'She's not going to get her library then. Her library for poets.' He put his hand over my own. 'Leave her to me, Phoebs old girl, *I'll* bring her round.' I stared at him. I doubted that.

'I could write more poems,' I said, smiling. 'As if that would help.' Gwilym looked bored.

'Yeah, why not.' He got to his feet. The car was like a drug to him. 'We need to get back. I'd like to give her one more spin.' I sighed.

'If you insist.' Gwilym grinned and took my hand.

On the way back, he drove too fast and it should have been fun. I liked the dangerous side of Gwilym, most of the time. As we headed towards The Rogues where the fair was held, I held on tight. The road was narrow and hard to navigate, but Gwilym didn't care. We headed down and across the junction with Midden Lane South without stopping, just as a man stepped out from the curb. I screamed, alarmed, but Gwilym just laughed, swerved and kept going. The man leapt back, just in time. If he hadn't, we'd have hit him. The man shook his fist and several people stared. I averted my face.

As we bounced along the road towards home I swore. 'You should have stopped!' I hissed at Gwilym. Gwilym just shrugged.

'I thought you didn't want people to see you.'

'If you'd have killed him then they'd have seen me!'

'Now you're being silly, I wouldn't have killed him.' Gwilym laughed and turned to me. 'He should have waited.'

'Didn't you recognise him? That was the vicar! He was the one who buried my sister.' Gwilym slowed down.

'You never told me you had a sister.'

'I don't have a sister, she died as a baby. Now I only have two brothers. For God's sake, Gwilym, look at the road!'

Gwilym grinned and came to a halt not far from the manor.

'Go and get Flora to make us some tea. I'll park up.' I frowned.

'I'm not your servant and don't you forget it.'

But I did what he said.

When I got in I looked for my cousin but I couldn't find her. Gwilym appeared.

'Cake, great!' he said, grinning and headed for the table. As if we hadn't had scones already.

'No, wait!' I took the plate out of his hand. 'I want to try something.'

'What?' said Gwilym, staring at the cake.

'When I arrived Clara insisted I walk round the house with a blindfold on. She said it would help me get to know it. Did she do that with you?'

'No, thank God.'

'Good,' I said, 'because I'm going to do it.'

'You've got to be joking!'

'Close your eyes and *no* peeking.'

'But I already know what the house looks like.' I sighed.

'Not like this. You're the artist, Gwilym, not me. It's about imagining your work, first, before you've created it.'

'Hurry up then, woman. The tea's getting cold.'

I laughed then, and took his hand. Then I lead him around the room slowly, stopping to ask him what he'd discovered, an ornament here, a picture frame there, the smooth wood of the door handle.

Then I stopped. 'What about this?'

Tracing his hand down my face, touching his finger to my lips. 'You can open your eyes.'

Then I let go and waited for Gwilym to pull back. Instead, he stayed still, then he slipped his hand down to my neck and ever so lightly traced my collarbone. I couldn't breathe. We stared at each other.

'Well, Phoebs,' Gwilym said, softly. 'This is interesting.'

I nodded, unable to speak. Then Clara walked in.

9

1911 – Clara

Gwilym pulled his hand away, but not quickly enough. Clara knew what she'd seen. She chose to ignore it.

'Tea?' she said, smoothly, pouring herself a generous cup then doling more out. 'Just what I need. How was the drive?' Watching them closely.

Gwilym rushed to fill the gap. 'Great, great, if a little bit bracing. She's a racer, that car.'

'Gwilym drives too fast,' said Steph, looking rather flushed. 'We nearly hit someone in town but the man jumped back just in time.' Gwilym looked embarrassed.

Clara frowned. 'How fast is fast?'

When he told her she was shocked into silence, but today had been a day of shocks. Starting soon after they'd gone out.

After they'd gone, Clara went down to the Lucienne Hall room. Her father had given the room that name. She could almost hear him.

'If Steph is like Jacob, she'll be wayward, into scrapes, Jacob was always getting into trouble. I bet his girl will be just the same.'

Clara wondered if that was true. A lot of the time, Steph *could* be wayward, like wanting to go in the car with Gwilym. Sometimes, however, she wasn't so sure. Steph had another side that Clara couldn't place.

She turned the handle, but the door wouldn't budge. Surprised, she tried again. Then she called Burns.

'The door's locked,' Burns confirmed, peering down at the keyhole and the doorframe. 'Miss Steph will have locked it. She's done it before.' Clara frowned.

'Has she?' she said. 'I wonder why?'

'I think she likes the quiet, Miss Clara, when she's writing her poems.'

'But she's not writing now, is she?' Clara sounded sharp.

'I think she likes to keep things... safe.' Burns sounded worried.

'Safe from what, exactly?' Clara said, angry. 'That room was my father's, it's not up to her to lock the door.' She paused, thought. 'Do we have another key?'

'Of course,' said Burns. 'I'll go and get it.'

Shortly afterwards, Clara stood in the room, which looked much the same as she remembered it, if a little tidier. Everything in its rightful place. Clara sighed.

She shouldn't mind Steph being in here, or reading Hall's work, especially now her cousin was a poet. A junior poet. Everyone needed some sort of space and she had her study. But this wasn't Steph's room. *And it is my house!*

That was the rub. Technically, the house *wasn't* hers, not until she married Gwilym. And morally, of course, it should've been Steph's, Jacob being the eldest son. Clara smiled, sourly. *Not in my lifetime.*

She started going through the files. *Some of these are Lucienne's work. I might find a gem.*

Two hours later, dusty and weary, Clara stopped. *Plenty of notes but not one gem.* Nothing she could use. *Time for tea and scones,* she thought. *It's getting late.* She'd just get that package.

She walked across the room to the cupboard, which was old and shabby and needed replacing. Right at the back was a smallish package, stuck between two of the shelves. It must have slipped down from within a file. It was most likely nothing.

Clara leant across and tugged, finally freeing the captive parcel and tipped the contents onto the desk. It was probably more notes. But no, she was wrong.

Inside was a tiny oil painting, of a small house with shutters, with clumps of tall trees spilling over a wall. The front door was solid, with a strip of stained glass, yellow and thin. Clara was intrigued. What was this?

She studied the painting slowly, carefully, seeing it as an artist does, seeing the house rise up from the oils. She turned the picture over, wondering. Nothing there.

Then she looked inside the envelope and saw the small scrap of paper.

The poet Lucienne Hall's house, Issington Halt. Clara stared.

This wasn't a picture of Issington Manor, this house was much smaller and Clara didn't know it. But it must be in Issington, the words said so. *Her very first home.*

Clara stepped back and leant against the desk, stunned and disbelieving. If what she was seeing and reading was true, then the manor wasn't Hall's only home in the town, or even her first. The one in the painting was Hall's first home, this tiny little house.

Which meant their events and her father's dream, were built on a lie.

10

1911 – Clara

After they'd eaten, Gwilym left to go back to his lodgings and Clara breathed a sigh of relief. She needed to think. Steph wanted to talk.

'I'm sorry,' she said.

'Sorry for what?' Impatiently.

'For going out in the car with Gwilym. I'm sure he'd have rather been with you.'

'Are you?' said Clara. 'Look, it really doesn't matter. So long as you both enjoyed yourselves.'

'Oh yes...' said Steph, smiling as she said it. A dreamy sort of smile.

Clara felt the knot in her stomach. Had they been touching?

No, she thought. *I'm not going to think that.* She rose from her chair. 'I'm going upstairs. It's been a long day.'

'Yes,' said Steph, still sounding distant. 'Yes, it has.'

Clara sat in her room, pensive, trying not to think about Gwilym. She knew he could always win people round, it was part of his charm. Part of why she liked the man. It didn't mean anything. The painting she'd found, now that was a worry. She studied it closely.

Did it look real, genuine? Yes, it did. Could it have been Lucienne's house? Yes, but it could have been anyone's house. So why did it have her name with it? Clara frowned.

She wondered where the house was located. It looked to her like Whitborough Walk but she didn't remember a house like that. She couldn't be sure.

What she *did* know was that if the painting *was* Hall's house, their plans for Hall's library were built on a lie. The manor hadn't been Hall's first home, she'd had another house before this, the one in the painting. Clara got up. She wanted to scream.

The next day, she rose early. Apart from Flora, who was cleaning the grates, the rest of the household were still in their beds. She slipped on her coat and left the manor, hurrying down the path to the road. Then she made her way down Whitborough Walk.

Clara was wearing a thick headscarf and had raised her collar to hide her face. She needn't have bothered. Apart from some men taking goods to the barges, she didn't see anyone. Nor did she see Hall's first home. But just before she reached the town, she stopped by a wall. This was it, she knew it was. There was no house behind the wall, instead there was a memorial garden, with a small brass plaque.

Stop here and pause a while
Before returning to your home.

Refreshed, restored and giving thanks
To nature and peace, and to the stranger,
Who left this place, in time, for you

Clara paused. The words didn't feel like Lucienne Hall's, but the space felt right, that was hers. What had happened to the house? She walked around the beautiful garden, searching for a clue, some yellow stained glass. She knew it wasn't likely and she found nothing. Clara smiled.

The house was gone, there was nothing to show it had ever existed and decades had passed since Hall had lived here, if she had. Her secret was safe.

Then she felt guilty. The painting made Hall's home look sweet. But better if it didn't exist.

She strolled back to the manor, considering. What should she do?

She doubted anyone else had a copy. *I could get rid of it.* Clara felt her cares fade away.

When she got back, she tiptoed up the stairs softly. Steph was such a late riser. And, thank God, a sound sleeper.

Always better to rise early, Clara had told her, then you can make the most of a brand new day.

You wouldn't say that if you'd had my... Steph had stopped and she'd looked scared. *What had that meant?*

Some old secret, best left hidden. Clara had let Steph's words go. Now *she* had the secret and it was hard. She studied the painting. It was quite good.

She was an artist. She couldn't destroy it.

Damn it, she thought. *I'll have to hide it.* But where, exactly? She couldn't leave it in her rooms, Mabel might find it. Or in Hall's room where Steph might see it. Clara needed somewhere else.

Light, when it came, was instantaneous. Clara smiled.

She went down to breakfast.

Steph was eating toast and marmalade. Clara poured tea. Steph smiled.

'Is Gwilym coming over today?'

'Yes, probably. Why do you ask?'

'Oh, no reason.' Steph took another piece of toast.

I wonder why she eats so much? Clara glanced at her cousin. 'Could you do me a favour?'

'Anything,' said Steph.

Clara doubted that was true. But in this case, maybe...

'I've got some urgent letters to write. So when Gwilym arrives, do you think you could keep him occupied, perhaps take him out for a walk or a drive?'

Steph looked delighted, then her face changed, becoming confused and then wary. Then, very slowly, the smile came back.

'Sure, if you wish.'

'Good. Thanks. And the other thing Steph... please don't lock the door to Hall's room. I had to get Burns to open it for me which, as you can imagine, was rather embarrassing. It *is* my house.'

Steph paled.

'Although, I'll admit it, you're the poet,' Clara added to soften her words.

Steph nodded. 'Yes, sorry, I forgot.'

You forgot? 'Just as well there's a second key then. But *I'll* have the other, when you're ready.'

'Yes, right, I'll get it now.' Steph jumped up, almost colliding with Burns as she went. Then Gwilym walked in.

'What's up with her?' Gwilym sat down and helped himself to coffee and toast. Clara frowned.

Don't they feed you at your lodgings? 'Nothing,' she said, 'just a storm in a tea cup.' She got to her feet. 'I'll see you later. Steph will explain when she comes back.'

Ignoring his protests, Clara left and went up to her room, locking the door, the irony of which didn't escape her. She stared at the painting of Hall's house. It was beautifully done but also small, which was lucky for her. How could she have thought of getting rid of it? But she did have to hide it.

By the time the others returned, the painting had been dealt with. Life could go on and no-one would know what she had discovered. The manor had been Lucienne's home, her *only* home and one day it would be a great library, for poets and scholars. And maybe for writers like Marie Corelli. Clara smiled to herself.

She was pleased she'd kept the tiny painting, given its history that had been right. But it would remain *her* secret.

11

1911 – Phoebe

I won't pretend it didn't annoy me, coming downstairs and seeing her portrait in the hall.

Seeing that ring on her finger, it was larger than the real one and it sparkled a lot more. I was furious.

The trouble with me pretending to be Steph was that I almost believed it. I talked like her and dressed like her and sometimes I even acted stupid, although that was harder. Because I'd known her, I could play the part to perfection. Even with Gwilym.

Ah, Gwilym.

When I'd first met him, I'd believed that *I* was in charge. I'd thought I could twist him around my little finger but it turned out I'd been wrong. Gwilym had managed to out-fox me *and* with Clara. That was a shock. I had to win him back.

I can't deny I found him attractive, but it was the manor I was after. Issington Manor was Steph's birthright, she was the daughter of the eldest son. And I *was* Steph. I went down to the poetry room.

I needed some space, some time by myself. I really enjoyed 'writing' my poems, perhaps today I'd write some more. Clara had gone into town already, once a week she visited the poor. Hopefully not in Chesterton Court.

Ma's house was getting quite crowded with all the things I'd brought from the manor.

'Can't you find me somewhere else?' This was on my last visit.

'No, I can't!' I'd told her, sharply. 'Clara gives me a small allowance but not enough to rent a house.' *Or I'd have nothing.*

Steph, of course, should have had an income, but being estranged from her mother, Thirza…

Ma was still going on. 'What about all that silver in the manor?'

I laughed. 'Are you mad? What would you like me to do, Ma? Sell it all off to the highest bidder, so you can be happy? Then when Clara notices it's gone, which she would, the servants would be sacked and I'd probably be out on my ear, back in this cramped, tiny house. Is that what you want?' Ma sniffed.

'Since when have you cared about the servants? I'm the one you should be thinking of, I'm your ma.'

'As if I'm ever likely to forget it. You know I do loads!' But I knew I should do more.

Ma gave me a bowl of soup, it was hot and thick with chunks of veg, just how l liked it, unlike the gruel Flora served up. I ate hungrily. 'You'll have to wait until I get married. Then things will change.' Ma grunted.

'How's that going? '

'Slowly,' I'd said, thinking of how Gwilym had betrayed me. Ma's face dropped.

I was in the poetry room, rifling through the shelves again and hoping to find some inspiration. I knew I'd have had more luck in the kitchen, rifling through the pots and pans. But that was a night job. Lately, though, I'd had some luck, as some of 'my' poems were going to be published, thanks to an editor, a Charles Jefferson. He was the man Clara had contacted. She'd been thrilled.

'I'm *so* proud, and you'll write more, I know you will.' She'd smiled at me. 'And, guess what? I've more good news. I've got a commission, for another river landscape.'

I grinned. 'Of course you have.' Clara was a talented artist and loved to talk about her work. As did Gwilym. Artists could be *so* boring.

I sat at my desk and sifted through papers, looking for something I could use. Scraps and snippets of faded verse, difficult to read. I wanted words that I could transform, turn into magic. Hall's music made into mine. I loved doing this.

As the daylight started to fade, dusk arrived early in December, I discovered a roll of paper, tied up with ribbon. *This could be something*, I thought, smiling.

Slowly, I untied the ribbon, it wasn't easy. Blowing a cloud of dust away, I unfurled the paper, reading what it said. I gasped.

Later that evening, when it was quiet, I pulled on my cloak and twisted my hair under my hat, and walked across the lawn slowly, slipping through the five-bar gate. The huge iron gates to the town being locked. I hurried along the road quickly. This trip was private.

Issington Halt was lovely by day, with walks by the river and places for tea. But at night, the river was very different.

I was used to the streets, but Whitborough Walk was darker than most, being close to the water. I raced down the road, weaving my way in between the warehouses, most of them empty. Most of their men were in the pubs, drinking and flirting with the girls of the night. *At least I've never gone that far.* My heart raced. *You're getting soft.*

When I arrived at Midden Lane Bridge, I paused for breath, remembering when I'd last seen Steph. Then someone grabbed me from behind and I shrieked, wresting myself out of his grasp.

'You stupid fool!' I rounded on Gwilym. 'Do you want the whole town to hear us, and Clara to know?'

Gwilym shrugged and then he laughed, pulling me close. I fended him off.

'No-one calls me a fool, Phoebs. I'll have a kiss, just for that.' He stepped even nearer.

'No, you won't,' I said, sharply, trying and failing to free myself.

'Come here wench.'

I cursed and I struggled and I kicked his foot but he held on and as I was stuck between him and the bridge, there wasn't much choice, it was him or the river. The river didn't beckon.

'Damn you!' I said, hot with exertion, and with kissing, when he released me. Gwilym just laughed.

'I didn't come here for that,' I said, smoothing myself down. 'I'm a lady.' He gave a hoot.

'You, old girl? That'll be the day. As for the kissing, you enjoyed it.'

'Ha!' I said, but he was right. I'd even enjoyed the dash down the road, my escape from the manor. Freedom at last.

'There's something I have to tell you,' I said, sobering up. 'That's why we're here.'

'Couldn't it wait until morning, girl?'

'No,' I said. 'I had to see you alone, without Clara.'

Gwilym winked but I ignored him. 'Right, bring it on, then.' He leant against the bridge waiting. The moon came out.

'I've been busy.'

'Writing poems to make money?'

'Yes, some, but never mind that. I paused. 'I've something to tell you.' I hurried on.

'According to the will, now Jacob's dead, Clara and I can live at the manor until one of us marries, then *she* gets the manor.'

Gwilym smirked. 'I know all that. Clara's going to marry me, then as her husband, *I'll* own the manor. But there'll always be room for you, *cousin*.'

I shook my head. 'I haven't finished. Today I found a *second* will, that Frederic's father made *after* the first one.' Gwilym paled.

'What? You're joking.'

'Do I look like I'm joking?' I paused.

'In this new will, Frederic's father left everything to Jacob as the eldest son. He obviously changed his mind later. And to Jacob's children, namely Steph.' I grinned.

'Or rather, me.'

12

1911 – Phoebe

Gwilym and I were still on the bridge. It would have been safer *under* the bridge, but here was warmer and I still shivered down in the shadows. It still bothered me that Thirza didn't know what had happened to her daughter. That felt wrong. I shook it off. Steph was still dead.

'It's not as if we killed her, Phoebs.'

Gwilym said that quite a lot, I reckoned the boat bothered him too, not that he would admit it. I felt for Jacob's watch in my pocket, the watch proved to me that Jacob was dead, that he'd died in the house. As Jacob's wife, Thirza ought to have it, but the watch meant a lot to me. I knew I'd never pawn it, no matter how desperate I was.

Gwilym was staring at me, stupidly.

'Are you sure about this will?'

'Would I have dragged you out here if not? Of course I'm sure.'

'Right, okay. So where is it?'

'Under my mattress.' Gwilym looked shocked.

'Christ, Phoebe, anyone could find it! Don't your maids turn over the beds?'

'*Maid*, remember, and yes she does, twice a year. It's not the right time.'

'Never mind that, it can't stay there. We'll have to find somewhere else to hide it. Once I've seen it.'

'*We?*' I said. 'I'm the one who found it, Gwilym.' I pulled my cloak around me more closely. I shouldn't have chosen the river for a meeting, it was too damn cold. I looked Gwilym in the eye. 'Are we going to tell Clara?' He scowled.

'How do I know you're telling the truth?' I laughed.

'Why would I lie? I thought you'd like to know, that's all. Just in case...' He knew what I meant. He said nothing.

Then in a move that caught me off guard, he swept me up and swung me round, high and up and over the river. I squealed. Gwilym put me down.

'You could show me the will *now*, if you were willing.' I laughed, shakily.

'Not on your life. You're not coming back to the house at night.'

'Only to see the will, Phoebs, because,' he paused, 'it might not exist. Or,' he grinned, 'it's the river for you.' Moving towards me once again. I ducked out of his reach.

'I *don't* lie.'

Gwilym laughed, and I knew I'd give in.

'Damn you!' I said and he bowed, gracefully.

'Dearest Phoebe, shall we go?' He held out his arm. But I shook my head.

'If you insist, you *can* come back, but I'll go first and you can follow. I'll let you in through the Palm House door.' Gwilym shrugged.

'If I must.'

The rest was a nightmare.

I tiptoed back across the lawn and let myself in through the French windows. Then I went upstairs, grabbed the will and crept back down, feeling like a thief. Which of course I was. Then I walked through the hall to the Palm House and waited. And waited.

A number of times I almost gave up, going to the kitchen for water and snacks, but I always went back. Pacing and waiting. Where the hell was he?

Finally, when I'd almost given up, Gwilym appeared and I let him in.

'Where the hell were you?' I hissed. I was seething.

'Sorry, I had to go back to my lodgings.' Waving some matches. 'Then I saw a mate.'

I stared. He was unbelievable!

I'd brought a candle, I didn't dare use the electric light. Together, we spread the will on the floor. Gwilym studied it. He looked up.

'Well, Phoebe, damn it, you're right. The house and land are Jacob's irrevocably, his and his children's. I can't believe it.' I couldn't either.

'Which means me, now that I'm Steph.' There was no way he was forgetting that part. Gwilym ignored me. He jabbed at the will.

'There's no provision for Clara in this. Even if she doesn't get married.' I didn't care.

Why was he worrying about Clara? 'The manor's mine. I can do what I like.'

'But,' said Gwilym, 'you're not Steph.'

'True,' I said. 'But who knows that, apart from you?' Had I made a mistake, trusting him?

'Very few people, surprisingly. There's Thirza, of course.'

'I've been told she's upped and gone.' The lie tripped off my tongue, easily. 'But even if not, she's miles away.'

'Not if you've got a car,' said Gwilym. I snapped.

'Whose side are you on? You *could* tell Clara I'm not Steph, but what good would it do you? She'd never trust you, ever again.' Gwilym shrugged.

'*I* didn't push Steph off a ladder.'

'Neither did I!' I jumped up, angry, frustrated. '*I* was trying to save her life. Which is more than you did.' Gwilym laughed.

'Honestly Phoebs, you're such a pushover.' Reaching out to pull me to him. I shoved him away.

'No, Gwilym! I was the one who found the will and this is *my* house, or it will be soon. I just thought you'd like to know.'

Gwilym grinned, it was more of a smirk. 'I won't blow your cover, Phoebs. But I think we need a change of plan. *And* we have to hide the will, properly this time.'

I nodded, and then I looked up. 'I can smell burning.' Gwilym shoved me out of the way. The candle had fallen, the will was on fire. *Oh, God!*

Gwilym grabbed the glass by my side and flung its contents over the will. 'No!' I yelled but it was too late. Fire *and* water. I could have wept. All my dreams gone up in smoke. Literally.

Gwilym dropped to his knees, quickly, and using his hanky, wiped the water off the will. The fire was out. Most of it looked alright, amazingly. But would we still be able to read it, after it dried?

'We'll have to wait and see,' said Gwilym. We were both upset.

I gathered my things, including the will. I couldn't believe no-one had heard us. The Palm House stank of acrid smoke, reminding me of the Cross Saddle fire. I felt sick.

'I'm sorry Phoebs,' said Gwilym, solemnly. I turned away.

'Forget it,' I said. 'Just see yourself out.'

13

1911 – Gwilym

Gwilym sat in the drawing room, a room he disliked. The house was old-fashioned, the room was too small. It was downstairs and next to the library. Who needed libraries, or poetry? The drawing room had a porch outside, so even if you were sitting quietly, planning your next portrait, the chances are there'd be someone out there, creaking in that damned rocking chair. Or maybe the someone was his own ghost.

Gwilym knew he'd have to leave.

When he came back, things would be different, here *and* there. He'd have to tell her, both of them, and then there'd be no turning back, because finding that will had changed all their futures. Steph, Phoebe, she was the one and that meant saying no to Clara, which was a damned awful shame. He liked Clara, a *bloody good woman*, if a little dull. He'd always thought there was more to her than met the eye. But with the new will it had to be Phoebs, which was fine by him, more than fine. Phoebe Slater was his kind of woman. Gwilym stared out at the garden and grounds.

This will would change his life for good. He wanted to be his own man, instead of being subject to other people's whims, but for that he needed money. Serious money. The will made it all possible. Better too, that Phoebs wasn't Steph, she'd know he could always call time on her. It would keep her sweet, well sort of sweet. Gwilym grinned. Hard luck for Clara but good luck for him.

Gwilym leant back. He knew he could always destroy this new will, but why would he want to? Phoebe might tell, and if she did he doubted Clara would still want to marry him.

Married to Clara, he'd be expected to stay at the manor, which wasn't his plan. Marrying Phoebs was a much better option. Once they were married, he'd sell the manor and buy somewhere else, a place that was his. If Clara continued to be nice to him, he'd buy her a house, a small one of course, so she could still paint. Gwilym frowned. He knew Clara was a much better painter. She could even paint portraits.

Ah, portraits.

Gwilym got up, picked up his paper and walked to the door. Burns appeared, the man never smiled. 'Would you like some more tea… sir?' he said.

Gwilym smiled at the word. Even though Burns was being sarcastic, he liked to hear it, almost as if he was master already. He smiled, condescendingly.

'No, thanks. I'm going for a walk.' Burns left.

As Gwilym strolled across the lawn towards the gates, he mused on his future. *A couple of weeks and that ought to do it. A commission down south, the excuse didn't matter, no-one here would be any the wiser. Perhaps over Christmas.* Gwilym frowned. He couldn't stand Christmas.

When he came back, things would be sorted. *If* he came back.

Gwilym knew he would come back, he wanted the life Phoebe offered, the manor and the money. He also knew the woman was right, they were well-suited. She was the one who needed convincing. But all the same, he *liked* Clara.

As for the other, and the boy, that would be hard. *Gwilym* sighed. *Women*, he thought. *Always trouble.*

He turned around and walked back to the manor. Time to leave.

14

1911 – Clara

Hall's room always beckoned.

Since she'd found the tiny painting of Hall's first home, Clara felt restless. Even though she'd hidden it well. Then Gwilym had told her he was leaving.

'It's Christmas!' she'd said, but he'd been adamant.

'I have to follow the work, Clara. That's how it is, I go where the work is.'

She'd been upset but she hadn't said much. At least he wasn't a lazy man, or a spendthrift like Jacob. But Clara wasn't happy.

Without Gwilym, the days dragged. Christmas passed with too much food and not enough wine. She and Steph were bored with each other. The weather was cold and there wasn't much to do.

Steph wandered around, restless, as if she was waiting.

'Haven't you any poems to write?'

'I can't,' said Steph, 'the words won't come.'

'Sometimes you have to sit down and work, instead of just waiting.'

'I'm not in the mood for a lecture from you. I'm going out.' Steph stormed out.

What the hell's up with her? Missing Gwilym? Clara felt cold.

She wandered down to the Lucienne Hall room. Since she'd found the unwanted painting, she couldn't keep away, it was as if she was looking for something more. She didn't know what. Another part of Lucienne's life? Something that make sense of it all? She found nothing.

'What are you doing?' Steph said.

Clara jumped. 'I thought you'd gone out.'

'I forgot my hat.'

'You're not going to find it in here, are you?'

Steph ignored her. 'What are you doing?' she said again, as if it was *her* room.

Clara swore, but under her breath. *It is my house!* She took a deep breath.

'Trying to get a grip on all this. It's still so untidy.'

Steph seemed about to speak, but then she just shrugged. 'Fine. I'm off.'

Clara watched her climb the stairs, wondering what she really thought. Sometimes she felt Steph watched her, though that was probably just paranoia. But lately Steph seemed different from before, less grateful, more impatient. *She's probably bored,* Clara thought. *And she never seems to have much money.* She didn't like to ask.

She carried on searching through the papers, checking to see there were no other time bombs. She found nothing.

Mabel brought her cups of tea and Clara drank them thirstily, then carried on working. She needed to check everything.

Next year, 1912, she'd be getting married and she wanted to start the year afresh with no secrets, *well, only the one.* She knew she should have destroyed the painting, she still could. *But I just can't do it.*

In the late afternoon it started to snow and the sky grew dark. Thanks to her father's electric light, she could still see, but the room was getting colder now. Clara shivered, she'd have to stop soon. Thinking about going upstairs, she moved some boxes onto Steph's desk and knocked a file onto the floor. Paper went everywhere, all of Steph's poems.

Clara sighed and bent down to get them. She picked up some scraps, scribbles or notes and came across an unread poem. It was really good, sharp and well-formed. Steph's work was just like Hall's, great to have such an inspiration. Clara smiled. *I need to paint and focus more.*

Gwilym had taken her mind from her work. That shouldn't happen.

Peering out of the snow-smeared glass, Clara felt a glimpse of hope. Steph and Gwilym were *so* exhausting. She needed more time alone, by herself, time to draw. She picked up a poem.

She knew it was Hall's straight away, she recognised her slanted style. But wait, no, the words were Steph's, she'd seen them before. She found the copy of Steph's work she wanted and studied them both. The cold from outside crept into the room.

Clara stared. Steph's words were Lucienne's words, changed a little here and there, but even the rhythm and the line length matched. More than simple inspiration, this was theft! She read a few more.

Hall's first home laid aside, Clara had another new task, to match Steph's words to Lucienne Hall's. What she found nearly broke her heart. Her cousin was a fraud. She grabbed some of the best examples, mostly Hall's early work, then went upstairs, her heart heavy. This was how illusions were shattered.

Steph was late getting home.

'It's snowing out there,' she said, laughing, shaking a shedload onto the carpet as she pulled off her gloves.

'Yes, I can see that,' Clara said, coldly, staring at her. It was cold in the room, despite the fire.

'I need to get warm.' Steph walked towards the hearth, kicking off her boots and warming her red-raw fingers on the flames. 'Oh, this is lovely. Toast and heat. I'm so glad I'm home. '

Clara knew she'd have to say something, it was now or never.

'You're not a poet, you stole Hall's poems!'

'What?' said Steph, surprised and puzzled, and just for a moment, Clara hoped she'd been wrong. But then, just as quickly, the moment passed and she watched as a shadow crept over Steph's face, the shadow of guilt. So, it was true. Steph was a thief. She felt the hurt, all over again.

'How could you?' she said.

Steph stood up and held herself tall, moved away from the fire. She looked defiant. 'What does it matter? Nobody knows. I only borrowed the older ones.'

'That's what you call it, *borrowing*?' Clara couldn't speak.

'I only changed the poems a little, to make them more modern. No-one will care.' Steph sounded anxious.

Clara walked to the fire. '*I* care. And have you forgotten, we made those poems public, bound them for sale? Worse still, an editor's seen them, he wants to turn them into a book. But they're not your poems, they're Lucienne Hall's. What am I going to tell him now? And someone *will* know, someone always finds out. Then we'll be ruined!'

Steph moved towards her. 'No we won't! Nobody knows apart from us and I won't tell and neither will you. I like writing poems and you ought to be grateful because no-one cared about Hall's work, the early stuff anyway. I've given it a chance.'

'Under your name! I'm the one who gave you a home and I ought to be grateful? For stealing Hall's work? Not on your life. Please leave, I want to be alone.'

'If you insist. I'll be in my room.' At the door Steph turned.

'Soon it'll be for good, anyway.'

'What do you mean?'

'Gwilym's changed his mind about you, he's going to marry me, and then you won't have to see us again, if you choose. But then you'll lose your precious home.'

'What?' said Clara, shocked into silence. *She's making it up.*

'You heard,' Steph insisted and left the room.

Clara, stunned, sank into a chair. She couldn't believe it. She knew Gwilym liked Steph, but liking and loving were two different things. And he was engaged! She'd asked him about her several times, but all he'd said was, 'Steph's good fun.' And a lot more too…

Clara needed to talk to Gwilym, but he wasn't here. She jumped up and paced the room. Could Steph be lying? Clara didn't think so.

What else had she said? That she'd lose her home. Well, of course she would unless she chose to live with them. *I can't do that.*

She looked around her lovely room, full of the things her father had bought, saw all of it gone. She imagined her house empty and bleak, peopled by strangers she'd never know. Clara couldn't bear it. All of Lucienne's work erased, her father's library never built, and all because of a primitive lust. She couldn't have that. *Never!* she thought.

She went for a walk.

As she walked Issington's streets, coated with snow turning to slush, Clara asked herself over and over, was her cousin telling the truth? She knew that she was.

She wondered what would happen next, when Gwilym came home and how she could bear it, losing her home and her father's dream, not to mention losing Gwilym. She was so *angry*.

But never once, as she paced the streets, did she think about the lies *she'd* told since she'd found the painting, and how they both loved the same man.

Clara and Steph, so very different, but when it came down to it, much the same.

15

1911 – Phoebe

Gwilym returned the very next day.

The night before, I'd paced my room, distressed, in a state.

Why did I say it? What will Gwilym say when he finds out? I'll be the one who's out on my ear, because I'm not Steph.

But Gwilym just laughed. 'Clearly I can't leave you alone.'

'Obviously not,' I said, scowling. 'I couldn't help it, it just came out.' I didn't tell him why.

'And did you mention the will as well? That *would* have been stupid.'

'No,' I said, rubbing my hands to get them warm, we were outside so we could talk. 'I didn't go that far.'

'Just as well, or there'd be trouble.' Gwilym's eyes twinkled. 'Don't worry, Phoebs, we can sort it out.'

'Can we?' I said. 'Clara's not speaking to me. We used to be friends.'

'She'll have to get used to it. You're the heiress.'

'But I'm not,' I said and Gwilym frowned.

'You are now, *Steph*, you can't go back.' I shivered.

'God, I'm cold.' I stamped my feet, and we made our way to the Palm House slowly. It had become our favourite place.

'Soon we'll have a whole house to ourselves.' Gwilym grinned. 'Your ma can move in.'

'Really?' I said. I'd given up hoping on Ma's account. And on my brothers'.

'They can have their own annex, in our new home.'

I stopped pacing. 'You're not serious, about moving from the manor?'

Gwilym was sprawled on the chaise longue. He smiled at me. 'Of course I am. You didn't think we were staying here? I want a home that's mine, Phoebs, designed to suit me. A brand new home.'

I paused, thought. 'Clara won't want that, the manor's her home.'

'She won't have a choice, now you've found a second will.' He pulled me to him, to silence my protests. Then he smiled. 'My visit down south, in case you're wondering, was very satisfactory.'

'What do you mean, s*atisfactory?*'

'I mean, Phoebe, that I made loads.' Patting his jacket which bulged with something, probably cash. But I was suspicious. Gwilym changed tack.

'Shall we go for a drive?'

'What? Now? In this awful weather?'

'It'll be fine, if you wrap up. The snow's all gone.' Gwilym frowned. 'Do you remember that day we went out and I nearly ran that man over?'

'The vicar you mean.'

'Yeah, right. Well, I got a fine for going too fast.'

I couldn't help smile. 'Serve you right. Though it is bad luck, you never go fast…'

Gwilym grinned. 'It was your influence.' I laughed.

'I expect it was.' Staring at him. Gwilym wouldn't be selling the manor, I wouldn't let him.

It was then that I realised I didn't need him, not if I was Steph, the heiress.

Nobody knew I wasn't but him. Apart from Thirza, miles away and Ma of course, but she wouldn't talk.

I kissed him again and we went out.

16

1912 – Phoebe

We were engaged. Gwilym talked to Clara at length and nothing was said to me about it, but it can't have been pretty. Clara wouldn't look at me. I wasn't happy.

Now, at last, I had what I wanted, and yet I didn't. Gwilym wanted to sell the manor and so far he was sticking to his plan, and Clara, well, she looked so sad.

I'd hear her cry *every* night, like I used to cry for Steph, in the long weeks after the fire. Nobody knew how upset I'd been, after we'd put her body in the river. Not even Gwilym. I went round to Ma's.

'That woman's got her comeuppance,' said Ma, making the tea. 'Steph should have had that house not her and now *you're* Steph. It's rightfully yours.'

Maybe, I thought, *but not for long, not if Gwilym has his way. And if I marry him, he'll be the owner.* I glanced around. Where's Alfie?

'Sweeping Miss Corelli's step, or that's what he said when he and Seth left. He says she pays well. Seth was going down to the river, he sells sticks to the paupers.'

But what are we, if not paupers? I looked around Ma's tiny room. It was dank and cold, almost colder than outside. So the boys had gone out. 'Ma, it's snowing!' Ma sighed.

'It gets them out from under my feet. And it brings in money.' She sat on the stairs, put her head in her hands.

'Ma, what's up?' She raised her head.

'What do you think? It's this place, girl. Every year the damp gets worse. I can smell it, even in the summer, and now it's so cold, and the things you bring just aren't enough.'

'Things are going to be different Ma, when we get married.' Ma almost laughed.

'If I had a shilling…'

'But this time it's true! Gwilym even said so himself, I didn't have to ask him. Once everything's sorted you can move in, you and the boys.'

Ma frowned. 'That's what you said about Jacob, girl, but that never happened. Talk's cheap.' She sighed, weary. 'The boys are getting bigger each day and harder to house. This place is a dump.'

I couldn't deny it. Ma sniffed.

'If it wasn't for the dripping Dave Smith gives me, along with the bread we get from the Co-op, I couldn't manage. Even with taking in other folk's washing.'

'I do my best,' I said, sharply. 'I get what I can.' I stared at Ma.

'You do want me to marry Gwilym?' Ma shrugged.

'It's up to you. Do you love him, girl?'

'Yeah, I guess, we're two of a kind. Clara loves him more, I think, but in the end I'm doing her a favour.' Ma laughed.

'How do you work that one out?' She went to the sink to peel the spuds. My brothers would soon be home for tea.

'Gwilym's keeping something from us. I don't know what.'

'It's probably a woman,' Ma said, sagely. 'It usually is.'

'Oh,' I said, my heart sinking. Maybe I cared more than I thought. I looked at my ma.

'You know that when I marry Gwilym the manor will be ours?'

'Yes, so you said.' Ma glanced up.

'The house should go to Clara, really. Steph's dead.' Ma sighed.

'Are you getting a conscience, girl? Because if you are, it's far too late. Clara won't be on the streets, she'll still have a home.'

'Not if there's a second will and Jacob inherits. Then she'd be homeless.'

Ma stopped peeling. 'Is there one?'

'No,' I lied. 'But if there was...' *How could I let her lose her home?* 'I couldn't have that.'

Ma sighed. 'I don't know what you're on about. You know what I think?'

'What?' I said.

'Steph's been dead a good while now. You say you want to be her, but up to now you've been *playing* at being her. If you want to *be* Steph Gilchrist, you've got to be Steph *all* the time and not keep running back to me.' I stared.

'Is that how you see it? I thought you liked me coming back here, wanted the things I bring for you, the blankets and stuff. I come back home because I care, not because I'm lonely or anything...' I stopped.

'Are you sure of that, Phoebe?' Ma folded her arms.

'Maybe you don't know why you're here, but I'm fed up with it. As far as I'm concerned you left years ago, when you started going with Jacob. All this time, I've put up with you playing the lady, like that woman down the road, *Miss* Corelli.' Ma sniffed. 'Of course I'm grateful, I won't deny it, for all your gifts, we've needed the things, but now you want me to be your conscience, well I won't do it, not anymore.'

'That's not fair!'

'Isn't it, Phoebe? You say to me you care about us, but when did you last play with your brothers? I'll tell you when, when you lived here, and that was a long time ago. And every time you come to visit, you always say that things will get better but they never do. Time's moved on and I'm still here. I'm tired of your lies.'

I felt sick. Ma went on.

'There's something else I need to say, you've got a secret. I haven't asked what, but I will say this, secrets mean trouble and frankly, girl, I've had enough trouble to last a lifetime. I don't want more. You'd better go.'

'Ma, please, this is my home.'

'Haven't you heard a word I've said? It's not your home, it hasn't been for ages. It's mine and the boys, such as it is. I'd like you to leave.'

Just like Clara. I couldn't speak. Ma frowned.

'I'm not saying you can't come back, I'm not that hard. Just leave it for a while, that's all I ask. I need some time alone for a change. Bringing the boys up here is hard.'

I left without another word.

I trudged home, in the dark, it was still snowing and my feet had gone numb to match my heart. Was I as selfish as she said? I'd thought Ma and I understood each other, but I had been wrong. I didn't spend that much time with my brothers but how could I even go out with them, when I might be seen?

She was right, I decided, secrets change lives and not for the better. I'd rejected my family.

That'll all change, I told myself, *after I'm married. She and my brothers can live at the manor. Then she'll forgive me.* Then I remembered, Gwilym meant to sell.

I reached the gates, which Burns had left open. The lights danced across the snow, meeting the sky and a brilliant moon. I stared down through the grounds at the manor, it was all lit up and looked stunning.

It was such a wonderful place to live. I couldn't give it up, or let Clara's dream of a library die, not even for Gwilym. It was then that I knew.

I'd write more poems, and this time they would be my own, not Lucienne Hall's. I'd write and write, until I was good enough. Then we'd see.

I walked down and stepped into the porch, shaking off a load of snow and hanging my coat and scarf on the hook. For the first time in ages, I felt warm. I loved Gwilym, as much as I could, but I knew in my heart, the house came first. The house and the dream. And they always would.

17

1912 – Gwilym

Gwilym frowned. Phoebe was being especially annoying and he didn't know why. *She'd got what she wanted, so what was the matter? Damned women, always so changeable!*

After he'd spoken to Clara at length, the first thing Phoebe had done was move her portrait out of the hall. Which Gwilym thought was rather mean. She'd put it in the drawing room.

'Nobody ever goes in there,' Phoebe had said. 'That's how I know who she dislikes.'

'Really?' he said.

'Really,' she smiled. She stared at the portrait. 'I hated seeing it in the hall, in pride of place. That ring was the worst, it sparkled too much, it was far too big. Much bigger than the real one.' Gwilym had laughed.

'I'll get you a ring that's twice as big.'

'Damn the ring, Gwilym, it's the house I want. You're *not* going to sell it.' Gwilym had scowled.

'You'd better shut up. Clara might hear.' Phoebe spoke louder.

'What is you don't want her to know? That you're selling her house?' Gwilym could have slapped her.

Later that day, Phoebe abandoned him, she went down to the basement, to that stupid little room. He couldn't understand what she saw in poetry, compared with painting, it was nothing. And even painting could be tedious, if you *had* to do it. That's why Gwilym wanted to be rich. So he didn't *have* to paint. He smiled to himself.

Once they were married, he'd be in charge. He'd be able to sell the manor and neither of those women would be able to stop him. He'd buy a house that suited *him*. Gwilym glanced at the clock. It was time to go home.

Gwilym lived on Whitborough Walk, so it didn't take long to get to his lodgings. His rooms were near the Riverboat Inn, a double-edged sword. Yes, he could get a pint when he wanted, but late at night the place was a riot. Nights were when he did his best work.

First, he'd sketch the image on canvas, mark out maps of light and shade, then at night he'd fill them with colour. Gwilym liked his double life, artist by night and almost Lord of the Manor by day. And the rest.

Having a glass of ale later, he thought about the first portrait he'd painted, he still had it now. He almost laughed, remembering how it had been ripped off the wall and thrown at him recently, when he'd left Dorset. Now it was torn beyond repair, but Gwilym still loved it. He didn't do pieces for free anymore, giving away his work for a pint.

I've come a long way, and I mean to go further. After I've married Phoebe Slater. Or Steph Gilchrist. Gwilym grinned.

Later still, he strolled round to the manor. Phoebe was in the library, reading. She smiled at him, as he walked in.

'What have you been doing then?'

'Painting, Phoebs. What else do I do?'

'Having a pint or two, I'd guess.' She stared at him. 'Will you paint *my* portrait?'

Ah, so you're jealous! 'Yeah, sure,' he said, amused. Was she afraid he'd change his mind and go back to Clara? He knew he wouldn't. 'I think you need cheering up.'

'We're not going out in that car again?'

Gwilym shook his head. 'I've been thinking about where we'll go after we're married.'

Phoebe scowled. 'Nowhere, Gwilym, that's where we'll go. This is my home and I'm not leaving.'

That's what you think. But Gwilym wanted a quiet life, at least today. 'That's not what I meant. I meant on honeymoon. How would you like a trip to New York?'

'Wouldn't that cost an arm and a leg?'

Gwilym thought of the money he'd earned. 'I can afford it. We can go by sea.'

She didn't seem thrilled. Gwilym frowned.

'Isn't it time you got over all that, not liking the river? I know what we did, but damn it Phoebs, Steph was dead. It's not as if we actually killed her.' Phoebe sat up.

'Shut up, Gwilym! Clara might hear. And it's not that easy.' Gwilym shrugged.

'It's up to you. Frankly, I'd like to move on with my life and I thought you'd want to do the same.' Phoebe said nothing.

'What if we went on a luxury voyage, like a floating hotel? Something quite special.' Still she was silent. Gwilym ploughed on.

'Imagine it Phoebs. Fantastic views and marvellous food, maybe even sitting at the Captain's table. And all the while being treated like a queen, which of course, is no less than you deserve.' Gwilym grinned and Phoebe relented.

'Maybe,' she said, 'if you book the tickets. So that I know you won't change your mind.'

'As if I would.' Gwilym gave Phoebe a cool, hard stare then he threw the packet onto the table and nodded at her. 'Go on, open it.'

Phoebe stared back, clearly amazed as she opened the envelope and saw the two tickets. 'Damn you, Gwilym, what if I'd said no?' But she was laughing.

'I guess I took a chance.'

'A pretty expensive chance, I'd say.' She stared at him coolly. 'I suppose we'd better have a good time, then.' Just for a moment she looked sad.

'I promise you, Phoebs, you won't forget it.' He put the tickets back in his pocket and smiled to himself, he could charm any woman.

Especially with two tickets for the *Titanic*.

18

1912 – Clara

Part of her wanted to howl and scream. Sometimes she did, when she was alone. Part of her wanted to scream at Gwilym. She did that too, and he just took it. Part of her wanted to kill the man. *Damn him to hell.* And as for Steph…

When Steph had told her late last year that she was going to marry Gwilym, she'd known it was true, even before speaking to him. And now they'd set a date for the wedding and even planned their honeymoon.

'We'll be gone some time,' Steph had said. Meaning she'd have time to get used to the marriage. And as for the wedding, she'd go away, she'd go to Aunt Vi's.

Her aunt had not been pleased when she'd heard. 'You ought to throw that woman out!'

'What's the point? She'll be back, and so will Gwilym. I'll have to get used to it, and to the manor not being mine. I'm lucky to have a home at all, though it pains me to say it.'

'Is there nothing to be done?'

'No, sadly.' *Apart from throw myself off the bridge.*

Her aunt's opinion was clear from her silence and hardly a letter had followed since then. Clara felt both betrayed *and* abandoned.

Venting her rage on Gwilym had helped.

'How dare you marry Steph! And after everything I've done for you.' Gwilym had shrugged.

'Things change,' he'd said. 'You know how it is.'

'No, I don't,' she'd screamed, lashing out with her fists. While he just stood there.

'I never meant to hurt you, Clara.'

'Well you damn well have. I hope you drown!'

Gwilym raised his eyes at that. Clara didn't care.

'You know your fiancé's a thief and a fraud?'

'What?' said Gwilym, looking concerned.

'She stole Lucienne Hall's poetry, changed the words and called them hers. She even let me send them out and Charles Jefferson bought a few. She's made me part of the whole damn thing.' Gwilym relaxed.

'You don't need to worry. She's writing her own poetry now. And I'm not marrying the woman for her poems, as I'm sure you know.' Grinning at her.

Clara shrieked and threw a book at him, a very heavy book. Gwilym ducked and the book hit the wall, then fell to the floor. Nobody came.

'You've turned me into a harridan!'

'You're much more interesting when you're angry.'

'Oh, how I hate you!' Clara was despairing.

'No you don't.' Gwilym looked sad.

Clara worked at staying sane.

'Look, Gwilym, when you get married the house will be yours. Yours and Steph's.' *God, it was hard.*

'Yes,' he said, suddenly wary.

'You know about my father's dream, his plans for a library. I want you to promise me you'll carry on, and put it in your will. You owe me that at least.'

Gwilym said nothing. Clara went on.

'I'm still going to hold the Hall events, whatever you say, so there'll be a library, one day, for the people who come after. Promise me you won't stop my plans.' She grabbed his hand, but Gwilym pulled away. He looked embarrassed.

'It's difficult Clara.'

'No it's not. It's what we agreed when we were engaged.'

'But now things are different…' He seemed about to argue the point but then he gave in, smiling at her. 'If Steph wants to write her poems and you've got all of Hall's old work, it's fine by me, it's just not my bag. I don't want to be involved.' He walked away and Clara stared after him.

It was far too easy. *What wasn't he saying?*

Clara stood alone in the empty room, unsettled and angry. Something was afoot. She didn't trust Gwilym, not one bit. Feeling cold, she stoked the fire and paced the room. She knew she was helpless. With all the strength of her pent-up rage she picked up a vase and threw it against the wall, violently. The vase shattered and fell on the floor beside the book. Still there was silence. Nobody came.

Exhausted, defeated, she sank in a chair.

The tears would come later.

19

1912 – Sadie

After the snow, came the rain. It rained until the river burst its banks, and water seeped within and through the gaps between buildings, past the sheds, to Whitborough Walk. Soon the streets were more than a puddle. Still the water kept on rising. Nobody liked it.

Higher up, on Bakehouse Lane, the water drifted around, slowly. It crept into alleys like Chesterton Court, but because the Lane sloped down to the river, it didn't get far, or into the houses. Unlike the ones down at the bottom. But it was still damp.

Sadie Slater, Phoebe's ma, had boots that leaked and she had to lift her skirts higher when walking across the wet cobbles. It wasn't much fun. But Alfie and Seth thought it was great.

'We're off down to the river to play,' said Alfie, and Sadie, being tired, she was always tired, let them go. The brothers were always somewhere, together, playing or cadging, the dangers from people being less than poverty.

Sadie ambled round the town, bought some bread and cheese for tea, but mostly she just talked to people. Some of the people had known Phoebe.

'How are you coping on your own?' Meaning, without a daughter to help her. Sadie just shrugged, what could she say? Some of the braver said, 'have you heard anything?' Meaning, had her body been found?

Sadie tried to avoid such people and after a while she knew who they were. She was tired of lying, making up stories, sometimes she wished Phoebe *had* died and then she felt

197

guilty. What kind of mother feels like that? No wonder she'd left.

Sadie made her way towards home, taking the route that went past the river, barely aware that she'd gone the wrong way. The river had flooded up to the bridge and all of Whitborough Walk was closed, it was one big pond. Sadie sighed. She'd have to turn back.

It was just past five and getting dark. Sadie stopped and stared out at the river. Something small was thrashing about. *Oh God, it's a child!* The child who looked about Alfie's age was clearly in trouble. Dropping her shopping, she clambered in, pulling her boots off as she went. Her feet stung on the cold, hard pebbles and the weight of her skirts dragged her down. As she struggled towards the child, she yelled and screamed as much as she could. 'Help! Please help me!'

A man appeared and pulled her back, not understanding. Sadie fought back and pushed him away but not before she'd grabbed his shirt and gasped, hoarsely. 'See, over there! I think that's my boy.'

The man leapt forward and started to swim and soon he'd reached the child in trouble and grabbed the boy. Sadie was still wading towards them. She couldn't swim.

The man brought him back and handed the child over to her. Seth was still struggling. The gasping, dripping man looked grim. 'I've got to go back.' Another man followed.

Seth started to struggle again and Sadie knew she'd have to get out. She daren't let him go. Climbing out by the bridge she handed him over to a woman she knew and went back to watch. The river was a lake overlooked by the bridge.

As darkness fell, more men came, adding their weight to the search for the boy, her older child, Alfie. She had been wrong, it hadn't been Alfie she'd seen, but Seth. By now a crowd had gathered around her and when the curfew sent them home, Sadie still stood there, numb with shock. She knew she'd never see Alfie again.

Yet even so, a part of her thought, *at least that's one less mouth to feed.*

And Alfie would be safe forever. Nothing to fear, no cold for him. Not anymore.

20

1912 – Phoebe

So this, then, is what happens when it rains.

When Ma came to Issington Manor to tell me the news, I knew it was bad. My ma *never* comes to the manor, unless she's invited, she knows I don't like it. She stood at the door, silent and ghost-like, her scarf blowing around her face. Her hair was still wet.

Clara was there, behind me, hovering, I wanted to snap and push her away. Yet we'd reached a truce.

'You'd better invite the lady in.' And then to Ma, 'We've a good fire lit, why don't you come in? It's cold out there.' Ma looked ill.

Once I'd installed her in the drawing room and ordered some tea, I grasped Ma's hands. 'Whatever's the matter?' She didn't waste words.

'Alfie's gone, he drowned in the river.' I couldn't believe what I was hearing.

'What was he doing in the river?' I said. 'It's winter out there.'

'Playing,' said Ma, 'messing about, you know how they do. And, yes, Seth's fine, Alfie probably saved him, that's why he drowned.'

'But Ma…' I said, and stopped, faltered. There were too many questions, it didn't seem real.

'Haven't you seen the river?' said Ma. 'You do live next to it.'

Of course I'd known the river was high, but I'd stayed inside, avoided the rain. I hadn't been near the town lately. I should have gone down to Chesterton Court to try to see Ma, despite our row, but I'd chickened out. I had been selfish and look what had happened. Ma probably blamed me, I certainly did. If I'd taken more interest in them…

Ma refused my offer of food, she didn't even drink Mabel's tea and although I offered to show her the house, she refused that too.

'I have to go,' she said, terse. 'Seth's with a neighbour. I just thought you ought to know.' *Though you're not one of us.* She didn't quite say it.

I walked her to the door. Halfway down the steps she turned back to face me.

'Only today, somebody asked me how I manage without my Phoebe. Thinking, of course that you were dead, instead of living here. I was talking, gossiping and laughing, while your little brother drowned. Alfie's dead and you're still alive.' I knew then, she wished it was me.

'What happened to Alfie wasn't my fault,' I snapped, hurt, wishing the words back in my mouth as soon as I'd said them. Ma sniffed.

'Are you coming to the funeral?'

'Yes, of course, I'm coming…' Then I remembered. Going round town with a headscarf on, late in the evening or in a fast car is not the same as going to a funeral with people who've known you all your life. I knew I couldn't risk it. I rushed on.

'I'll pray for his soul, every day. And I'll pray for you too – they might yet find him.' Ma swore.

'A fat lot of good prayers have done. And it's too late, Phoebe.'

'Shh, Ma!' I said, horrified. Ma stared.

'I was right, wasn't I? Your brothers and I are nothing to you. All that matters to you is this house.'

I reddened, shamed. 'Is Seth alright?'

'He is,' said Ma, 'but no thanks to you. *Goodbye*, Phoebe.'

It felt like we'd come to the end of the road, another chapter closed for good. But I was wrong.

Later that month as the water subsided, they found Steph's body.

21

1912 – Sadie

Sometimes life could be hard.

First, she'd had to bury Alfie, whose body they'd found the very next day, knowing his death was her fault. She shouldn't have let the boys go out on their own, even though they'd done it before, loads of times. What a fool she'd been.

And now she had to bury her daughter, knowing the body wasn't hers.

She'd have to tell the vicar lies, say this was Phoebe even though she knew it was Steph, and having been in the river for so long, it could have been anyone. Thankfully. She felt sick to the stomach.

She'd already had to swear that a ring, probably Steph's, had belonged to her daughter, a darling girl she'd loved and lost. Well the last bit was true. She didn't know this new Phoebe.

She'd do this last thing for Phoebe and Steph, and for Steph's ma, Thirza, deprived of the right to bury her child. Of all the things that Phoebe had done, this was the worst. And now she was going to marry the painter and her lies would go on, into the future.

Alice had been right after all.

Sadie walked up the aisle, slowly, the church was still empty. She'd arrived early to gather her thoughts. But as she walked towards the pulpit, Sadie saw she wasn't alone. A woman sporting a large black hat sat at the front. Sadie wasn't a regular churchgoer but according to gossip the woman was, and she always chose the very same spot. Which annoyed the vicar, those pews were allocated.

Hearing her footsteps, the woman turned round. Sadie gasped. It was Alice. Sadie nodded.

'So you're the one. I'd never have guessed.' Alice looked blank.

'The woman who always sits at the front, even though the vicar doesn't like it.' Alice laughed then covered her mouth.

'No, laugh. It'll cheer me up. Why the front row? Can't you see?'

'That's not it. You don't come to church often?'

'No,' said Sadie, *though, perhaps I should have done.*

'The verger hands out bread to the poor. If I'm up front, I've got a chance.'

'But you're not poor, you've got a job.' Alice smiled.

'I give the bread to the people who need it, not just those who come to church.'

So that's why the vicar didn't like her. Sadie nodded. Alice was kind, if rather eccentric. 'I see the river's gone down a bit.'

'Yes, right, and all over town, people are claiming for the things they've lost, even if they haven't lost anything. Like old Mrs Smith, who claimed for a table she'd taken upstairs. And she's not the first.'

Sadie chuckled, her first laugh in ages. It felt good. Alice went on.

'I was sorry to hear about Phoebe, Sadie, you've had it hard. That's why I've come to church today, to show my respects.' Sadie nodded, she couldn't speak. Alice smiled.

'Did Steph Gilchrist come to see you?'

'What?' said Sadie, her heart thumping.

'I thought I saw her at yours once, quite a while back. But I could have been wrong.'

'Yes, right, a long time ago. But not since Alfie...' Sadie couldn't speak.

'They're saying *she's* going to marry the painter, instead of Miss Clara.' Sadie nodded.

'That's what I've heard.' The church was filling up at last and the vicar was walking towards them, slowly. *Hurry, please hurry.*

Alice leant over the pew towards her, keeping her voice low. 'If you see her again, will you give her a message?' *God, what now?*

'Tell her she's not to go on that ship. That journeys can be dangerous. Do you hear me, Sadie?' She gripped Sadie's arm so hard that it hurt.

Sadie felt dizzy. She heard the babble of voices around her and smiled at the vicar as he passed. 'Journeys, what journey?'

Alice shook her head. 'Just give her the message, please Mrs Slater, it's very important. Do you understand?'

Sadie nodded and Alice released her arm at last, turning back towards the front. Music was playing and the vicar was talking. Sadie sat back. She took a deep breath.

She knew Alice had warned her of something, something important, but at that moment she almost didn't care. Sadie Slater was *so* tired.

22

1912 – Phoebe

It's not long now until we're married, then the manor will be mine. And we won't be leaving, I'm determined on that. But there's one small problem. I can't find the second will. I was shouting at Gwilym.

'Where have you put it?' And trying to keep calm. Gwilym smiled.

'Why assume I've put it anywhere?' He was sitting outside on the porch, drinking tea and drawing the church. It was far too cold to be outside. Gwilym gestured at the sketch. 'It's a new commission.'

'Good for you. Damn it Gwilym, where's the will?'

'How should I know?' he said, bored and I swore at him. Gwilym laughed.

'You're getting rather repetitive, Phoebs.'

But I was angry, very angry and afraid.

Three hours later, having searched *everywhere*, I was still seething. I didn't know what to do next. I couldn't ask Clara, she didn't even know the damn thing existed. I tried to remember when I'd last seen it, who'd put it where, after the mattress. Gwilym *must* have it. He'd told me he'd hide it, for safe keeping. *But where, exactly?* I asked him at lunch.

'Perhaps, Phoebs, I *have* hidden it,' Gwilym admitted, wiping his mouth on a fine napkin. Only the best at Issington Manor. Clara was out.

'I knew it!' I said. 'Where the hell is it?' Gwilym wagged his finger at me.

'Patience, Phoebs. I'd love to tell you where it is but the light is perfect for painting right now. When the muse calls I have to be ready. Would you like to see my sketch?'

'No, I damn well wouldn't!' I jumped up. 'Tell me where the will is.'

'Shush, girl, Burns might hear. Why don't you go out for a walk? It's a lovely day. Maybe we can find the will later.'

'Ha!' I said. 'I'll hold you to that,' and stormed out, leaving him to it. Gwilym was just playing with me. Damn the man and his stupid games. I decided to risk a visit to Ma.

Today was Friday, the day the carts came into town and Issington Halt was full of people. Jacob and I used to come here on Fridays, leaving the carriage at The Royale, while we walked by the river. Jacob ate candyfloss, I couldn't stand it. Then we'd go for tea somewhere, usually at the Old Cottage tearooms. I can't bear to go there, anymore, it's far too sad.

Today, the air was sharp, with a bite, a typical bright March day. Everyone else was in a hurry. I'd chosen the long way, I couldn't face going down Whitborough Walk and seeing the road after the flood. Like the river, it was full of debris, bits of tree and broken chairs. Going back home was bad enough. Today, I'd brought money, cash he'd obtained from one of his commissions. Sometimes even Gwilym could be kind.

Ma sniffed as I walked in. 'Oh, so it's you.' I glanced around.

The house seemed smaller every visit and today it felt as small as a doll's house, though not so pretty. Ma looked sour.

'I can't take much more of this, having to lie to people in church. Pretending you're dead, when I know you're not. Everyone felt so sorry for me.' I stared.

'Would you rather I was, Ma? It's not as if you go to church, most of the time. Soon my death will be yesterday's news. People will forget.'

'What about Alfie? Do you want them to forget him too?'

'No,' I snapped, 'of course I don't.' I held out the money. 'This is for you and Seth, Ma. I got it from Gwilym.' Ma took it, grudgingly.

'I'm taking it for Seth, not for me.'

I sighed. 'I'm doing the best that I can, Ma.'

'Well right now that's not good enough. If you'd been at home with me, instead of down there playing Lady of the Manor…'

If you'd kept the boys with you. But I didn't say it.

Ma sank into a chair. She'd lost two in the flood, but she hadn't bothered to claim either of them.

'I'm taking in sewing. Alice has arranged it.'

'Sewing?' I snapped. 'I've already told you, I don't want you to do that, it's bad for your eyes.'

'And I've told you, I can't manage. I need to buy food, and clothes for Seth. Work is work and this is from home. I could do worse.' I sighed.

I knew I'd never get her to agree, or to forgive me for forging a life outside these walls. I nodded at her. 'I'll be back in a couple of days.'

'That's up to you. But before you leave you ought to hear what Alice said. About going on a journey.'

'What?' I said. *How did Alice know?*

'Is it true that you're going on a boat for your honeymoon?'

'Yes,' I said. 'We're going to New York, on the *Titanic.*'

'Across the Atlantic!' Ma looked worried.

I laughed. 'It's a floating hotel, Ma. We'll be fine. What did Alice say?'

'She said not to go on the ship. That journeys can be dangerous.' She grabbed my arm. 'Please, don't go.'

I shook my head. 'Honestly, Ma, the ship's brand new, and it's the best. They'll have checked everything. It'll be fine.' Ma sniffed.

'Suit yourself, you always do. But you know Alice has second sight?' I laughed.

'I don't believe in second sight.'

'There's something else.' I sighed.

'Go on then, if you must.'

'Alice said *her*, meaning you. But, she never mentioned Gwilym.'

I stared at my ma. Now, *that* worried me.

I didn't tell Gwilym what Alice had said. I was more worried about the will.

'So where is it?'

Gwilym ignored me, he was still painting, his sketch had turned into multiple colours. It wasn't half bad.

'Please Gwilym,' I said, wheedling. I was feeling desperate. Gwilym didn't answer.

'Fine,' I said, 'if you won't help me, I'll have to talk to Clara. I'll tell her I've lost a document and then I'll get her to help me to find it. And, believe me, we will, I'll even search your lodgings if I have to. Then,' I said, 'it'll all come out. Then where will you be?'

'Exposed, like you. It's a test of wills.'

'Ha!' I said, 'but Clara and I used to be friends. She might forgive me. She won't forgive you. Then you'll have nothing.'

Gwilym frowned, getting up. 'Fine, you win. Of course I've got it. You asked me to keep it for you. Don't you remember?'

'No,' I said, knowing he was lying. 'Where is it?'

But Gwilym just smiled. 'Never you mind. I promise it's safe, you don't need to worry. Now give me a kiss.' I stepped back.

'Not until I know where you've put the will.'

Gwilym leant forward and pulled me to him, running his hands down my dress. My heart quickened. Sproat strolled past with a barrow full of plants. I shoved Gwilym off.

'No!' I said. 'Not until you tell me *where.*' He touched his finger to my lips.

'When we're on our honeymoon, Phoebs.' I pushed him away.

'I'm not waiting until then. That will's mine. I was the one who found it, remember, and I'm the one who's meant to inherit.' Gwilym laughed and shook his head.

'Not in my book!' His voice softened. 'Look, Phoebs, you don't need to worry. It's safe where it is and no-one will find it, especially Clara. When we're married and on the ship, *then* I'll tell you where it is. I wouldn't want you to change your mind.' His eyes twinkled.

'Ha'! I said, and turned away. But I was still worried.

It wasn't me he loved but the manor, and only that for the money it brought.

23

1912 – Sadie

Sadie struggled up Midden Lane South, Seth trailing along behind her. For all it was March, the day was cold and her shopping was heavy. She always took Seth everywhere now and that was a burden, him being so young. He always wanted to be somewhere else, playing with the lads or down by the river. Despite what had happened.

'No,' she said, repeatedly. 'You're coming with me.'

'Aw, Ma...'

'You can help me carry the shopping,' she said, 'otherwise you'll be sleeping in the yard.' Sometimes you had to be cruel to be kind.

'At least I've got my own bed now.' Sadie turned and stared at him. There wasn't much she could say to that. She swallowed her pain.

They seemed to have more money too, that was the hard thing. Weighed down, she struggled up the road.

At the top she paused, watchful, waiting for the carts to pass. Fridays were always so busy in town. It was then that she spotted the two men, the painter and another man, one in a suit. She'd seen him before. *What was he called?* She struggled to remember.

Seth tugged at Sadie's arm. 'Ma, come on, it's time to cross!' Sadie batted her son away.

'Wait, just a minute, Seth.' Knowing that she was getting in the way, she studied the men as people passed by. A couple of them tutted at her. Sadie ignored them.

What was he called? Thomas, no, Tommins, that was it! The man was a builder, quite successful. What did the painter want with him?

Sadie had a nose for trouble and those two meeting just didn't feel right. She didn't want Tommins or Gwilym to see her. So she turned around and hurried back the way she'd come, dragging a reluctant Seth with her. When she reached Whitborough Walk she kept her eyes firmly fixed on the ground. God, it was hard.

She walked past the Riverboat Inn and the bottom of her street, still clutching Seth and the shopping, and made her way to the five-bar gate, pushing it open. She hurried up the path to the manor and banged on the door, praying it wouldn't be Clara who answered. Instead it was Burns.

He glanced down at her and the boy, he hadn't been there the last time she'd called. 'We don't have any work,' he said. 'But thank you for calling.'

Sadie felt her face flush. She hadn't gone to the manor for work, she'd gone there to help, to warn them of something, she wasn't sure what. Then she saw red.

Damn them, she thought. She'd gone there to help, but not anymore. She jerked Seth around and hurried away, seething with rage. *Who did that man think he was?* Not even able to visit her daughter…

She remembered saying the same to Phoebe after Alfie had died. 'I can't even call on you, unless it's in secret.'

'That'll all change, after we're married.'

Sadie didn't believe that now. How could Phoebe explain her to Clara, and to the servants? As a charity case? She wasn't having that. She leant against the gate, bone weary. Her daughter was dead, at least to her. She needed to face it.

She'd wanted to warn them about George Tommins. The man had bought land and sometimes houses then knocked them down and built others. Multiple dwellings, shabby and cheap. She knew the sort of man he was. She'd gone to the manor to warn her girl.

Now she knew about the will. The second one. Phoebe had told her.

'Look Ma, you've a right to know. The second will leaves everything to Steph as Jacob's heir. The manor will be mine.'

'It'll be Gwilym's after you're married. Why wait until then? Tell Clara now.' Phoebe said nothing.

'You're afraid Gwilym would tell Clara you're not Steph and you'd lose everything. Or maybe you just want to marry him.'

Phoebe shrugged.

'Fine, so marry him. *Then* your brother and I will move in. And about time.' Phoebe looked grim.

'You don't understand. Gwilym wants to sell the manor and buy somewhere else. A place that's his own.'

'I don't mind where we go, so long as it's out of here, and soon.'

'But Clara and I don't want to sell.'

Sadie frowned. 'So you think, but you can't be sure, because you haven't told her about the will. You don't trust her. Or me, either.'

'That's not true!'

But Sadie thought it probably was. She sighed, heavily. She only had herself to blame, bringing the girl up with fancy ideas. But she still felt bitter.

She recalled all this, staggering up Bakehouse Lane with Seth and the shopping, thoughts of her meeting with Burns simmering. Phoebe had chosen a different path, well so be it. She wouldn't be going with them when they moved. *She'd* had her fill of deceit.

If Phoebe wanted to know about George Tommins, let someone else tell her.

24

1854 – Lucienne Hall

Augustin returned early in the spring, as he'd said he would. He'd brought chocolates and wine.

She held out *her* gifts, chocolates and wine. The wine was the same. Augustin laughed. 'Your chocolates look better.'

'So they should, they've been made for you. See, this is a house like the manor.' Augustin smiled. They were still in the porch.

'Aren't you going to invite me in?' For once the weather was better than rain. Lucienne paused.

'That depends.'

'Depends on what?'

'On how long you're staying.'

Augustin grinned. 'A week if you like.'

'Maybe,' she said and opened the door. 'If you behave.' But Lucienne was smiling.

Later, at dinner, they talked about houses. Augustin poured more wine.

'Only a small mansion this time. And, of course, not a patch on this. It's hard, you know.'

'What is?' she said, handing him coffee and adding small cakes.

'Knowing I've done my best work so young.' Lucienne laughed.

'You're *so* arrogant.'

'Maybe I mean it.' Grabbing her hands across the table. 'I'll build more houses and they'll all be as good as the one I've just finished. But this, darling Lucienne, will always be best, just like you.' Lucienne laughed.

'Your charm doesn't work on me, *darling*.'

'Are you sure?'

A few nights later, after supper, they were sitting in Lucienne's study in the basement. Augustin shivered.

'It's cold down here.'

'It helps me work.' She handed Augustin one of her poems. 'What do you think?' Augustin shrugged.

'It's no good asking me, Luci, I know nothing about poetry.'

'While I, of course, know loads about buildings.' She turned and wrapped her arms around him, pulling him close. 'Where are you going for your next commission?'

'London, I think, somewhere in Greenwich. It could be a good one, there's money down there.'

'But, that's not where you're going next week. Otherwise you'd know. So where, then?' Augustin faltered.

'I'm going home. I need a break.' Lucienne sat back.

'You're having a break now, with me.'

'It's not the same.' Augustin got up and paced the room, not very easy in the space. It was too small. 'I need to be on my own sometimes, just like you, when you write.' He opened the door.

Lucienne stared. 'But that's when I'm working!' He was walking away from her. 'Augustin, wait!' He stopped on the stairs. She took a deep breath.

'I've been thinking...' knowing as she said it that it was the wrong time.

'What?' he said, climbing again. She ran up the stairs after him.

'That you could make your home with me. The manor could be your permanent home.' Hurrying past him to the top, so she could look at him, say it to his face.

He didn't look happy.

'Look, Luci, I need to be on my own a lot, to have my own space.'

'You could have some space here, there's plenty of room.' Augustin sighed.

'That's not what I meant.' He stared at her. 'I don't understand what the problem is.'

'There isn't a problem,' Lucienne lied. 'I just want to see a bit more of you. Why is that wrong?'

'Don't be silly. Of course it's not wrong. We have a great time when we're together. But if we spent our *lives* together, it could get b...'

'Boring. You were going to say boring.'

'No,' he said. 'I wasn't going to say that. I don't think that.' His voice sounded strained.

'Augustin, you were!' Wishing she hadn't started this.

'I just like having time alone. It's how I am.'

I've put myself on the line for you and you don't care.

Lucienne felt her rage grow, she'd been a fool and all for a man. 'Damn you to hell,' she yelled, angry, upset and ashamed. She felt like an idiot. She gave him a shove, a hard shove, forgetting they were on the stairs. He overbalanced.

She watched him tumble down the stairs and land at the bottom, saw him crack his head on the floor, it was cold, stone, heard him cry out and then – nothing. Lucienne stared. Then, as fast as she could, she raced down to the basement.

As she got near him, she saw that blood was dripping from his head, but it didn't look bad, a large gash. Until she felt *behind* his head and her hand came away covered in blood. Lucienne shrieked. She grabbed his wrist and felt for a pulse, but she couldn't feel anything. Then she put her head on his chest but she couldn't hear a heartbeat. Augustin was dead. *No*, she thought, *I'm not going to think that.* She needed a doctor.

Hating to leave him alone like this, she raced back upstairs, grabbed a lamp and left the house, making her way up

Whitborough Walk. A quick right turn took her to the doctor's. Dr Rolfe was out.

Oh, God. What shall I do?

Then she remembered the nurse, Mrs Cam, who lived not far away. The woman was a gossip and not very clean, but even she was better than no-one. The doctor could be hours yet and Lucienne couldn't afford to wait. Lifting her skirts so she could run faster, she turned around and headed back the way she'd come, past the manor, stopping for breath outside her old home on Whitborough Walk. Now, which house was Mrs Cam's?

Standing outside her old front door, uncertain and scared, Lucienne longed for simpler times. She saw that the door to the garden was open. She couldn't resist.

Knowing she ought to head for Nurse Cam, Lucienne checked each of the windows, saw no-one was in and slipped down the passage. *Just for a second. No-one will know.* Seeing her old garden would calm her. But it was all changed.

Gone were the trees and the flowers she'd grown, instead there were slabs and shrubs in pots. It was stark and bleak and no longer hers. She'd been wrong to come here.

Then she glanced across at the wall, was that the clematis she'd once planted? A little unhinged with stress and fear she hurried towards it, swinging her lamp, no longer afraid that she'd be seen. Lucienne didn't care. The climber was close to the kitchen window, which was open. That was rather odd...

Lucienne stopped, bemused and tired. *What's that smell?* It wasn't very pleasant. She bent down to look at the climber, intent on her task and dropped her lamp.

She didn't get to see anything else.

25

1912 – Clara

Clara was packed and ready to go. Burns was taking her to the station. But Clara was finding it hard to leave.

When she came back, Issington Manor wouldn't be hers. They'd be married and Gwilym would be here all the time. That would be hard. She'd be invisible in her own home.

But it won't be yours, not anymore. The thought sickened her.

If it wasn't for Father's dream, she thought, *I'd leave now and never come back.* But Clara loved Issington Manor and she'd promised her father she'd fulfil his dream. If only *they* would leave.

Burns appeared. 'Are you ready, Miss Clara?'

Clara was going to stay with Aunt Vi, but first she had to say her goodbyes. She'd already spoken to Steph last night. Wishing Gwilym well would be a lot harder.

Her ex-lover was in the drawing room, reading the paper. It annoyed her how he was here so often, almost as if he already lived here. It wasn't right, before they were married. Not that she cared.

He didn't look up as she walked in.

'I hope you enjoy your trip to New York.' She'd be damned if she'd wish him a happy wedding day.

Gwilym nodded and got to his feet and. He didn't look happy.

Are you wondering if you've made the right choice? She didn't give a damn.

'I'll see you after your trip, Gwilym. I trust you'll be back for the Hall events?' She wanted him to know she wasn't giving up.

Gwilym looked grim.

'Yeah, sure, but you ought to be aware that after this year, there won't be any more Hall events.'

'And why's that exactly?' Clara felt her heart quicken.

'Because we're selling the manor, that's why. We're going to buy a new house, something that's ours, but you needn't worry, I'll make sure that you're provided for. Maybe a nice little home by the river, where you can still paint?'

Clara gasped, white with rage.

'Where I can still paint? You're talking as if it's some sort of hobby instead of my work. When I'm a better painter than you!'

Gwilym laughed. 'You *are* a good painter, and maybe one day you'll be better, but right now you haven't half my experience or my expertise. You're still learning.'

Clara stared at him, opened-mouthed. The insults were bad enough, but what he'd said was filtering through and not about the painting. She stepped towards him.

'Did you say, you're going to sell the manor? Over my dead body! You might be marrying Steph, Gwilym, but I'm damned if I'll let you take my home.'

'It won't be your home after I'm married, it'll be mine. I can do what I like.' He stepped towards her and Clara stepped away.

'No you damn well can't! You might be the owner after you're married, but I'm still entitled to live here and you can't sell it. It's in the will. So put that in your pipe and smoke it.' She closed the drawing room door, quickly. Burns mustn't hear. 'I'm not leaving until this is settled.'

'Yes Clara, but which will?'

'What did you say?'

'Steph found a second will, a later one, and in this version everything is hers, as Jacob's child, including the manor. And Steph's going to marry me.' He stared at her, coldly. 'You might as well know, we're going to have the house demolished. It's prime land, suitable for building and I've got a man who wants to buy it. He's going to put up several houses.'

'What?' said Clara. She couldn't believe it.

'The man's called Tommins, we've already had a brief meeting and he's shown a lot of interest. "Homes by the river, they'll fetch a packet," that's what he said.' Gwilym smirked.

It was all too much. 'A second will?'

'Yes, it's true, there's a second will. I've seen it.'

'Where is it?' She forced herself to walk towards Gwilym, this was the man she'd wanted to marry. This... scoundrel. Gwilym shook his head.

'Oh, no. You can't see it yet. When we come back, *then* you can see it.'

Clara wanted to scream and hit him. 'Where is it?' she repeated, her voice rising. 'If you won't tell me, Steph will.' She opened the door, ran into the hall and raced up the stairs, pounding on her cousin's door.

'Steph, get up! I need to speak to you. Right now!'

Gwilym had followed close behind. He grabbed Clara's arm. 'You're wasting your time asking Steph, she doesn't know. I thought it was better if she didn't. Though you can ask if you like. If it's any consolation, she was cross too.'

Clara turned around to face him. 'I'm not *cross*, I'm angry as hell. I'd like kill you and you ought to know, I will if I have to, if push comes to shove. That will belongs in our family, it's not yours to hide or to steal.' She laughed, unsteadily. 'You're a liar, Gwilym. For all I know you're making it up.'

'You wish. Steph's seen it, as I said, *she* found it, in the Lucienne Hall room. If you'd kept that room tidy, *you* would have found it, think of that. Then you could have got rid of the thing. And all for the sake of your precious Hall library.'

'I wouldn't do that!'

Gwilym grinned. 'So you say. Like I said, when we sell, I'll make sure you have somewhere to live, and near the river, although it won't be here.' He paused, grinned. 'You ought to be grateful, because in this will it all belongs to Steph, so we don't have to give you anything.'

That did it. Clara screamed, a piercing scream and grabbing hold of Gwilym's shirt she half-pulled him down the stairs, along the hall and out of the front door. He didn't resist. 'Get out,' she said and don't come back!' Gwilym laughed and raised his hands.

'Okay,' he said. 'I'm going now, and I won't be back until after the honeymoon. But the will exists, and we'll be selling, whatever you say. Why do you think I told you now? So you can get used to it.'

'You're poison,' she said, but Gwilym just laughed and walked away. She almost thought she could hear him whistle.

Heart pounding, she leant against the door frame, wondering what the world was coming to. That man had taken everything, her cousin, her home and her father's dream. She'd be damned if he would!

She turned around to see Steph, bedraggled and flustered and still in a night wrap. Burns was behind her, cool as anything.

'Excuse me, Miss,' he said to Steph.

'Sorry,' said Steph, moving away. Burns stared calmly at Clara.

'I think you've missed your train,' he said.

Clara and Steph had coffee upstairs, away from the servants.

'So Gwilym told you about the will.'

'Yes he did, and also that you're selling the house, taking away my father's dream and leaving me with a small cottage where I can paint pictures. And for all that I ought to be grateful!'

'Hell,' said Steph.

'I couldn't believe it when he first said it, that you and he had joined forces against me, to sell off my home. *Our* home. And you didn't think to mention this?'

'That's because we haven't joined forces. I don't want him to sell off the manor, I like living here, in Lucienne Hall's house.'

One of her houses. At least they don't know about Whitborough Walk. Clara wondered why she cared. Perhaps she should take the money she'd get and leave this place, go far away. *Never!* she thought.

'He's going to have the manor demolished. Did you know that? He wants to sell the land to a local builder, someone called Tommins, who'll put up more houses and make more money. It's a get rich quick scheme.' Steph looked worried.

'No. I didn't. He said he wanted to buy a new house but I was against it. I thought I'd change his mind eventually. He never mentioned demolishing the manor.'

'I'll bet he didn't,' Clara said. 'You know, once you're married, the man can do whatever he wants.'

Steph frowned. 'I wish I'd never found that will.'

'You and me both. How would you feel if you were me? Your cousin appears and steals your fiancé, then both of them take your family home and your father's dream.' Steph looked down.

'You could let me see the will,' Clara said, softly. 'I wouldn't tell Gwilym. I just want to see what it says, Steph. I wouldn't do anything.' Steph sighed and shook her head.

'I've no idea where he's put it. He took it away for safe-keeping, it was so fragile, after we... He said he'd checked and there wasn't a copy so it had to be kept somewhere safe. I've asked him several times where it is, but he won't say.'

'He'll have to produce it eventually, if he wants to sell the house. Then when I've got it, I'll destroy it – and him too, if he gets in the way.'

Steph gasped and Clara smiled.

'I let you into my lovely home and this is how you both repay me. By stealing my inheritance. Your father was right to keep us apart. I wish I'd never met you.' Steph looked strained.

'Don't say that.'

Clara smiled. 'And why not?'

'Because I'm your...' Steph stopped.

'Why do you want to marry him, cousin?'

Steph shrugged. 'God knows,' she said.

In spite of herself, Clara laughed. 'I often felt like that,' she said.

Clara cancelled her trip to Aunt Vi's, she wanted to stay in the house while she could. The thought of the manor being demolished was too much.

She and Steph carried on talking but only about everyday things. The rest was too hard.

At the end of the month, before Steph left, to meet Gwilym and get married, Clara tried again.

'Do you know if he's taking the will with him? Have you looked?'

'Of course I have. I've searched everywhere, Clara, including his pockets and his artist's bag. I've found nothing. But he won't be taking it on the ship in case it gets stolen.'

'Maybe a solicitor's then?' Steph shook her head.

'He's very suspicious, he doesn't trust anyone.' Steph sighed. 'I'm out of ideas.'

'It must be in his rooms then, on Whitborough Walk.'

'Gwilym left his rooms last week and the landlady's rented one room out already. Lately he's been in lodgings in Upper Fell Street. He wouldn't leave it there though, it wouldn't be safe. It must be somewhere in this house. God knows where.' Steph looked at Clara.

'After tomorrow, you'll be alone, apart from the servants. You'll have several weeks to search this house, with no interruptions. If I was you, that's what I'd do. Tear the house apart.' Clara frowned.

Steph went on. 'And if you find it, what you do then, that's up to you. I know what I'd do.'

The two women smiled at each other.

26

1912 – Clara

Steph left on the London train. That was it, they were both gone. The house was quiet, empty of drama. At least for a while. *Thank God,* thought Clara leaning back in her chair.

She hadn't asked about their wedding or where it would be, apart from in London. She didn't want to know. The way they were doing things seemed underhand, but Steph obviously didn't care. Perhaps she only wanted to be married. And get the manor. Clara frowned.

Damn Jacob *and* his daughter. If Jacob hadn't come back to the area, none of this would have happened. *Then I'd be the one getting married to Gwilym.* Did she still want that?

Clara went to ring for Mabel, then realised she wasn't there. None of the servants were in tonight, Burns and Mabel were visiting their families, and Flora had said she was staying with a friend. *In Pooling Road?* Not a good place.

She ought to know more about her servants. But did she care?

Forget tea, Clara thought. *I need a real drink.*

She poured herself a large whisky and put the bottle near her on the table. She'd be having some more of that. A whole lot more.

So, it was over. That brief, bright and glorious time of having the manor to herself, of building up the Hall events and meeting Gwilym, thinking he was the one for her. Then knowing he wasn't. All of her dreams had come tumbling down.

Clara rose from the chair again, and wandered out towards the Palm House, clutching her glass. It was one of her father's crystal ones, old and substantial.

Gwilym and Steph had met in the Palm House, once she'd even seen them together, whispering, talking. It had probably meant nothing, but why was he even in the house? She should have challenged them at the time but instead she'd done nothing. *God, I feel drunk!*

Clara stared out at the grounds, seeing the glass of the door sparkle, the moon was high. Recalling Steph that very first day, her face in the door. How she'd taken Steph round the house and how, later, they'd had tea. She remembered it all perfectly.

Then she recalled an earlier time, her first Hall event, pretty successful, thanks to Alice. She'd never looked back. Marie Corelli and all her acquaintances, walking across her lawn, laughing. Later that day, after everyone had gone, dancing alone with the music blaring. She'd been so happy. Still dancing in the rain, not knowing then what she knew now. Promises broken, secrets unearthed. *Damn them to hell, Gwilym, Jacob* and *her grandfather and his stupid second will!* Clara laughed.

She threw her drink at the orangery wall and the glass shattered, tiny fragments raining down, slivers of ice, glass tears, falling like rain.

But tonight, Clara wasn't dancing.

PART FOUR

1

1912 – Stella

In several weeks the *Titanic* would sink. On its maiden voyage, on the way to New York. No-one believed that a large, luxurious liner like *Titanic* could sink. But Stella had never heard of *Titanic*, even though she was going on a journey. Hers was only across England, from Dorset to Issington, a place she'd never been to before. Or expected to visit. The journey itself was uneventful.

Arriving in the early evening she found a room in a lodging house, close to the river.

'You're lucky my dear,' the landlady said. 'I had a young man in here before, but he's just left, he's gone to get married. The room's free, if you'd like it.' Stella did.

She never thought to ask who the man was, she was more concerned about her four-year old child, who was tired and whining. She glanced at the woman.

'He's normally good. We've come a long way, I'm *so* glad to have found this room.' Mrs Moore smiled.

'Don't you worry. I know what children can be like. I'm a mother myself, and a grandmother. Will you be staying with us for long?' Stella paused.

'I don't know, that depends. Probably several weeks, I think, but I'm not sure. Can I let you know?' Mrs Moore nodded.

'Yes, dear, but I'll need two weeks' notice. It gets busy in the summer.'

I doubt I'll be here by the summer, thought Stella, wondering then if that was true. She didn't know what was going to happen. But *if* she stayed, she'd need to find work and get someone to look after Jack. It wouldn't be easy. Stella sighed.

What she'd seen of the town so far looked good, it was pretty and quaint. Bigger than Malden, the place she'd come from, but still small, which would help with her search. If she failed, she'd have to go back and that would be hard. Stella had burnt her bridges there, including with Roland.

'I'm happy to take you, you and the boy,' he'd said to her, a kind older man with plenty of money. As if she was just a stray dog.

I can do better than that, she'd thought. *But could she?* she wondered.

When Mrs Moore had gone downstairs, Stella unpacked and put Jack to bed. She stared out of the tiny, cracked window.

A man was striding down Whitborough Lane, his dog by his side. It cheered her up. The sun was setting, low in the sky. Stella smiled. She closed the curtains.

Tomorrow would be better.

2

1912 – Clara

Clara glanced at the clock and sighed.

At last that door was finally closed, Steph and Gwilym would be married by now, and soon they'd be on that huge ship. Sailing across the Atlantic Ocean. Enjoying the trip, enjoying each other... *Ah, well.*

The will problem wasn't so settled. Clara had searched the house thoroughly but she still she hadn't found it. She'd tried all the obvious places but none had been right. Then one day she was staring at the paintings in the drawing room and had an idea. Maybe he'd hidden the will in a picture. Not in her self-portrait, it wouldn't be in that, but maybe, perhaps, in one of the others. Clara smiled.

Several days later she'd proved herself wrong. Dusty and weary, Clara was desperate. In a few short weeks the couple would be back. Time was running out. The will must be somewhere.

The only place she hadn't searched was Lucienne Hall's room. Her heart sank at the thought of going through all that paper. Yes, it was tidier, thanks to Steph, but all the same... And Gwilym never went down there. But that's where Steph had found the will, so maybe he thought she wouldn't check.

She ran her mind around the room. Mountains of paper, shelves piled high, an old cupboard and a desk with drawers and maybe even some hidden compartments. *But it could be anywhere!* Her mind ran riot, drifted away from the poetry room.

Clara stepped out into the garden, the weather was changing, spring was here. She could almost smell it. The early bulbs were beginning to bloom. Better to look at the plants and trees, enjoy the river, than worry about her future life. Clara stopped walking. *Maybe*, she thought.

Whitborough Walk was one of her favourite routes into town. Out of the gate and round to the right, strolling along, as if by the river. Not that she could see the river, or her house, the trees hid them. Walking slowly down the road, the tiny houses on the left with the trees peeping out, the memorial garden, and to the right a different view, the smell of activity, barges and sheds, the work of the river. Clara loved this walk so much. It felt like hers. She stopped by a three-storied house on the left.

A large woman emerged from the house. 'Miss Clara,' she said. 'I didn't expect to see you here.' The woman looked wary and Clara smiled. She wanted to put her at ease.

'Hello Mrs Moore. I hope you're well? Mr Lawson asked me to call to see you. He left something in his room and he asked me to get it, if you don't mind.' *And even if you do*, she thought.

'And what's that?' *Clearly this wasn't going to be easy.*

'It's personal,' said Clara, looking away. *The things I have to do for the manor.* 'I know it's a bit of an imposition, but please Mrs Moore, it won't take long. I just want a look.'

Mrs Moore moved towards her.

'I've rented one of his rooms out now, to a nice young woman with a small child. I don't think I could let you in, not with her things there, it wouldn't be right. The other room, fine, although there's nothing in there. I'm having it painted.'

Damn, thought Clara, cursing the stranger who'd moved in so quickly. She needed to get in the room with the desk. She took a deep breath.

'Gwilym and I were engaged once. And as you'll have heard, he changed his mind.' She swallowed, looked up. 'But when he comes back he'll still be the owner of Issington

Manor, a man of great wealth.' She smiled at Mrs Moore. 'So, I know you'll want to help me with this, you'll be helping him too, and I know he thought a lot of you.' *Lies, all lies.* The landlady sighed.

'Well, yes, alright, but only for Mr Gwilym's sake. I'll have to stay in the room with you because it's been let. Lucky for you, the young lady's out.'

As if Clara wasn't a lady. But what did it matter, she'd got what she'd wanted? If only her wiles had worked on Gwilym. *Still, never mind. Now, for the will.*

She followed Mrs Moore upstairs.

3

1912 – Stella

Stella was at the town hall offices. The fair young woman stared at her.

'You're looking for Mr Gwilym Lawson? Why, exactly?' Stella stared back.

'I'd like him to paint a portrait for me, of my son.' The fair woman smiled.

'Then I'm afraid you're out of luck. He used to have lodgings in Whitborough Walk but he's no longer there. You'll be able to find him at Issington Manor, but not at the moment, he's out of town.'

Damn, thought Stella. 'How long for?' The young woman shrugged.

'It's no good asking me,' she said and shouted behind her. 'When are they coming back, Theo?'

A young man emerged from behind a cabinet.

Nice, thought Stella, smiling at the man. The man smiled back.

'I'm not sure. End of April, possibly May. I don't keep track of Steph's movements.'

'Well you should, Theo. She is Clara's cousin.' The young man winked.

'That's Alice for you. Always telling me what to do.'

'Who's Clara?' Stella said. 'And who's Steph?'

'Clara's my niece,' the man explained, 'although we're similar in age and we don't really speak. And Steph is, well...' he glanced at Alice, 'she's Clara's cousin and she's just got married. To the man you mentioned, Gwilym Lawson.'

'What?' said Stella, feeling faint. She reached for a chair to steady herself. Had she heard that right? She knew she had. *Oh God*, she thought. *I've arrived too late.*

4

1912– Clara

It hadn't been hard to get rid of the woman. Clara mentioned a knock at the door, an imaginary knock, but it sent Mrs Moore scuttling downstairs. She was only gone minutes. Then Clara mentioned the smell, and Mrs Moore disappeared again, muttering something about scones in the oven. Clara had to be quick.

She'd only come here to look at the desk. Clara opened each of the drawers, as she'd expected, there was nothing inside. Then she pulled each of them out, felt behind them, but again, nothing.

Then she sat on Gwilym's chair, the chair he used to sit at while painting. Clara felt sad. She put her feet on the bar at the bottom, pushed a little and something moved. She bent down and looked at the back, lifted up the sliding panel. *This must be it.*

But, no, *damn it*, the cavity was empty. Clara panicked. She needed more time. She could hear Mrs Moore, climbing the stairs.

Clara hurried to the door, took the key and locked herself in. The woman wasn't pleased.

She rattled the handle and yelled at Clara but Clara ignored her. She knew she didn't have much time left. She stared at the desk. There must be more to the space than this. Then she noticed a tiny brass ring screwed into the wood. She gave it a tug and the panel moved forward and fell on the floor, leaving another, larger space. In the space was a bag. Clara grabbed it.

She stuffed the bag inside her own and quickly put the panels back. Then she stood up and smoothed herself down.

Some of her hair had come loose from its pins. She took a deep breath and opened the door. Mrs Moore looked livid.

'And to think I thought you were a lady – you're no better than a common thief! Locking me out of my own rooms! If this gets out I'll lose my licence.' Clara smiled.

'I had to lock the door, Mrs Moore. I was afraid your lodger would come back and find me. I didn't want to cause a scene.' Mrs Moore sniffed.

'You should have let me in straight away.'

'Yes, true, but I was still looking. And I've found what I wanted. Here, look.'

Clara showed her a picture of Gwilym and her, from when they'd first met. It was one of the new photographs and had cost a lot at the time, but it had been worth it, then *and* now. Even though she hated the thing. Seeing the photo Mrs Moore softened.

'Dear Miss Gilchrist, you should have said. Of course, you'd want your picture back, who wouldn't? It's incredible isn't it, what they can do now?'

It's all that girl has left of him, that's what Mrs Moore would be thinking. *Damn the old bat.*

Clara kept a calm demeanour.

'I've tried to put things back as I found them, but if your lodger makes a complaint, send her to me and I'll reimburse her.' Wondering then if this was wise. Mrs Moore wasn't above a scam. Clara smiled and eased past her.

'Thanks for all your help, Mrs Moore.' She made her way down the stairs slowly, trying to resist the urge to hurry. Mrs Moore followed.

When she finally reached outside, she turned to the woman. Now for the hard bit.

'If you could pretend I'd never been here… I'd be so grateful.' Making her face as sad as she could. It wasn't hard. Saying the words really stung. But if they worked…

Mrs Moore nodded and Clara stepped down onto Whitborough Walk. Waving goodbye, she hurried away, back to the manor.

Now for the will.

5

1912 – Clara

Clara couldn't wait to get rid of the servants. When she got in Mabel appeared.

'Would you like lunch, Miss?'

'A sandwich in my study, please. And strong coffee.'

The girl hurried off.

Clara carried her bag upstairs, carefully, closely, as if it held something close to heaven. Which it did. She stood in her study, stared out at her grounds, wondering if she'd be able to stay. Wondering when her food would come. She needed privacy. When Burns had gone, she locked the door and taking a quick gulp of the coffee, she opened her bag and took out the other one. Her hands trembled, it had to be the will. When she finally opened the bag, Clara swore. It *was* paper, but not the will. The bag held money. Loads of it.

She tipped the notes out onto the desk, she couldn't believe how many there were, and that he'd left them. All that money just for portraits. Thinking about how little *she* earned. She searched the bag one final time and a note fell out, thanking Gwilym for one of his paintings. The note had an address in Dorset. Then she heard a noise below. Clara got up.

Shoving the money into a drawer, she walked out to the landing and peered downstairs.

'Someone here to see you, Miss.' Burns looked solemn. Whoever it was they were still outside. Clara smiled.

He really was the perfect butler, trained by her father.

Just about to close the door she spotted something on the floor, the thank-you note. Picking it up, she hurried downstairs and out to the front. A young woman stood on the doorstep, slight with dark hair, her hair straying out of its pins. Like hers had been, just hours before.

The girl looked flustered, somewhat embarrassed. Was she here for a cause?

'Yes?' said Clara, wanting to be kind.

'You're Clara Gilchrist?' Clara nodded.

'I'm Stella Dunne. I understand Mr Lawson lives here.'

'Not *yet*,' Clara snapped, all her kindness falling away. 'Mr Lawson married my cousin. This is *her* home. *And mine*.'

'Yes, right.' The girl shifted her feet. 'Alice and Theo said he was away.' The young woman hesitated. 'On his honeymoon.'

Theo? thought Clara. *Aunt Vi's brother? Who is this woman?*

'How can I help you? Were you his model?'

'What? No. Well, sometimes I was.' In spite of her nerves, the young woman laughed. 'I'm currently lodging at Mrs Moore's house, on Whitborough Walk.'

Then it all made sense. *She wants some money for being in her room.* Clara felt bitter. Mrs Moore and the woman hadn't wasted time. *Well, they wouldn't get much.* Thoughts of the cash in the drawer upstairs flashed into her head. 'So you want compensation?'

The woman looked puzzled. 'What? No, you've got it all wrong. I only want to know when Gwilym's coming back.'

'So you know him then? He's never mentioned you.' Clara was puzzled.' You'd better come in. I'll order some tea.' She went to usher Stella inside. But the woman shook her head.

'I don't want tea, I just want to know when Gwilym will be back. When he told me he was leaving, I never imagined a place like this.'

Clara felt cold. 'You've only just moved into Mrs Moore's lodgings. Where were you before?'

'Malden, Dorset Why do you ask?'

'It wouldn't be 53 Byrd Lane, Malden?' The woman looked shocked.

'Yes, that's right. But you said he never mentioned me.'

'No, he didn't.' Clara took the note out of her pocket and gave it to Stella. The young woman paled.

'Are you his sister?' Clara knew the answer already but she still had to ask. Stella smiled and shook her head. She stood a little taller.

'No, Miss Gilchrist. I'm the mother of his child.'

6

1912 – Clara

Clara ordered coffee instead, she needed a cup, even though she'd had some already. Mabel brought enough for two and Stella Dunne drank most of hers. She'd finally agreed to sit in the drawing room. They sat there in silence.

After Stella had drunk her fill the woman got up and wandered across to Clara's self-portrait, the one with the ring. Clara hated it.

That's what I get for tempting fate. But it had been of use.

The young woman turned. 'I heard you were the one he chose first.' She smiled, ruefully, staring at Clara. 'When Gwilym told me he was leaving, I was so angry. Not that he ever said it was a woman. But I knew that it was.'

'"I'm taking up a position," he said. Then he told me he was sorry, but that he knew I wouldn't stand in his way. "I owe it to myself to be somebody, Stella, instead of being just a portrait painter." And the man has a son!' Clara said nothing.

'I didn't believe him at first, you know. I thought he might have been making it up, like he did, sometimes. But in fact he told the truth. Then he ditched you too.' Clara swallowed.

'Yes, he did.'

'Worse for you than me, I think. She's your cousin, after all. Is she very beautiful?' Clara laughed.

'I wouldn't call her beautiful, no. But she does have something, attitude, character.' Clara smiled. 'Much like you.'

Stella Dunne said nothing.

'Coming up here, searching for Gwilym *and* bringing your boy, that must have been hard, taken quite a bit of courage.

And as for Gwilym having a son, we didn't know. How could Gwilym leave his boy?'

The woman's eyes flared. 'He didn't leave Jack, he abandoned me. He came here to improve his prospects. He wouldn't desert his only child. Or so I believed.' Stella Dunne sighed. She stared at Clara defiantly. 'It was me he left, and only me. And just for the money. He doesn't love her.' Clara stared.

Was that true? Then she leant across and grabbed Stella's arm, as a thought came to her. 'You've got a child, tell me, are you married? Properly married, as in a church.'

The woman shook her off. She looked uncomfortable. 'Yes, we're married, *in my heart*. Not, that it's any of your business. But then I discovered he wanted out and wanted *this*.' She looked around her.

Clara sighed. It was no good. If Gwilym had been married to Stella, his marriage to Steph would have been bigamy. She had another thought. 'Did he leave any papers with you?' Stella frowned.

'What sort of papers?'

'Legal documents, that kind of thing.'

Stella shook her head. 'When Gwilym left, he took everything with him, not that I realised at the time. He said he'd be back to see Jack. Gwilym's had other women before, but he always comes back. This time, when I searched, I found he'd taken everything. That's when I knew.'

'How did you know he was here?' said Clara.

'He used to talk about Issington a lot, he said it was lovely. Which I thought was strange, there are plenty of lovely places in Dorset. I knew he'd found work here, but I was naive. Then at the town hall they told me the truth, that he'd married your cousin. And that they'd both left.'

'He's not been gone long.' Stella looked grim.

'It's too long for me. And now Gwilym will have other sons and daughters and forget about Jack. And it's all *your* fault!'

'Mine? Why?'

'Because if he hadn't wanted to be lord of the manor, he'd still be at home with us in Malden, and Jack and I would be part of a family. A boy needs his da. I won't let you take him away from Jack.' Stella got up. 'When are they back?'

'I really don't know.'

Stella Dunne laughed. 'I'm sure you don't.' She got to her feet.

'Good day, Miss Gilchrist and thanks for the coffee.'

Once Stella had left, Clara ordered more coffee and went back to her study. What could she do? Gwilym and Steph were already married, and doubtless there'd be children eventually. What Gwilym had done wasn't down to her but the man had a child. Stella deserved something.

'Are you going back to Dorset?' she'd asked Stella as she was leaving.

'No,' said Stella. 'I like it here.' Defiantly.

So she meant to cause trouble. 'What work do you do?'

'Instead of being a lady of leisure? I look after my son, that's what I do.'

But how will you manage to pay the bills?

Still in her study several hours later, Clara had an inspiration. She couldn't give Gwilym back to Stella, nor could she even save her home, unless she found the wretched will. Clara was getting tired of looking. But she could do something much simpler. She could give Stella Dunne some of Gwilym's money.

Clara rose from her chair. Since Gwilym and Steph had left for London she'd barely eaten. But now, for the first time, she felt like some supper. It must be the thought of helping someone. Giving Stella Dunne some of Gwilym's money was the right thing to do, the woman had a child, Gwilym's child, or so she said. The plan pleased Clara.

Having the woman here in town, strolling around with her child on her arm, where Gwilym and Steph couldn't help seeing him, that would be a kind of revenge.

Clara smiled.

7

1912 – Stella

In order to stay, she had to find work. And Stella Dunne meant to stay, until she'd seen Gwilym. She was careful and she had some money, but she'd have to find more to pay the rent. Clara Gilchrist's words had stung. 'What work do you do?'

Damn her, thought Stella, *she's got a house, a bloody great house all to herself, instead of one room and a child to bring up. Stupid spoilt cow!*

Though to be fair, she hadn't seemed spoilt, rather, sad. She'd made Stella think.

Stella wandered into town, planning to call at the town hall offices, hoping to see Theo. She'd taken quite a shine to him. He was younger than Gwilym and seemed kind. *Damn Gwilym,* she thought, sourly, *the man was a cad, and who needs a bloke who paints for a living.* She needed a grafter. Theo wasn't there.

The fair-haired woman at the desk was frosty. 'Oh, it's you. What do you want?' Stella stood taller.

'I've come to talk to Theo,' she said. The woman's eyes narrowed.

'Theo's not in. Perhaps I can help?'

She didn't sound like she wanted to help and suddenly Stella felt afraid. The woman was cold and looked so smart. Whereas she was tired… but this was no good.

'I'm looking for someone to care for my son, so I can find work. Do you know of anyone, or any work going? And yes, I've got money.' Alice studied Stella.

'I could probably help with both of those. Unless you'd like to wait for Theo.'

Sarky cow!

Alice came out from behind the desk and gestured to Stella to follow her, quickly. *What a strange woman!*

They stepped out onto Bakehouse Lane and then into a passage called Chesterton Court. The place stank. The courtyard was small, and even though it was open to the sky Stella could still smell the midden. Alice turned round.

'It's better than some,' she told Stella, seeing her face, 'and Sadie's house is dark, but clean. She keeps a fire going. Your boy could do worse.'

'No,' Stella said. Her Malden home had been stone-built, it was freezing cold even in summer, but for all its draughts, the air smelt fresh. This place was different. She stared across the small courtyard, seeing the houses, all of them poky, a washing line strung across the yard. *God, it was grim.*

'No,' she repeated.

'You won't find better,' Alice insisted, 'not for what you can pay. You could, if you want, take your son to a village girl, but that'll mean walking there *and* back, the cart only comes to town on Fridays. It's not a bad walk in the warmer weather, but in the winter, it'll kill you. Especially after doing a day's work.' Alice sounded cheerful. Then she relented.

'Sadie Slater's a good woman. She's had a hard life, but who hasn't *and* she's got a son of her own. She'll know how you feel. Why don't you come inside and meet her?'

Stella sighed. What choice did she have? She made to walk towards Sadie's door, but Alice pulled her back.

'Before we go in, a word of advice. *Don't* mention Gwilym or Steph. Steph knew Sadie's daughter, Phoebe, and now Phoebe's dead. They recently found her body in the river. Everyone thought she died in the fire, but apparently not. Sadie *hates* being reminded.'

Fire? What fire? Stella was confused. Alice went on.

'One more thing. Sadie Slater takes in sewing. So if you need your things mending, or your boy's, Sadie's not bad. She's getting quite a bit of work.'

'I do my own mending,' Stella said, stiffly. 'Do you trust this woman?' Alice nodded.

'Yes, yes I do. Like I said, she's had it rough, and she's a worker, so I do what I can. If *you* work hard, I'll help you too. What do you say?'

'Maybe,' said Stella, wondering how her son would cope in a place like this. It needn't be for long. When Gwilym got back she'd make him help. She nodded at Alice. 'Fine,' she said. 'But only on trial.' She paused, went on.

'Where could I find some work, then?' Alice looked smug.

'The brewery's not that far from here. It always needs women for bottling work. It's tough and damp and in basement conditions. But I'm sure they'll take you.'

Stella smiled. *Sounds ideal.*

8

1854 – Lucienne Hall

Something must have woken him.

Augustin gingerly raised his head. God he felt ill. He felt around the back of his skull, his hand came back covered in blood. *Christ*, he thought. At least it seemed to have stopped bleeding. He sat up slowly, a little bit dizzy, forced himself further and climbed to his knees. Nothing felt broken, apart from his head. *Ha, ha*. He wondered then where Luci was. Augustin struggled to his feet and the world started spinning so he leant against the wall. *How had this happened?*

Then he remembered. They'd had a row and he'd fallen backwards, then, what?

Augustin dragged himself slowly into Lucienne's study and sank into a chair. Outside, he could hear people shouting. That wasn't right.

He got up again and poured himself some brandy. *God that's good.* Knocking it back, he crawled up the stairs and wandered through the hall and into the drawing room, feeling pretty rough. He had a tot of whisky, *now* he felt better.

Still no Luci.

Perhaps she'd gone to get some help. His memory was coming back slowly, in fragments. She must have been horrified when he fell. *But, wait, no, Luci actually pushed me!* In spite of the pain, Augustin grinned. If she was upset, serve her right. *What a spitfire she was!* He'd have to make it up to her, but not by moving into the manor. Where the hell was she?

Lucienne's absence worried him.

Topping up his empty glass, he staggered outside and took a deep breath. The cool air steadied him, made him feel better.

He stumbled along the path, slowly and out of the gate onto Whitborough Walk. It was just as well it was dark, he thought, they'd think he was drunk. He continued walking down the road, he didn't know where he was walking to. He needed a doctor. Perhaps that's where Lucienne was. It was eerily silent after the shouting, silent and cold. He ought to care what the noise had been about but he hadn't got the strength. He stopped, mesmerised. *So that was why!*

Across the road, where a house had been was an empty space, part of a wall and pieces of brick, clinging together. Debris everywhere. Near to it was a large group of people, all of them staring, some of them holding drinks in their hands. Augustin knew he was still concussed. He strained to remember. No, it couldn't be.

This was the place where Luci had lived, when he'd first met her, now it was gone. All he could see was rubble and smoke. What would she say when she found out? Troubled and anxious but not knowing why, he staggered towards where the house had been. He was stopped by a constable.

'I'm sorry sir, you can't go in there.'

He wanted to protest but talking was beyond him. He still felt fragile and broken, besides, he was drunk. He couldn't remember when he'd last eaten. And his head was still spinning. A man emerged from beyond the dust, carrying something, someone, a woman. Augustin gasped.

He couldn't get close, the policeman wouldn't let him, but he knew it was her, without even seeing her, he knew from the shape and the scraps of her dress, a pretty blue pattern. Luci, his love, the one he came back for, Luci was dead. Augustin felt sick.

There were others around, standing and staring, watching him moan and sink to his knees. Hearing him howl, just like a dog. The howling went on, and on and on.

But he was too bereft to see the woman behind him, standing in the shadows, and Miranda didn't know who Augustin was.

9

Clara – 1912

Clara went back to Mrs Moore's house. She wanted to see Stella. It felt sad coming back here. Mrs Moore wasn't pleased.

'Oh, so it's you.' Scowling at Clara. 'In answer to your question, Mrs Dunne's not here. And I'm not letting you into her room.'

Don't you mean Miss? Clara smiled to herself. Mrs Moore wouldn't like that, she thought herself proper. The woman went on.

'I'm looking after her boy today, but as I told her, it's only the once, I'll not be a soft touch. I've more to do than looking after kids. Mrs Dunne's out, looking for work.'

I'll have to come back. Clara turned to go.

'Would you like some tea?'

Clara blinked, caught off guard. *Who would have thought it?* 'Well, yes, thank you, that would be nice.' She smiled at the woman. Mrs Moore sniffed.

'I think we got off on the wrong foot before. I've just made some scones.'

'Scones would be lovely.' Surprised and amused Clara trailed down the dark hall after her, taking in everything as she went. *God, it's old-fashioned.* Mrs Moore's parlour was warm and cluttered. But the room was clean, with fresh daffodils. Mrs Moore nodded at the flowers.

'They're from the market in Lower Fell Street. A last minute bargain.'

Clara took the tea that was offered, the mug was chipped and the tea was strong. A lot stronger than she was used to.

'How long have you lived here, Mrs Moore?'

'Oh, ages, dear. Have a fruit scone.' Clara took one.

'I used to live at the house next door, where the garden is. The one with the rose on the plaque, you know. I tried growing roses myself once, but they never took. No green fingers, that's my trouble.'

'You used to live in the house next door?' *Lucienne Hall's house.* Clara couldn't believe what she'd heard.

'Yes dear, years ago. Then when it was demolished we moved in here. John and I were lucky to get it, this house is much bigger.'

'How did you manage it?' Clara felt faint.

'It was because of the gas explosion. When my old home was damaged, this one was too, so we got it for a song. My dear old pa had left me a nest egg, but not enough to buy this place until after the explosion. No-one wanted to live here then, they thought it might be dangerous. It took us years to do it up, then we took in lodgers. John had always hated his job.'

'But before, you lived in the house next door?'

Mrs Moore frowned. 'Yes, like I said.'

'What was it like?' Mrs Moore shrugged.

'Small, if I'm honest. Poky and dark, with only two storeys, this one has three. There was a lot more garden there, but it was all overgrown. So we chopped all the trees down and made it nice with slabs and pots.' Clara winced. Mrs Moore went on.

'We knew we'd need more space for guests so John started looking around. Then, after the explosion, when we moved in here, he did all the work himself to save on bills. Painted the rooms and fitted them out. They did look smart. We've never wanted for lodgers since.' Mrs Moore beamed.

'Who lived in your old house before you did?' Mrs Moore shrugged.

'A couple I think, but I never met them. The house was always rented out. I'll tell you one thing, though, they didn't like gardening.' Mrs Moore laughed. Then she leant in. 'Before the couple, it was a woman.'

Clara sat up. 'A woman?' she said. Mrs Moore nodded.

'The landlord owned a couple of houses, this one and that, and another down the road. He talked about the woman I mentioned as if she was special. Maybe he'd taken a shine to her.' Mrs Moore smirked. 'There was one thing.' She paused and went on.

'When John was clearing out our attic, years later, he came across a box I'd found in next door's debris. It was just an old box with a letter inside, I'd forgotten all about it. I reckoned it belonged to the woman who lived there. And what's more...'

'Have you still got it?' Clara interrupted.

'What? The letter, yes, I do. Do you want to see it'

'Please,' said Clara, feeling faint.

Mrs Moore got up and glanced at the clock. 'Oh dear, look at the time, it's after eleven. I'll have to put the dinner on.' Glancing at Clara. 'I'm sorry dear, you'll have to come back. I always do a hot meal at one, for two of my lodgers, as I did for Mr Gwilym once, until he met you.' Mrs Moore scowled.

'I'm sure he enjoyed your food much more,' Clara said hastily, knowing it was true. Gwilym had always hated Flora's cooking, he used to say it was far too fancy. But never mind that.

'What about the letter?'

'The letter will have to wait, Miss Gilchrist. I've a living to earn.'

Can I come back? It was all she could do not to say it out loud. *Damn*, Clara thought. She stepped down into the street, thinking.

The woman who'd lived at the now demolished cottage had to be Hall. But who was the letter from? Perhaps the landlord, Will Brookes, but it could have been from anyone. She should have asked. Clara sighed. She'd have to go back, and not just for Stella. Hall's house was *her* secret and that was the way it had to stay.

She walked briskly back to the manor, restless. As soon as she'd got her hands on the letter she would know more.

Then she'd destroy it.

10

1912 – Stella

Stella got a job at the brewery. She'd had to beg, although she didn't want it.

The manager looked at her and laughed.

'You're little,' he said 'and you don't look strong.'

'I'm tough,' said Stella, remembering how she'd struggled with Jack who could be a little tyrant. The manager frowned.

'Most of my women are bigger than you.'

She knew he was lying. Stella stepped forward.

'Give me a chance, Mr Thatcher, please. Put me on trial for a while if you like. You won't regret it.'

She started that day.

Gregory Thatcher didn't regret it but Stella did. *I'll kill that Alice Sewell when I see her.*

The women stood up to their ankles in water, and it was noisy, bottling beer and heavier work than she'd expected. Then there were the drunken men.

'You'll get used to it,' Lindy, one of the girls, said.

Never, thought Stella, but she didn't say anything. Like everyone else she needed the money. Then it was pay day.

'Look at them all,' she said to Lindy, happier than she'd been for ages, watching the wives standing outside, waiting for their men. 'Isn't that nice?' Lindy laughed.

'Aren't you naive? The women are waiting for the pay, not for the men. So the men don't spend it down the pub.' Glancing at Stella. 'Didn't your husband drink, then?'

Stella said nothing. She'd told the girls she was a widow, but the rest was true, she and Jack were on their own. And the money was rubbish.

'Is this all we get?' she'd said, incredulous. Lindy looked angry.

'When you first started, nobody thought you'd last the day. *"Up from the country, she won't last,"* that's what they said. I was the one who defended you, I told them you had something about you. Don't let me down.' Stella laughed.

'No chance of that, I need the work. I just don't think it's much, that's all, for what we do.'

'It's better than nothing, remember that. And no-one gives you something for nothing, not in this life.'

Stella agreed, thinking of Gwilym.

Until she got home and found the money.

11

1912 – Clara

Earlier that day.

'You know that girl who was here, Miss? The shabby looking one?'

Clara nodded and smiled to herself. Mabel might be only a maid but she had high standards, sometimes even higher than Clara's. She couldn't resist teasing the girl.

'There's more to a woman than what she wears.' Mabel frowned.

'She's working at Chesterton's.'

'Really?' said Clara. Mabel's sister worked at the brewery, and according to her the work was rough. *I was the clever one.* Mabel went on.

'Lindy says the girl's on her own, and has a small boy.' Mabel sniffed. 'If Thatcher finds out she's not a widow, she'll get the sack. I wouldn't have let her in here, if I'd known.'

'You didn't,' said Clara, smiling at her. 'Burns did. I'd have let her in. We have to be kind.'

'I don't see why,' Mabel muttered and turned away. Clara smiled again.

This was how it used to be, when her father was alive.

She knew she was far too soft on the servants, treated them more like friends than staff. But Aunt Vi was too far away, and there was no-one else she could talk to.

When she arrived at Mrs Moore's house, the kettle was boiling. 'I've made some fruit loaf.'

'Lovely,' said Clara taking a piece. *When do I get to see the letter?*

She thought she'd start her off gently.

'You didn't have lodgers, before you moved here?'

'The odd one or two, for a couple of days, but no more than that. The place was too small.' Mrs Moore frowned. 'That was the worst thing.'

'What?' said Clara.

'A woman had died, she'd been in our garden. The police said the explosion was gas but I already knew that, I could smell it.'

'One of your lodgers?'

'Bless you, no, we only took people late in the year. They came for the boating, then for the fair.' Clara nodded.

'The night that it happened, John and I were down the pub, the Riverboat Inn, just down there. We heard the explosion and we ran outside, terrible it was. The street was packed. Billy, the constable, he was there and he was trying to hold the people back. But he wasn't succeeding, not at first, everyone was running all over the place.'

'It must have been awful.' Mrs Moore nodded.

'It was for us, we'd lost our home and all our things. Not that we knew that at the time.'

'Then somebody said it could be our house, so John went down to take a look. He slipped past Billy when he wasn't looking. I wanted to go with him, but John wouldn't let me. He said it would be too dangerous.

'So I went there alone, the very next day, when he was at work.'

'That was brave,' Clara said. Mrs Moore shrugged.

'All of our stuff was inside that house. I wanted to see what was left and if there was anything I could save before someone stole it. Nothing lasts round here for long.' Mrs Moore sighed.

'Seeing the place in daylight was a shock. There was glass and debris everywhere, my best plates all over the street. Some of the things went as far as the river.' Mrs Moore frowned.

'People were picking up stuff from the road, helping themselves, as if they had a right. They even took the broken things like mugs without handles. It made me so angry. But I still managed to save some things.' She paused, looked at Clara.

'I never found out who the woman who died was. I'm not sure they knew, she was too badly injured. As well as the old place, where we used to live, a wall of this house was badly damaged *and* the foundations. Even now, there's a slope on the floor.'

It was true, there was. 'Didn't they try to save your old home?' Mrs Moore smiled.

'There wouldn't have been much point, dear. There wasn't much left, the roof had come down and most of the internal walls were rubble. And all my pots broken.'

Oh dear. 'Where did you live, until you moved here?' Mrs Moore grinned.

'We had to stay with John's old ma, she lived up Pooling Road then, well you know what that's like, or perhaps you don't. Eventually we moved in here but the place was a mess, it was just about safe. That's all that can be said.' She glanced at Clara.

'No-one wanted to buy this house, I reckon they thought next door was haunted, because of the woman. Brookes tried to sell next door but even when he reduced the price no-one would buy it. Then it became what it is today, a memorial garden.'

Clara looked up. 'Who did that?'

Mrs Moore shrugged. 'I wanted to buy the land off Brookes, it had been our home, but John wouldn't have it. He was always superstitious and someone had died there.'

'And you never found out who that was?'

'No, as I said it was just a woman, although there were rumours, quite a few women went missing back then. It wasn't as safe as it is these days. Here, dear, have some more fruit loaf.' Clara gave in.

'Billy and I used to be close, we even went out a couple of times before I met John. He would often tell me things, but not about this. Even years later, he still wouldn't talk, which I thought was strange, unless he'd been got to. That's what John reckoned.' She glanced across at Clara. 'And before you ask, I don't know why.'

'Wasn't she missed?' Mrs Moore shrugged.

'Obviously not, it's a bit of a mystery. Maybe she didn't have much family. I didn't, before I met John.' She got to her feet.

'I was going to show you the letter.' She handed Clara a folded-up page she'd taken from the dresser. It was yellowing with age. Clara's hands shook.

She glanced down, skipping over words and going straight to the bottom, searching for a name.

Not the landlord, Will Brookes, but a man who signed with the letter A, just like her grandfather had.

Augustin Gilchrist.

Before she left, Clara handed Mrs Moore a package for Stella. She told the woman what was in it and that she'd counted it. You couldn't be too careful.

'It's money she's owed.' Mrs Moore said nothing.

It was hard to think of Gwilym with Stella, that they'd had a son, even worse than thinking of him with Steph. *I never really knew him,* Clara realised, which was worrying now that he was part of her family.

Had she ever really known anyone? Clara wondered, hurrying home as the rain came down.

Including her grandfather, Augustin Gilchrist, she hadn't known the man personally, but she'd known of his dream, his library for poets, the one he'd passed down to her father. But her grandfather had divided his family with his will, and even though he'd changed his mind later and made a second will, it had come too late. And now she'd discovered he'd loved someone else before her grandmother.

When Clara got in she looked at the calendar, not that she needed reminding which day it was. Today was the 10th – Gwilym and Steph would be joining *Titanic* and sailing to New York. She envied them that, she envied Steph her inheritance, and perhaps even more. She couldn't think about Gwilym. But she was still here. It was where she belonged.

After Clara had read the letter she'd asked Mrs Moore something.

'Do you like poetry?' Mrs Moore laughed.

'Like the sort you have at your place? No, not much, not if I'm honest. I don't understand it.' Mrs Moore went on.

'There are people who paint, like you and Mr Gwilym, and people like me who take in lodgers. I know what I'm good at, I've never been any good with words. Why do you ask?'

'Because you kept the letter, I suppose. It's kind of poetic.' Clara hoped she sounded convincing. Mrs Moore shrugged.

'I kept it because... well, it seemed important. Poems, no, they're not my thing. Sorry.' Clara smiled.

No need to say sorry. She knew Lucienne's secret was safe. *There was only one house.*

But she still hadn't found the will.

12

1912 – Clara

Letter dated Spring 1854

Dear L

When I stood there, on Whitborough Walk and saw your home, your very first home in Issington Halt, broken, destroyed, I tried to believe it wasn't true, that I was concussed and I couldn't see straight. Which of course I was. But the house was still gone.

I tried to believe you weren't inside, that you were still walking, looking for a doctor. Or sitting by the river as you often did, writing by the moon.

But then they brought your body out.

Now it's *my* turn to write.

I couldn't be sure if it was you, but then I saw the shape I knew, the form I loved, *then* your dress. That was what clinched it. I stared at its simple blues and browns, the colours you'd worn earlier on, when we were so happy. Not that it felt like that then. If I could go back... But you can't go back.

I'll do what I can.

I'll make a memorial garden here, and no-one will know it's yours but us. I think that's how you'd like it to be. I'll carry your story to my grave and make your words and dreams my own. If I can manage it.

I'm leaving now, I can't bear to stay here, now that you're gone, and then there's work. Thank God for work. But one day, eventually, I'll come back, for good, like you wanted, and then I'll deliver your house of dreams. A library for poets. I'll pass it all down.

I hope you'll like the space I'll make, the memorial garden, and better still, the house of dreams, and if by any chance I'm wrong, and you do come back, you'll know where to find me.

I couldn't have stayed, I wasn't that man and I can't stay now, but one day I will, I promise you that.

And wherever I am, your words, you, will always be with me.

A.

Augustin's letter haunted Clara.

He'd turned the remains of Hall's first home into a memorial garden. Then later on, he'd bought Issington Manor in Lucienne's memory and forged the dream that had haunted their lives. She'd known that this had been Lucienne's home, but she hadn't known that Hall and her grandfather had been lovers until Hall died, and before Augustin had married her grandmother. Nor had she known about the memorial garden. *Now* it made sense.

Nobody knew about Hall's first home apart from her and nobody would. She held the letter in her hand and smiled to herself. Then she frowned.

The memorial garden might be forever, but the manor wouldn't last if she didn't find the will. Why had Augustin changed his mind and made a second will? She'd probably never know. But she had to find it, and that was a problem because she'd looked everywhere, including the Lucienne Hall room. Maybe she wasn't meant to find it. Clara sighed.

Then she heard a knock at the door.

PART FIVE

1

Now/1912 – Miranda

It's hard to think that Alice is dead. I walked down that darkened road and felt the blast of the explosion happening, then I saw them carry her out. It could have been Alice, it probably was. But it could have been someone else instead. That's what I tell myself, *not* Alice.

Whoever it was, the house was demolished, like Issington Manor and I want to know what happened next. Maybe I can change the past, I've done it before. But Alice went back, and now she's dead. No, I can't think that.

Today, I'm back at Judy's workshop and, this time, I've come prepared. I'm wearing a dress. I don't often wear dresses, I much prefer trousers. But if I'm going to Edwardian England, I have to look right. I also have a headscarf.

This time I get the timing right, the house is there and it looks like it's lived in. Staring down from my churchyard view, the bank drops down then rises again to a small parterre, surrounded by a low balustrade. I'm proud I even know the words. Curdizan, where I used to live, is a world away, there are no parterres or balustrades there. Beyond the parterre is a path which leads to a low verandah, and then to the door. I run down the hill.

This time the manor looks cared for, its stone tubs are filled with flowers and the lawns are just mowed. At the back is an orangery, most of it glass. *Better get on.* I join the path, pass the verandah and head for the porch. I climb up the steps and knock on the door but nobody comes. I turn the handle and, surprisingly, the door opens. Of course I go in.

The hall is paved with colourful tiles and *very* thin rugs. *Not warm enough here.* There's a table for post, and beyond the hall, stairs leading upward. They also go down. I'm transfixed. *I'd love to live in a place like this.* Then somebody coughs.

'What do you want?' a woman says sharply, and I spin round abruptly, knocking the tray with the cards on the floor. There are only two, I pick them up. I stare at the woman. She's probably not much older than me, but she looks severe with her hair pinned up. I try to remember what I had planned.

'This is Lucienne Hall's home?' I say. The woman looks sad.

'It was, yes, but not anymore. It's my house now, although not for long. Nobody keeps this house for long. My father died.'

'Oh,' I say. 'I'm sorry to hear that.'

'It was quite a while ago now, 1910.'

I don't know what to say to that. I want to ask what year it is, but of course I can't. 'I'm sorry you're losing your home,' I say. Willing her to tell me why. She laughs, loudly.

'Not half as much as I am, Miss. My cousin Steph is throwing me out. She's found a will that makes my home hers, now that she's married to my ex-lover. Pretty bad luck, wouldn't you say?' I stare.

I'm wishing now I hadn't come, the woman's quite mad, but I can't just leave. 'Well, yes,' I say, 'it is, rather,' and then her face changes and she seems quite normal.

'Would you like a cup of tea? Then I can tell you the whole story, about the will and my ex-lover, Gwilym, who's now my cousin's husband. I'll ring for Mabel, she's the maid.'

In spite of myself I grin at her. The woman *is* crazy but what does it matter, she sounds quite fun and I'd like to hear her story. This is the past I would have liked, strolling into people's homes, drinking tea and chatting for hours, not like in the twenty-first century, where doors are always firmly locked. We did a bit of visiting when I lived in Curdizan, but we didn't have maids, and *I* was the one who made the tea. I follow the woman into a room, some sort of library.

'How lovely,' I say. Another faux pas. The mad woman frowns.

'This room was meant to be *part* of a library, one that filled the whole of the house. That little plan failed.' She hands me the tea. 'I'm Clara Gilchrist. Who are you?'

'Miranda Collenge. I'm not from round here.' Clara Gilchrist laughs.

'I'd never have guessed. I know most of the people round here. Are you calling on someone?'

I think of the card I picked up from the floor. 'The Leightons of Pinnet are distant cousins. But, right now, I'm looking for someone.'

'Lucienne Hall?'

I can't help smiling. 'No,' I say. 'A woman called Alice.'

Clara takes some time to think. 'I do know an Alice,' she says, slowly, 'she's helped me with the Hall events. But I haven't seen her lately.'

'It would have been just a few days ago.' But Clara shakes her head.

'The Alice I know works at the town hall. You could always go and ask.'

'Right,' I say, suddenly upset. *So it can't be her, then.* I put down my cup. 'I'd better go.'

'Do you have to?' says Clara, looking disappointed. 'I'm on my own here, apart from the servants and they can't talk to me, they're far too busy. I'd love to tell you about the manor, if you've got time.'

'Alright,' I say, trying to push Alice out of my mind. 'I do want to learn about the house.' Clara looks pleased.

'I'll tell you about my cousin first. Her name's Steph, and she and Gwilym, my former fiancé, are sailing to New York. When they come back, I'll have to leave.'

'Sailing?' I say, and suddenly I'm nervous. I still don't know what year it is. 'Sailing on what?'

Clara looks proud. 'The *Titanic*,' she says.

I knew it, I think and wonder what the hell to say. I could say she doesn't need to worry, the chances are they won't come back and then she'll get to keep the house. I could tell her that they need to get off, as soon as they can, but would she believe me?

'What day is it please?'

She looks at me as if I'm mad. I probably am. Then she tells me it's Wednesday.

Too late, I think, and my heart sinks. It's evening now and the ship will have gone and there are only two more stops on its journey. If I was able to reach the ship, which I can't, what could I do? Would anyone listen, let alone believe me if I tried to tell them what happens, in just a few days? No, of course they wouldn't. I feel helpless. Clara is talking.

'Some people I know say the ship isn't safe. Because it's so big and on its first trip. But Gwilym never listens.'

Gwilym, the cad she clearly still loves. *Come on Miranda, just stick to the house. Then you can leave and check on the web. Just ask the right questions, then you'll find out.*

Sounds like a plan.

After she's shared her past with me, Clara shows me round the manor.

'It's still my home,' she insists, firmly. 'It'll always be mine, whatever they do.' I think she's trying to convince herself.

'Where will you go, afterwards?' *Assuming they survive the Titanic.* Clara shrugs.

'I don't know. It doesn't really matter.'

We're still walking around the house. We wander into the drawing room, I don't like it much. All the walls are covered with paintings, most of them awful. I glance across the room at a picture. 'Oh, that's you.' Clara nods.

'Yes, I painted it, using a mirror. It was a challenge and harder than I thought. I don't usually paint portraits. It used to live in the hall once, when I was engaged.'

I stare at the painting.

'After Gwilym broke it off, Steph moved it in here, out of the way.' Clara looked at me and smiled.

'Sometimes I forget it's in here.'

It's such a sad story.

As soon as I can I go back to the present, get on the web and look up *Titanic's* passenger lists. The website I use has plenty of facts. As well as the names, sometimes it tells me who lived and who died. But some of the names have nothing against them, not everyone was accounted for. Many are still at the bottom of the sea. My heart's racing.

I look up the second class list first, that's the place to find them. I search under Lawson, assuming they'd use his name as they're married. They're not there. Then I search again under her name, Gilchrist, and finally search the first and third classes. I can't find anything. The records, though good are not complete. I sit back, annoyed.

Given what happened to the house later, one if not both of them must have survived and come back to the manor. Unless Clara finds that will, she'll lose her home, and Hall's library won't exist.

Which, I think, *is exactly what happened.*

I know then, I have to do something.

2

Now– Miranda

The next day I'm thinking of Alice. If it hadn't been for her I'd still be in Curdizan. I owe it to Alice, or my memory of Alice, to help Clara Gilchrist. *But how?* I think.

I'm still on the course and today's the fourth day. We're all on a visit to Henry's shop. He deals in antiques. I look around.

'I'm not sure your shop qualifies,' I tell him. Henry isn't the least bit offended.

'True,' he says, 'it's mostly junk.'

He's on the course to improve his income. *Anything would help.* I have an idea.

It came when I saw Clara's painting. I'd walked right up to the portrait and studied it. Clara had stayed close to the door.

'You've caught your likeness perfectly.' Clara looked bored.

'I *am* a professional a*nd* I used a mirror.'

I walked back towards the door, looking at the other pictures. 'None of these are yours, then?'

Clara looked angry. 'No, can't you tell? They're all from my grandfather's time. And dreadful to boot.'

'Why do you keep them, if you don't like them?'

'Because Father liked them, although God knows why. I keep them because they remind me of him. I don't even do portraits, I paint landscapes, views of the river. I did once paint Lucienne Hall, what I thought she might have looked like. It wasn't very good.'

I take a deep breath. 'You told me Gwilym's an artist too. And he does paint portraits. Have you tried looking in the back of a picture for the missing will? That's what I'd do, if I was him.' Clara went pale.

'There are none of his paintings in this house, I wouldn't have it.'

'There are plenty of others he could choose. What's to stop him choosing one of these, taking the back off, hiding the will, then sealing it up.' I walked across to a small, dark oil and took it off the wall.

'No, Miranda, stop!' Clara looked scared. 'You don't need to do that. I've looked at them all.'

Clara was lying. 'You've opened them all?'

'No of course I haven't. But I've looked at them all and I'm sure I'd know if one had been opened. Even if Gwilym had it reframed.'

I nodded and changed the subject. But I didn't believe her.

So now, today, I'm at Henry's shop. I glance around, it's *full* of stuff. Oliver, one of the students is picking up artefacts, putting them down. He's not really looking at them. The place is a mess, it needs a good clean *and* a good sort out. I'm not volunteering. Would anything here cover the bills? Henry speaks.

'As you can see, it's a hotchpotch of things, drawings and vases and people's old jewellery, most of it tat.' Judy, the tutor, looks amused.

'But, having said that,' Henry goes on, 'if I'm fortunate *and* I've chosen wisely, I'll find a piece that makes it all worth it.'

'Do you keep records?' Judy asks and Henry blinks. *Guess that's a no then.*

'Don't you have a computerised system?' Judy's clearly enjoying herself. I interrupt her.

'What's downstairs?'

'That's where I do my stock management,' Henry says, glaring at Judy. 'And my restoration work. Mostly old paintings.'

Paintings! I think, and we head for the basement, squeezing down some dodgy steps. I bang my head.

In the middle of the room is an old table and stacked on the floor are loads of old paintings. While the others gather round the table, I flick through a few, looking for any from 1914 when the manor was sold. It's a very faint hope. Henry is talking.

'Here we're looking at two paintings, both the same view but by two different artists. They're virtually identical – but one's a copy. They're both from around 1912.' The others are intrigued.

'Wouldn't a copy normally be newer?'

'This one is, but not by much. Copies are often fakes for money but not in this case, this is just a replica.'

Why would someone do that? I'm still looking.

'Who's the original painting by?'

'Clara McKinver,' Henry says and I look up.

'The woman who lived at Issington Manor.'

Henry nods and Judy looks at me, surprised. Henry goes on.

'Her real name was Clara Gilchrist. She took her mother's name for work. Clara McKinver was a landscape artist who became well-known, locally.' I smile. Henry points at the painting he's holding.

'This is the park where the manor used to be, next to the river. It's one of McKinver's lesser-known works and probably isn't worth much money. But this one here is a copy of McKinver's.'

'How do you know the original's McKinver's?' Cher pipes up.

'Because of the provenance.' Henry passes Judy a small piece of paper. 'Provenance traces the painting's history, it tells us if the artwork is genuine. Provenance could be a gallery entry, a catalogue record or a bill of sale. Finding such records makes my life easier.'

I cross to the table and look at the receipt Judy's holding. My heart stops. It's from the sale of the manor's contents in 1914. I pick up the painting. 'This is the original?'

'Yes,' says Henry. 'Such paperwork can, of course, be forged, but not in this case.' Cher chips in.

'What do you do if there's no provenance?'

'Testing the paint can tell us quite a lot. The oils artists used changed over time. I had the work tested.'

'Did that help?' Oliver adds.

'It confirmed both were painted around the same time. I also had some x-rays done, to check how old the canvases were.'

'Why would that matter?'

'Artists sometimes re-use old canvases. That can tell us more about the painting. And the artist.' Judy smiles.

'What about paint cracks? Can't they be distinctive, like fingerprints are?' Henry nods.

'Yes they can. Cracking, or craquelure, to give it its real name, *can* be very useful, but not in this case. It can be induced, but fake cracks tend to be uniform in pattern, rather than irregular.'

Oliver takes the copy off Henry. 'I'd swear they were both by the same person. Who was the artist?'

'A portrait painter by the name of Gwilym Lawson. He was more successful than McKinver, and in a different field.'

I stare. My heart starts to race. Henry goes on.

'He wanted to copy McKinver's style but I don't know why.'

'Bit of a mystery then,' says Judy. 'Maybe he just liked the view.' Henry laughs.

I turn the matching paintings over and stare at them closely. They both look untouched.

'You must have taken the backs off these to have the work done?'

'Of course,' says Henry. 'But those are the original frames.'

I want to ask the obvious question. *Was there anything inside?* But I say nothing.

'Do you have any others by Clara McKinver? Or Gwilym Lawson?' Henry nods.

'Yes, sure, over there.' He points to some paintings stacked on the floor. 'There's not much demand for McKinver now, a bit more for Lawson. Which is a shame. They were both popular artists once.'

'Especially as you've got some of their paintings,' Oliver adds and everyone laughs. But I'm not listening.

I'm leafing through paintings as fast as I can. Most of them are from the house sale. Many aren't hers, but I recognise some, I saw them on the walls just yesterday. *Was it really only yesterday?* None of them look as if they've been opened, but how would I know after all this time? I sigh, defeated, ready to give in.

And then I see what I'm looking for.

3

Now – Miranda

Eventually, it's time to leave but not before somebody asks.

'So what happened to Clara McKinver?'

Henry looks up. 'McKinver's cousin married Gwilym Lawson and eventually they all moved out. Clara McKinver moved to Upper Fell Street and carried on painting but she never painted the river again. The manor was demolished in 1914, with a view to the land being used for houses but they were never built. Then came the war.' Judy chips in.

'Once the war started, the builder's firm was taken over, and by the time it had ended he'd retired, so the council bought the land instead. Thankfully, for Issington Halt.'

'And what about Lawson?' Cher asks. Henry shrugs.

'I assume he and his wife moved elsewhere.'

'It's such a shame the manor was demolished.' This is Cher. Judy nods.

'Shame or not, we've got to get going.'

Henry and I are alone at last. I turn to him.

'When you opened up those paintings by Lawson and McKinver, did you find anything?'

'Apart from what I'd expect to see?'

'Yes, right, something hidden inside. Like paperwork, a document, and probably older than the painting itself.' Henry stares.

'No, I didn't. But now I'm intrigued. Should I have done?'

Damn, I thought and looked at him. 'Probably not.' I pause, take a chance. 'Look, Henry, this is confidential. I need you to look in the back of a painting, I think there's something valuable inside it. I'll pay you to do it. What do you say?' Henry laughs.

'So long as the painting's yours, why not? Bring it in tomorrow. And no, I won't charge you, although I probably should.' Henry sighs.

I bend down and pick up a painting. 'It's this one here.'

'Ah, right, *not* yours then. Another McKinver.'

I nod. 'Is it worth much?'

Henry laughs. 'I very much doubt it. Besides, I won't damage it, not if I'm careful.'

'Then you'll do it?' I could have hugged him.

'Yes, sure, on one condition. You tell me what you're looking for.'

The others have gone and Henry and I are alone in the basement. I watch him work.

He opens up the back of the picture, Clara McKinver's self-portrait. It must have ended up in the house sale.

I'm not sure we'll find the will. Assuming Lawson hid it in the portrait, if he came back, survived the *Titanic*, he would have removed it. Given that the house *was* demolished, he probably did. But I'd still like to check. *A masterful stroke*, I think, sourly. Hiding the will in Clara's self-portrait, knowing how much the painting upset her. I'm hating Lawson more every minute.

'Nearly done,' Henry says, releasing some tape and a cloud of dust. 'There's something in here,' he adds slowly, 'and it's wrapped in cloth.' I can't breathe.

'Careful,' I say, and he *is* careful, but the thing will be fragile, and I want to do it. I hold back.

Henry puts the package on the table and opens it up, with gloved fingers. 'It's not a will, it's a painting of a house and the house isn't Issington Manor.' *Hell*, I think. *What now?*

Some time later Henry speaks. 'Not what we thought, then?'

'No,' I say. *Obviously*. So out comes the story, without the part where I meet Clara. 'Research,' I lie.

'Thinking of the painting was a good idea,' Henry agrees. By now we've moved upstairs to the shop which has a small sofa in the space he calls his office. We're on our second bottle of rough red wine and I'm drowning my sorrows. I knew I'd been looking for a needle in a haystack, but I'd come so close, finding the painting. I'd *so* wanted to help Clara, and find Alice. I'd failed on both counts. I drink more wine.

Henry picks up the tiny picture. 'What's it of?'

'A house,' I say and he glares at me. I shrug and sigh. 'I don't even know who the artist is. Is it a McKinver?'

Sadly Henry shakes his head. 'The style's not right and it's not Gwilym Lawson's.'

'So why hide it?'

Henry frowns and studies it closely. 'I think this is Whitborough Walk, from an earlier time. Look, there's no tarmac.' I nod.

For all I don't know it, it *does* look familiar. Then suddenly I realise, it's the house from the explosion, I recognise the wall. *The house where Alice died.* I can't bear to look at it now.

'Never mind that,' I say, sharply. 'I have to find the will.' But Henry and I have run out of ideas.

'Have some more wine,' he says, calmly, pouring me another large glass. He hands me the painting. 'You have it, you found it. I'd still like to know why it was in there.'

Me too. I turn to him. 'Do you think it's worth anything?'

'Probably not, but if it is I'll have it back.' He grins at me. 'You can't have the self-portrait, that's part of my collection.'

'Yeah, sure, that's why it was sitting on the floor.'

Henry tops up my glass again. 'That's part of my filing system.'

'Judy *will* be impressed. I ought to go home.'

'What will you do?' he asks later, after we've finished the rest of the bottle.

Go back to Clara, I think, sighing. Although why I'm not sure.

4
Now/1912 – Miranda

Today is the last day of the workshop, but Henry's not here. I try not to worry, he's probably just got a huge hangover. But I doubt he feels as bad as me, I've failed Clara. The will could be anywhere.

Just after lunch Henry turn up.

'Where have you been?' I stop eating.

'Checking on something,' Henry says, pinching some of my crusty roll. 'But don't get your hopes up.' I pull out a seat.

'Explain,' I say.

'I wondered if I'd been wrong,' he says, 'and the self-portrait wasn't by McKinver. And maybe that's why the will wasn't in it. It's not as if I'd studied it closely. So I had a word with someone I know and he used IR, it's a special technique, to see if there was a sketch underneath, an under-drawing. McKinver never did them, she worked intuitively.'

'So *that's* how you knew Gwilym Lawson's copy wasn't by McKinver.'

'That was one of the reasons. But I was wrong about the portrait, she did paint it.'

'Damn,' I say. Later that day I go back to the past.

Clara was at the door to greet me. 'Miranda, come in! I'm *so* bored with no-one to talk to. I'm surprised how much I miss my cousin, all things considering.'

'Thanks,' I say. 'I love coming here.' Crossing my fingers.

'We'll have to sit in the drawing room today. Flora's in the library, cleaning or something. More's the pity.' We make our way slowly down the hall. Clara goes on.

'Last night I had supper with the Leightons, the Leightons of Pinnet.'

I stop. My cover is blown.

'It seems they've never heard of you. So why are you here?'

'Looking for Alice. I can explain.' Clara laughs.

'I look forward to that. But let me get us some tea first.' Clara walks out.

This is my chance to make an escape, but I can't do it. I look around the room wildly, see Clara's self-portrait and wish yet again that it held the will instead of a painting. Then I blink. Something's not right.

I get up and rush towards the painting. I see what it is. Her ring's missing.

In Henry's picture, Clara is wearing an engagement ring. In this version there isn't a ring. How can that be? I think fast.

Just suppose there were two portraits, as Henry had shown us the two landscapes, one by Clara, the other by Lawson. The original painting would have had a ring, but not Lawson's copy, because Clara wasn't engaged to him then. Or maybe just to tell them apart, or not upset Steph. Anything was possible. I thought a bit more.

What if Lawson had hidden the one Clara painted and it had been sold with the house contents? That would explain how it ended up with Henry. Then he'd replaced her original with this one, the one I'm looking at. Why would he do that? My heart starts to race.

Clara wouldn't have noticed the switch, she hated the painting. But I'd noticed, and now I know I've no time to waste. At least it's only a small picture. I glance at the door.

I lift the painting from its hook, and slide it into my oversized bag. Thank God I brought this one. I scribble a note.

Got to go but I'll be back. Sorry, don't worry.

I put the note on the floor where she'll see it and leave the room. I run down the hall. I can hear Clara's footsteps, not far behind.

I run out of the house and up the bank, rushing through where the wall is now. I find the grave and turn the post, and when I look up the wall is in place. I take a deep breath.

I clamber carefully onto the railing and peer over the wall. The manor is gone. I'm becoming quite an expert at this. But I'm still scared to look. I jump back to the ground and open my bag. The painting's still in it. I sigh, relieved.

But is the will inside the painting?

I need to find Henry.

5

1912 – Clara

When Clara returned to the drawing room, carrying the tea, Miranda had gone. *Damn, what a shame.*

I shouldn't have mentioned seeing the Leightons. The lie hadn't mattered, it had been fun talking to Miranda. Talking to a stranger, like she had with Alice. Clara put the tea tray down, feeling deflated. She was alone.

Flora had finished her work and left and she'd scared her guest away. *Wait, what's this?* She picked up the note.

Got to go but I'll be back. Sorry, don't worry.

Why should I worry? She glanced around the room, puzzled, then noticed the space where a painting had been. Clara felt cold.

So that's why Miranda had come to the manor, to steal her self-portrait. Clara remembered her oversized bag, the woman must have planned this. And to think she'd trusted her.

Not only had she stolen the portrait, she'd also stolen the painting inside it, the tiny picture of Hall's first house. Clara felt ill.

She'd told Miranda Collenge loads, all about Hall, *and* about her engagement to Gwilym *and* about his plans to sell. Lonely and bored, she'd poured her heart out to a stranger, a woman who'd cheated her, and now she'd left herself open to blackmail. And to the loss of the Hall legend. She'd been stupid.

Clara ran out onto the path, but Miranda, of course, was long gone. She crossed the lawn and stared down at the river. Today it was high.

I ought to jump, or walk to the bridge and jump off there. Nobody needs me, not anymore. Now I can't even hold onto the legend. And things will get worse when they get back.

But, still, she just stood there.

6

1912 – Phoebe

I stepped through the French windows of Issington Manor and into the library, stood there and smiled. As soon as I did it, I knew I'd been right. I dropped my bags on the floor. Home at last!

I'd have to go out, straightaway, to Chesterton Court. Ma would be wondering where I was. But I'd had to come home first.

Where was everyone?

I shouted for Clara, but nobody came. Then I went to find Flora but the kitchen was empty. I could have rung for the others, but old habits die hard.

Perhaps Clara had gone to the church, that could explain it. I still remembered reading the news, it had been such a shock. I realised then, that Alice had been right. I could still see the headlines.

'*Titanic* Sinks. Great loss of life. World's Greatest Liner Strikes Iceberg.'

So many deaths. It brought back all my horrible memories.

I took my luggage upstairs to my room. It was just as well Clara was out, I wasn't sure how she'd be with me. Strangely enough, despite what I'd done, the thought upset me.

After I'd put my things away, I grabbed my bag and went downstairs. I got a shock. A small, dark woman was standing in the hall.

'What are you doing here?' The woman stood taller.

'I could ask the same of you. Are you a servant?'

Am I a servant? At that I nearly snapped. 'I'm Steph, Clara's cousin, and if you don't answer my question now, I'm throwing you out.'

The woman smiled and softened slightly.

'Ah, so you're Steph. He obviously likes the same type. Haven't you noticed?'

I looked at her a little more closely, and saw what she meant. She looked like me and a bit like Clara, although Clara's features were much more delicate. *One of Gwilym's women then.* She was carrying luggage and a bag. *What did she want?* The woman laughed.

'I can see your cousin's not told you. You needn't worry, I'm not stopping. I only came to give her this. You can tell her from me, I don't take charity.'

She threw the bag onto the table and I opened it. It was stuffed full of money. I was astounded.

'This is from Clara? Whatever for, and where has she gone?' The young woman shrugged.

'I'm not her keeper. As to the why, your dear cousin tried to buy me off.'

I must have looked blank. The young woman sighed.

'I expect you'll find out soon enough. Gwilym, your husband, he's got a son. Gwilym used to be with me and while he's no loss, he is the father of my boy and that won't change. I came here to tell him that, to make him understand. And now your cousin wants me to leave – she even said it was *his* money. The cheek of the cow!'

'Excuse me?' I said. I couldn't take it in. Gwilym *had a son?* I thought then of all I'd been through: the Cross Saddle Fire, Steph, Jacob and Alfie's deaths, then the *Titanic*, but still this woman had managed to shock me. 'What did you say your name was?' I said.

'I didn't,' she said. 'My name's Stella Dunne. You can tell your cousin that I'm not taking a penny from her, I can earn my own money. And I'm staying right here.'

I glanced at her luggage. Stella gave a chortle.

'Oh, you wish! I've just come back, from Malden in Dorset. It's where I used to live.'

I stared at her. 'Don't they have any papers in Dorset?'

'I didn't have time to read the papers. I had to get back, I've work to go to, as I've just said.'

God she was prickly. 'Haven't you heard about the *Titanic*?'

'What? Oh. Yes, it's very sad.'

'Hundreds of people, children included, die on a ship and all you can say is, it's very sad!'

Stella blinked and looked surprised. 'Well it is very sad. What do you care?'

'I'll tell you,' I said. 'Gwilym, my husband, and your boy's father, was on that ship and he's probably dead.'

'What?' she said, and she paled slightly, looking around, as if for a chair. 'Tell me you're joking.'

'Hardly,' I said. 'Not much of a joke.' Stella looked troubled.

'Wait a minute, you're still here.' I laughed.

'Wish I'd drowned as well, do you?' She didn't answer. I took a deep breath.

'The reason I'm here, is that I decided not to go. I didn't know then if I'd made the right decision, but I do know now.' I handed her the bag. 'So take my advice and keep the money. If it is Gwilym's, you won't be seeing much more of it. Now, I have to go out.' Stifling her protests, I almost pushed her down the hall.

A few minutes later, I took the same route, strolling along Whitborough Walk, on my way to my ma's.

Feeling the freedom from Gwilym and others.

7

1912 – Phoebe

When I got back, the house was still empty. I was starting to worry about Clara.

I searched the manor looking for a note but found nothing. Then I went down to the poetry room – still nothing. Then, I made a cup of tea and took it to the library. I loved having the house to myself. I thought about Stella, *what a surprise*, and then about Gwilym. I'd thought I'd known what he was like but it seems I was wrong. I couldn't settle. *Where the hell was Clara?* Perhaps she'd gone to visit Aunt Vi. Then I thought about Ma.

She'd welcomed me with open arms.

'Thank God, you're alive! I've been so worried. Losing Alfie, that was bad, but to lose you too, I couldn't have coped. I've been all over the place.'

That was true, the house looked a mess. I gave her a hug and grinned at her.

'But I'm dead already. The river, remember?' Ma swatted me.

'That made it worse. Who could I tell?' She smiled, happily. 'Barely back and cheeking me already.' Then she grew sombre.

'What about Gwilym?'

I shrugged. 'I left him standing at the docks, I couldn't face going. I've checked the lists and his name's not there, but that doesn't mean anything. Loads of people died that night. I could have been one of them.' Ma stared.

'Why didn't you go?'

'I had a feeling, and when I heard what Alice had said, it started to niggle. Alice is strange, but the woman talks sense. And I'm not that fond of boats anymore, not since the river.'

'But still one for a joke, my girl, you haven't lost that.' I smiled.

'No, Ma, I've only lost Gwilym. I still can't believe it.' Ma nodded.

'But *if* he's dead, you'll be able to stay at the manor, you'll not have to sell it.'

I nodded, I'd thought the same. 'It's one worry less. Though I still don't know where the second will is, Gwilym wouldn't tell me. Not that it matters if he's dead. But it would've been nice to have been the owner, to have run the manor as *I* wanted.' Ma smiled.

'You're forgetting, you're not Steph.'

'Since when has that mattered? '

Ma sighed. 'I've done a lot of thinking lately, since the ship sank. The Gilchrists have brought us nothing but trouble.' I jumped up.

'That's not fair. Think of all the things you've had.'

'But what about your brother, Phoebe? Alfie's dead.'

'That wasn't their fault!'

No it was mine. She'd never say it, but she'd always blame me for Alfie's death, for not being there. I stared at her.

'If I was the rightful owner of the manor you could move in and things would get better.' I got to my feet. 'I've got to find that will before Clara does. For all I know she's found it already, but nobody's home. I don't know where she is.'

'That's strange,' Ma said and I agreed. I was still worried.

I didn't mention Stella Dunne. I just couldn't face it.

As Burns wasn't there, I had to lock up. After I'd locked the large iron gates at the end of the grounds, I walked to the

Palm House. Finally I closed the French windows. Now there was only the front door to do. I stepped into the porch.

A tall woman was standing outside. By now it was late. I stopped, shocked. *Yet more strangers.* I didn't mince words.

'What do you want?'

The woman smiled. 'I'm Miranda. I'm looking for Clara.'

'Aren't we all?' I said, sourly. 'I'm Phoe... Steph,' I said. *God, I'd almost dropped my guard. That's what comes of visiting Ma.*

'Stephanie Gilchrist, Clara's cousin?'

'What *exactly* do you want?' The tall woman smiled.

'I've already said. I've come to see Clara. Isn't she in?'

Obviously not. I walked into the hall and sank into a chair. It was all too much. I stared at the woman. What did she want? 'I don't know where Clara is. I'm only just back.'

'From the *Titanic*?'

Who the hell was she? I didn't trust this woman one bit. Miranda, though friendly, was watching her words. 'What's that you're holding?'

'What? Nothing.' Shoving the parcel into her bag.

'Is Clara expecting you?'

'She probably wasn't expecting *you*.' Miranda gave me a piercing look. 'You weren't on the lists.'

So, they'd been looking. I was *so* tired. I threw her a wild card. 'Have you met Stella?'

Miranda shrugged. 'Who's Stella?'

I sighed. 'Look, Miranda, it's been a long day. I don't know where my cousin is, or when she'll be back. You can leave a message if you want, but after that I'd like you to leave.' Miranda didn't move.

'Did... Gwilym survive the sinking?'

'That's none of your business!'

'Yes, true, I shouldn't have asked. I'll leave you alone. But when you see Clara, tell her I've got some news for her and that I'll be back.'

News? What? I had to know. I knew she wouldn't tell me. I walked Miranda to the door and down the porch steps. She stumbled slightly, helped by a shove.

'Whoops look, you've lost your shawl.' I draped it gracefully over her shoulder, easing her bag back up again. Then I waved goodbye. 'Watch out for the tree roots.'

Then I locked the door behind her, fast.

Smiling a little as I put her parcel on the table.

Thanks, Ma, you did teach me something.

8

Now/1912 – Miranda

Almost at once I see what she's done. My bag's too light.

I tip it onto the lawn, quickly, but the portrait's not there. Steph has stolen it. That woman's outwitted me. *Damn her to hell!*

I think of going back but I know there's no point.

I sink down onto the lawn. She has the portrait and something else. I can't believe I've been so stupid. I've made things worse. *Much* worse.

When I'd got back to Henry's on Friday, I'd shown him the painting. Clara's portrait, *without* the ring. Henry smiled.

'This is Gwilym Lawson's work. He obviously copied Clara's self-portrait.'

'Like he did with the landscape. That was probably practice for this.' I nodded at the painting. 'Can you see how it's different?'

'You mean there's no ring?'

I nodded. 'He'd be engaged to Steph by then. What better place to hide the will than in his own painting, a portrait he knew Clara wouldn't look at. The original had been moved to the drawing room. Steph saw to that.'

'It's a clever idea,' Henry agreed. 'Assuming you're right.'

I stared at him. I had to be. I glanced at Henry. 'Lawson must have hidden Clara's version somewhere in the house. Then it was sold with the house contents. That's how it ended up in your shop.'

Henry nodded. 'So how did you find this one, then?'

I shook my head. 'Don't ask.'

When we unpacked it, there was the will. It was hard to read, but as we expected, it left everything to Steph and whoever she married. I was ecstatic. Now I could give the will to Clara and she'd get rid of it. Steph wouldn't inherit the manor, so Lawson wouldn't be able to sell it and the manor would be saved. It might even be here today. I was so proud.

But you know what they say about pride and a fall... I'm not proud now.

Now, today, Steph has the will and the manor could be sold and then demolished, perhaps even if Lawson is dead. Before, the will was hidden in the portrait – I should have destroyed it or left it there. I should have told Clara. All I've done is made things worse. Issington Manor doesn't exist and it's all my fault. What can I do to put things right?

9

1912 – Phoebe

I couldn't believe it, I'd found the will! I opened the package and found the portrait *and* the will. I was astounded!

I had a glass of wine or three, thinking about the things I'd do once the manor was mine. I'd ask Ma to move in along with Seth and I'd change things round and have some fun. It'd be better than Cross Saddle House and that had been great, until the fire. I drank too much.

I woke with a start to the sound of footsteps in the hall. I hadn't meant to fall asleep. I was still in the library, the will on my lap. It was morning now, and just after seven.

Burns poked his head around the door. 'Morning Madam. Welcome back. I'm glad to see that you're alright. We've been worried.'

Worried? I thought. *I could have died!* I smoothed back my hair.

'Any chance of some coffee, Burns? And where's Miss Clara?'

'She went to see her aunt in Pomphret. She's due back today, along with the others.' He paused, coughed.

'I'll make you some coffee, but Flora won't be back until later. I trust you'll be eating out for lunch?'

I couldn't help smile. This was *so* like Burns, everyone in their proper place. He didn't do cooking. It was great to be back. Then I glanced at the floor.

The will! I thought, and picked it up, quickly, folding it up and putting it away. It mustn't leave my sight again. I glanced up at Burns.

'I'll have my coffee in here, please. And I'm not accepting visitors today. Whatever they want.'

It was after four when Clara returned. Flora had already made up a fire, despite it being April. I was so damn cold.

I couldn't stop thinking about Gwilym and what he must have gone through. *Could he be alive?* I wasn't sure how I felt about that. If I'd gone on that ship, I'd probably be dead. How many lives can one person have? The door opened.

'Clara!' I said and leapt to my feet.

'Steph!' she cried and hurried towards me. 'Thank God you're alive!' She couldn't stop smiling. 'It's so good to see you. We'd heard nothing. I was so worried. Are you alright?'

'Yes, I'm fine, just a bit shocked. I didn't go, I changed my mind. I know it seems mad, but I just couldn't do it.' Clara went pale.

'But what about Gwilym?'

'I left him at the docks. He's probably dead, not that I know.' Clara sighed.

'I know I shouldn't care, after all he's done, but it's strange, I do.'

'Perfectly natural, if you ask me. The man was a charmer.' I glanced at the bell. 'Mabel's back, I'll ring for some tea. I'm absolutely starving. Burns told me he didn't do lunch.'

Clara laughed. 'Burns is very traditional. That's why I like him.'

After supper I knew it was time to mention the will.

'Did you ever find it?'

'No,' said Clara, 'and while I'm sorry Gwilym's… gone, at least it means that nothing has to change. Things can go back to the way they were.'

At once I felt angry, things *had* changed. She couldn't have everything all her own way. Not anymore.

'*I've* got the will.' Holding it up. Clara looked stunned.

'Where did you find it?'

'A friend of yours had it, *if* she is your friend. She called herself Miranda.' Clara nodded.

'She's more of an acquaintance, but yes I know her. How did she get it?'

'Never mind that. As you know, with this will I'm the rightful heir, but I won't sell the manor. This will always be your home. There'll be a few changes, but nothing to worry about.'

'Really?' said Clara, reaching for the will. 'I think I'm starting to worry already. Let me have a look at it.'

'Why?' I said. 'I'm telling the truth. Don't you believe me?'

Clara laughed and got up from her chair. 'If you think I'll hand the manor to you, without even seeing the evidence of ownership, you must be mad. And I know you're not.'

I handed it over.

Clara studied the will closely and seconds went by although they felt like minutes. Then she looked up and smiled at me. 'It all seems in order. And as you've made your terms clear, I'll do the same. You can live here under my roof, just like before. Before that man came into our lives.'

I didn't understand.

Then she ripped up the will and tossed the pieces into the fire.

I stood there, stunned. Clara smiled.

'Lost in the flames, like Cross Saddle House. Rather apt, don't you think?'

10

1912 – Miranda

That night, after losing the portrait, I don't go back to the twenty-first century. Instead, I sit in the churchyard, thinking.

I think about all the mistakes I've made, not just now but in my past, including with Ben, my old lover. I think about Ma and the Keepsake Arms, should I go back there? But life in the twenty-first century is easier. What can I do?

I'll have to explain to Clara what happened. That it's all my fault she'll lose her home. *Oh God.*

Just after four I fall asleep, propped up against a gravestone. No wonder I'm thinking of Ben, and Alice. Who wouldn't, of course, have made my mistakes. *Damn Alice.* For once, I smile.

Just after eight, I walk into town, via Whitborough Walk, hurrying past the memorial garden. Then I turn up Bakehouse Lane, it doesn't look that much different from today, apart from the horses. Then I blink, I've seen a ghost.

'Alice!' I yell. The woman turns round.

'Miranda,' she says and grins at me. As if she hadn't come back from the dead. 'This *is* a surprise.'

I race up the road. 'I've been looking for you.'

'Well here I am.'

'Have you time for a coffee? '

'I can make time for you. Fortunately, I've got my purse. The money's rather different here. And we don't have a Nero's.'

We? I think. I've a lot to catch up on.

'I thought you were dead,' I say to her, once we're in a tea shop. Alice sips coffee.

'The explosion, yes, I heard about that. One of the town's pieces of history. But no, it wasn't me.' Then we talk about the will.

'I've messed things up. What can I do?'Alice shrugs.

'Probably nothing. The will's not yours.'

'But that cow stole it from me!'

'That cow, as you call her, is the heir to the manor. She's entitled to have it. Apparently.'

My eyes narrow. 'What do you mean, *apparently*?' Clutching at straws.

Alice winks. 'Someone told me something once, about Sadie Slater. What was it?'

'Who's Sadie Slater?' Alice loves to wind me up. But she shakes her head.

'That doesn't matter. But what I heard made me think.'

'Think about what?'

But Alice just smiles and shakes her head.

'You'll have to wait, it'll take a little time. Come on, let's go.'

11

1912 – Phoebe

Seeing the will shrivel and burn made me mad. All my dreams, up in smoke. Like Cross Saddle House.

I leant across and slapped Clara.

'Oh!' she said, and touched her face.

'How dare you!' I said, wanting to shake her and hit her again. Instead, I banged my fists against the wall. It hurt like hell. 'Damn you!' I yelled.

I stormed out through the French windows into the garden, running as fast as I could to the river. I hated the river. All I could see when I looked at the water were images of Steph and images of Gwilym, and Cross Saddle House, burning forever. Fire and water, a never-ending death. Now I hated Clara too. I screamed and screamed into the night.

Everything I'd worked for, had dreamt of, was gone.

I'd never be able to bring Ma to the manor, I'd never see Alfie or Gwilym again. Perhaps I even cried for Jacob, for all of the people I'd wanted to save and hadn't been able to.

Then I heard her footsteps behind me.

'Steph,' she said.

'Leave me alone.'

'I had to do it, Steph,' she said. 'I had to save the manor for us, for my father's dream, Hall's library.' I stood up.

'You knew I wouldn't have sold the house. You didn't need to burn the will.'

'I couldn't take the chance, Steph. You can't imagine what it's been like, knowing I'd lose my family home, having to give up on my father's dream, being forced to move out. You don't understand.' I blinked.

I did understand. I stood there and faced her.

'Damn Lucienne Hall,' I said. 'The woman's long gone, but I'm still here, and so is my mother and your aunt. It's the living that matter, not a dead poet.'

'I'm sorry you feel like that,' said Clara. 'Hall matters, at least to me, and so does my father, even though he's dead. I promised my father I'd save the house for future generations and that's what I'll do. That's what I've done.' She softened slightly. 'Your mother's welcome to visit anytime.'

Of course she meant Thirza. I said nothing.

'Please come back to the house, Steph.'

'I love the manor too, Clara. Probably more than you do, actually. Please leave, I want to be alone.'

Clara went.

When I'd calmed down, I thought about how it would be in the future.

Much like the past, but without Gwilym. More thefts of blankets and money, trying to keep Ma and Seth afloat. Ma getting older. I couldn't bear it.

The next day, after tea, we sat in the drawing room. I knew Clara hated the room, so why were we in here? Maybe she liked to play the lady and that's where ladies sat after dinner. Maybe she wanted to be in charge. I felt trapped. I hated her then.

Then I smiled. There was one way I could get my own back. I took a deep breath.

When Miranda left the will, she also left you something else. I picked up the package I had by my side and a painting fell out. A painting of a house.

'It looks important. What do you think?'

And watched as Clara's face went white.

12

1912 – Clara

Time had passed, but things were no better. Clara sighed. She was trying to plan the Hall events but not getting far. She couldn't even think. She didn't trust Steph, but Clara was tired of living a lie. Did it matter that the manor wasn't Hall's first home?

Clara glanced up. Burns looked worried.

'There's someone at the door Miss. You'd better come.'

'Yes, alright.' Clara got to her feet, reluctant. Was it some sort of beggar, or perhaps Stella Dunne? Or maybe Theo had called at last. It didn't seem likely.

She went into the hall and walked towards the porch, slowly. She could see it was a man. Clara gasped and held onto the doorframe. *No, it couldn't be.* But of course it was.

'Gwilym,' she said.

Gwilym smiled. 'Hello dear cousin. I expect you're surprised to see me here. Or perhaps disappointed.'

'Cousin-in-law,' Clara snapped, and leant against the wall. 'I thought you were...'

'Dead? Yes. It's hardly surprising, given what happened. But never presume, that's what I say.'

Clara felt cold. 'Will you come in?'

'Of course I'll come in. It is my house.' He pushed past Clara into the hall. 'Where's Steph?'

'We need to talk. Let's go into the drawing room.'

Gwilym laughed. 'You haven't changed. We can talk if you like, but not before I've seen my wife.' He followed her into the drawing room. Neither sat down.

'Steph's out. She'll be back later. How was the *Titanic*?'
Gwilym flinched and Clara felt a twinge of guilt. It soon
passed.

'Cold, and wet. I'd rather not talk about what happened, if
you don't mind.' Clara shrugged.

'Fine by me. Have you just got back?'

'Yes, this morning, and I've no luggage. I lost it all, apart
from some cash.'

And a bit of that too, Clara thought, thinking of Stella. She
smiled, briefly.

'I hear Steph abandoned you, at the docks.' Gwilym
grinned.

'Just temporarily. Steph doesn't like water.'

'Shame you booked a sailing then.'

'Yes, so it seems.' Gwilym looked downcast. 'Look Clara, I
know you must hate me, but Steph and I are married now,
and believe me, I've had the most God-awful time. Can't we
be friends?'

Not on your life. 'You mean you want some sort of truce?'

'Yes, if you like. I thought I'd stay at my old lodgings, just
for a while. It'll give you time to get used to the changes.'

Meaning, she thought, *the manor being sold.* Clara smiled.

'You won't be able to move back there. It seems Mrs
Moore has a new lodger. And things have changed. We found
the second will.'

'Oh,' said Gwilym, looking surprised. 'I'd never have
believed it. Well done you.' Clara frowned.

'You really are the limit, Gwilym. As it happens, you're
right, I didn't find it, someone else did and she gave the will to
Steph. But I took it off her and burnt it in the fire. And, just in
case you're wondering, I tracked down the solicitor who
handled the transaction, the firm's long gone and he's in the
churchyard, so I don't think you'll be getting a copy.'

Gwilym looked grim. 'You really went to town on this.'

'Well, yes, I did, it is my home. And while we're on the subject, Gwilym, as Steph's husband you're welcome here, but don't think you can be my friend. And according to the will that exists, you can't sell the manor. Now, I must get on. If you want to see Steph you can come back later.' Clara walked to the door. 'I'll see you out.'

She glanced back at Gwilym but he hadn't moved.

'You know that will you destroyed? Didn't you notice anything about it?'

'No, what?' She was starting to feel anxious.

Gwilym smiled. 'That was a copy. I've still got the original.'

13

1912 – Phoebe

So Clara and I both had our secrets. And, what a secret!

Getting the truth hadn't been easy. But today, coming back from a stroll round the grounds, had felt like the day. For ages Clara had refused to talk about it.

I walked in and found Clara in the library. I sat down.

'Tell me about the painting, Clara. The one with the house.' Clara sighed.

'There's nothing to tell.'

'So what's it of?'

'It's a house, clearly.' I frowned.

'I can see that. I also know it's on Whitborough Walk, I recognise that bend in the road. Was it something you painted? It looks pretty old.'

'No, I didn't paint it, I don't know who did. Look, Steph, I've told you already, it's just a house.'

'That painting was in Miranda's bag, it must mean something.'

As soon as I'd said it I wished I hadn't. Clara pounced.

'I knew it!' she said. 'Miranda didn't give you the will, or the painting, you stole them from her. You're a thief, Steph, a mean little thief. Well what a surprise!' Meaning my poems. I held my ground.

'Yes,' I agreed, 'I wanted that will. Because I'm the heir.' Clara looked angry.

'Not anymore. I'm not sorry that I burnt it.'

'No, I can see that. But, in return, I want an answer. What does the house mean?'

Clara said nothing. I went on.

'I've just been to where the house should be and guess what I found? A memorial garden. And some really crappy verse.'

'That's rich, coming from you.'

'My work's getting better. I've been practising.' Clara laughed.

'All the practice in the world wouldn't make you a good poet. Unless by practising you mean stealing.' I scowled.

'Don't be horrible. Then I went to the Issington Star and did some research. That house was damaged in an explosion and a young woman died. I wonder who she was? Let me guess…'

'Yes, alright, it was Lucienne Hall. That's where she died and that's why the painting matters.'

No, I thought, *that's not it.* 'How come Miranda had it?'

'She must have taken it from my portrait, that's where I hid it.'

'After you found it, in the poetry room.'

'Yes, if you like.'

'It must have been important then, for you to hide it. How do you know she died at that house? It wasn't in the paper.' I shook my head. 'I don't think that's it. I think the house was Lucienne Hall's home, before she lived here.'

'No,' whispered Clara.

'Yes,' I insisted. 'No-one moves into a place like the manor straight away.'

'She used to live on Upper Fell Street.'

'They were just lodgings. Hall had been writing for several years before she moved into Issington Manor. I found some old verse in the poetry room. They're only scraps, but they've got dates.'

'You never said.'

'Why the hell should I? You resented me being down there. You thought she was yours.'

Clara leapt to her feet. 'Well, so she was, mine and my father's. We had a dream, the Hall library, and you and Gwilym were going to take that away. *That's* why I burnt the will, and as for that house on Whitborough Walk, the place was a ruin after the explosion. There's nothing to prove it was *her* house.'

I smiled. I knew she was lying.

I tipped the package into my hand. A small slip of paper fell into my palm.

'Apart from this. And, no, Clara, you're not going to burn it.' I read out the words.

'The poet Lucienne Hall's house, Issington Halt.'

Clara gave a strangled cry. 'Why go through all that if you already knew?'

'I wanted to hear what you would say. You needn't worry, I'll keep your secret.'

She stared at me. 'There's something you ought to know. I was going to tell you before all this. Gwilym's alive, he turned up this morning, after you left.'

'No,' I said. 'You're making it up.'

'If only,' she said. 'And he's coming back. He wants to see you.'

But do I want to see him? I thought.

'I told him about the will,' she said. 'And that I'd burnt it. He didn't seem bothered.' I interrupted.

'Look, Clara, it'll be fine. The second will's gone so the manor is safe. That's all that matters. We'll find a way to deal with Gwilym.'

'You don't understand. Before he left town, he had the will copied and that's the one Miranda found and I got rid of. He still has the original.'

'No,' I said, faintly. 'That can't be true.'

'That's what he said, Steph, and I believe him.' Clara picked up the picture.

'The painting isn't the issue here. Gwilym means to sell the manor and everything in it, unless he's stopped. Or unless we stop him.' Clara paused.

'So, cousin. Whose side are you on?'

14

1912 – Phoebe

The next day I went to see Gwilym. He hadn't turned up the previous evening. Then, I'd been pleased. Now I was anxious.

The weather was good and I walked the back way, passing some builders putting up houses.

Will they be working on our land next? The thought sickened me.

As I crossed Lower Fell Street to get to Gwilym's lodgings, I glanced across at the rectory. Another lovely house and grounds. *At least that's one that won't be demolished.* Then I was there.

'Phoebe,' said Gwilym, emerging from the house. Then he rushed toward me and scooped me up, swinging me round like he used to do, holding me close, not letting me go. There in the street. We were alone.

'Hi,' I said, feeling the pull of the old attraction, grinning at him. But I had to be strong. *Damn you*, I thought. *The manor is mine.* I narrowed my eyes.

'Aren't you glad to see me, old girl?'

'Not if you're going to sell, no.' But Gwilym didn't care.

'Needs must, I'm strapped for cash.'

'That's such a lie! Besides, you can work. I thought you liked painting.' Gwilym just laughed.

'Yeah, sure, but not all the time. Painting's more fun when you don't *have* to do it. We'll all be rich when the manor is sold, including your ma.' I stared. Gwilym went on.

'I'll see she's alright *and* little Seth. Maybe I'll give him a bright future, in some sort of trade.' I glared at him, angry.

'You've obviously thought of everything, Gwilym. But aren't you forgetting, I'm not Steph and it's not your house. I'm not going to let you sell, I'd rather tell Clara the truth, first.'

'And you think she'd let you stay there, afterwards? You lied to her, then married her fiancé *and* you put her cousin in the river. She'll be thinking you murdered Steph. Not that I would mention the body, not unless I had to.' Gwilym winked. Then he went on.

'No, Phoebs, you'd be out on your ear and, unlike me, you wouldn't have a job. If you betrayed me I wouldn't want you, and would happen to your dear ma then? You'd have to go back to Chesterton Court *and* find work. If anyone would have you.'

Later, that evening, in my room, I remembered the letters Steph used to write. Well, I could write letters, and unlike her, I usually sent mine. So I wrote one then, and waited for the post to come.

15

1912 – Phoebe

I went to see Stella. I knew it was a risk but I had no choice. She didn't look happy.

'What do you want?'

'Can we please talk in your room, Stella, and not on the doorstep?' She folded her arms.

'You're lucky I'm here. I should be at work, but Jack's sick.'

'Oh. I'm sorry.'

'You're obviously not, but it's just a cold. Jack will be fine. What do you want?' I showed her the bag.

'You forgot this.'

'I've told you before, I don't want the money, I'm better off without it.'

I doubted that, but I went on. 'What about Gwilym?'

'What do you mean?'

'If he came back, would you still want him?'

Stella looked angry. 'Why are saying this? You told me Gwilym was dead.'

'That because I thought he was, but I was wrong. He's back in town. Wouldn't you like to know where?'

Stella went pale. 'Does he know I'm here?'

'I haven't told him.' Then I leant in. 'When you saw Clara, you lied, and I know the truth. Do you still want him? Because I don't and you've got a son.'

Stella's face crumpled. 'No,' she said, 'not anymore, not after everything that's happened. But I've Jack to think of, and working in the brewery's hard, standing in water for hours on end. God, how I hate it!'

I dropped the bag on the step in front of her. 'Well take the money then.' I smiled, remembering being on my feet for hours at Milsom's, being nice all the time. I had some sympathy. But Stella wasn't smiling

'God, how I hate you, you and your cousin *and* bloody Gwilym, you're all so alike, so self-satisfied. And I don't want *that*.' She glared at the bag. I nodded.

'You think Gwilym chose me over you, or that he liked Clara? You've got it wrong. Gwilym chose a house, not a woman, that's what he wanted, the manor, the lifestyle. Being a painter wasn't enough, it'll never be enough.'

Stella looked sad. 'Yeah, sure, but he made so much.'

'Yes, by your standards, and even by mine. But not by his own – he wanted it all and now he thinks he's got what he wanted. But he hasn't, I promise you, now that I'm sure.'

I picked up the bag and gave it to her. '*Now* are you going to take the money?' Stella sighed.

'Maybe,' she said.

I smiled.

That afternoon, Clara and I walked by the river. On the other side for once. It didn't make it easier.

'The manor's always been my home. I don't think I could bear to lose it. All my work on Hall lost.' Clara looked up. 'Where did you go, when you went out earlier?' I sighed.

'I went to see Stella, and then to see Gwilym. It didn't go well.'

'So he's not going to change his mind, then? No, of course he's not.' Clara scowled. 'I knew I shouldn't have trusted Gwilym, but for once I was reckless and look where it's led us.' She sighed, heavily. 'Think of it, Steph, our lovely grounds turned into houses, lots of little boxes. But why should I worry? We'll soon be dead, like Lucienne Hall.'

I stopped, shocked. 'You're only young and so am I. We've got our whole lives. Anything could happen.' Clara looked angry.

'Don't you understand, my dream has died? At least you're married but I'm on my own and I'm going to lose my home, the only one I've had. And I've let Father down.'

'Nonsense,' I said, 'it wasn't your fault. And you'll always have me.' Clara didn't answer. I tried again.

'Suppose something has changed?' I said. 'Something Gwilym doesn't know about yet?'

'You haven't found the will?' she said. Hopefully.

No,' I said. 'I'm expecting a baby.' Clara frowned and turned away. I jumped in quickly.

'I knew you wouldn't be happy,' I said, 'because the child's Gwilym's, but it does mean the manor has a future, if we decide it. *My* baby can be *our* future. A Gilchrist descendant to take on the dream.'

'My father's dream,' Clara insisted. 'But we've still lost the manor.'

'It's a pity,' I said, 'that we need Gwilym.'

'Do we?' she said, just as I'd hoped.

'Sometimes,' I said, carefully now, 'people just vanish, if there's a reason, like on the *Titanic*. Especially when they won't be missed.'

'But Gwilym didn't die.' I sighed.

'How many people know that he didn't? Very few people know he's here. He *could* disappear.'

'He's not going to do that.'

'He might if we made him.'

Clara frowned. By now we were standing under the bridge and people strolled past, people and dogs, chatting away, sharing their lives. No-one came near us. Clara considered.

'Why would you want to do that, Steph, make your husband go away?'

It was on the tip of my tongue to tell her. But I held back.

'Because the manor means more to me. Just like you.' Clara smiled and I rushed in.

'We'd need to be sure, and we'd need... resources.'

'Are you sure it's *possible*?'

I smiled. 'It's possible, alright, and I'd be happy to handle it, if I was certain you would support me.'

Clara nodded. 'I think I could do that.'

'That's good. Let's talk about the details later.' We walked a little further.

Clara looked up. 'I've always wondered why you went as far as the docks but didn't sail?'

'Someone told me I shouldn't go. I just ignored it, but when I got down there I knew she was right. And, I don't like water, or boats. Though both can be useful.' Clara stared.

'Do you remember them finding that tart? Uncle Jacob's woman? It was quite near here.'

'Yes,' I said, holding my breath. Had I been rumbled?

'I always thought she'd died in the fire. But instead she'd drowned. How did that happen?' I shrugged.

'I don't know. Though bodies can rise to the surface,' I said. 'It's not very pretty.'

'That was because of the flood,' said Clara. 'I doubt we'll have another, soon.'

'No,' I said. 'We probably won't, not for a long time.' We stared at each other.

Clara turned away from the river and took my arm. 'You're right, of course. We have to look to the future now. Now there'll be three of us.'

16

1912 – Clara

Everything was peaceful now. Clara felt she'd lived through hell, these past few years, but now it was over. It was all for the best and she and Steph had got through it.

Steph came downstairs. 'I'm going for a walk. Do you want to come?'

Clara frowned. 'I think I'll stay inside today and do some more sketches, if you don't mind.' Steph shrugged.

'Just as you please. I'll see you later.' Her cousin left.

A few minutes later the doorbell rang. Burns appeared.

'A man called Tommins to see you, Miss.' Clara sighed. She'd known it would happen.

'Show him into the drawing room, please. And bring us some coffee.' *I need coffee. Or, rather, a brandy.* Burns left.

Tommins was balding, with a pompous manner.

'I've an appointment to see Mr Lawson.'

'Are you sure Mr Tommins?' Tommins looked shifty.

'Fine, so I don't, but he's missed more than a couple of mine, so I thought I'd follow up on it.'

'Is it about the sale of the manor?' Tommins went pale.

'He's spoken to you?'

'I know of his plans and we're not selling.' Clara went on before he could argue.

'Gwilym's not here, he's out of town, I expect you know he travels for work. I'm not quite sure when he'll be back.' She raised a hand. 'And before you ask, I don't have his current address, but I'll take your card, just in case. Although I wouldn't hold your breath.'

Tommins swore. 'So Lawson's wasted my time then? When I've spent months working on him... working with him and I've got customers ready to buy.'

'Really?' said Clara, smiling at Tommins. 'That's such a pity. Lots of little boxes, all much the same, after you've demolished our family home, the house my father and grandfather cherished.' Tommins went puce.

Burns walked in and Clara smiled.

'Thanks Burns, but Mr Tommins is just leaving. I'll have a coffee.' Clara stood up and stared at Tommins.

'Mr Lawson won't be back, at least not for a while, so please don't call again Mr Tommins. We won't be selling the manor to you, or selling at all, in my lifetime. Burns, please show the *gentleman* out.'

Tommins hurried towards the door, growing more red with each step. Clara glanced across at Burns. He was trying not to smile.

17

1912 – Miranda

Alice has thought up some sort of plan. It took quite a while. Eventually she borrows a carriage. How does she do it? Alice just laughs.

'A coach would be useless. Where we're going is out in the sticks. And as we don't ride… What do you think?'

I stare at the carriage. It's small and once inside it's airless, surprisingly cold despite it being spring and bumpy like you'd never believe. I feel every pothole.

'Stop moaning!'

I haven't said a word, but Alice just knows.

Annoyingly, I'm still in awe of her, despite her being younger. Our Curdizan story binds us together, but I prefer the twenty-first century. So why I am here? The carriage stops and we get out.

I stare, mesmerised. There's a house in front of me, or what's left of a house, stripped and bare, with lots of charred wood. Cross Saddle House.

Still in a mess, a year later. Alice looks at me.

'Still angry with Steph Gilchrist?'

'I wasn't…' I mutter, but Alice is right, she's always right. I *had* been angry. *Damn her*, I think. Alice, not Steph.

We climb back in the rickety thing, trundle along and arrive at a cottage, much smaller than the house, well-maintained, with a nice front garden. An ideal home for a couple and their daughter. Now, only the wife lives there. This is Thirza's home. I turn to Alice.

'What are we going to say to her?'

'Why are you whispering?' Alice replies, looking amused and not answering. She walks up the path and I hurry after her. Why am I always following Alice? Thirza opens the door to us.

She's well-turned out. Her hair is held back in a graceful bun and she's wearing a plain, dark blue dress, with lace on the sleeves and across the bodice. The sort of dress that would last a while.

'This is Miss Collenge,' says Alice. 'May we come in?'

Thirza nods and we go inside. The woman is expecting us, but she's not exactly welcoming. Alice is talking but what she's saying doesn't make sense. Nor is she making much progress with Thirza.

'Clara Gilchrist isn't my family. I don't even know her.'

'She is your husband's niece,' says Alice, 'so legally, she's your niece too.'

'By marriage,' says Thirza, folding her arms. 'And as you know, my husband left me. For *that* woman.'

'Well, I heard you threw him out.' Alice leans in and smiles at Thirza. 'I would have done the same,' she says.

Thirza thaws and laughs, self-consciously. I sit back and drink my tea. *How does she do it?*

'It would only be for a few minutes, and only the once, I won't ask again.' Alice stops and takes a biscuit. 'These are delicious. Did your maid make them?'

Thirza starts to answer her, then stops and laughs. She smiles at Alice. 'Alright, you win, but just the once. Although I can't see why one visit would help.'

'You'd be surprised. I'll arrange for our carriage to pick you up.'

Thirza shakes her head.

'You're very persuasive, Miss Sewell. But this time, the answer is no. I'll take *my* carriage.' Thirza smiles. 'That way, I can leave when I want.'

332

Once we're on our way back to Issington I have to ask.

'What did you say in your letter to her? To make her agree to visit the manor.'

'I told her Clara wanted to see her, to talk about Steph.'

'But that isn't true,' I say, alarmed, 'and once Clara opens the door, Thirza will know that. What happens then?' Alice just smiles.

'We'll make sure Steph is in and then we'll see.'

Then she winks at me in that way she has.

'Trust me, Miranda, it'll be fine.'

18

1912 – Phoebe

The manor felt more like home each day. I didn't want to leave it. The weather was warm and Clara and I were on our own. Sometimes I felt queasy with the baby.

'That's only to be expected,' said Clara. She didn't seem daunted.

I was sitting, working, in the library, rattling out a couple of poems. They were all my own work, not Lucienne Hall's and they weren't half bad. Clara and Ma didn't agree.

'It's boring,' said Ma, when I read one out. 'It's all about houses, gardens and trees. And it doesn't even rhyme.' I'd laughed at her.

'Honestly Ma! Would you like me to write about bodies in the river?'

'Well, at least that would be interesting.'

But what about Alfie?

I wondered then if I'd changed, if Clara and the manor had got to me. Or maybe the baby had. I still hadn't worked out how I'd get Ma and Seth to move in, two complete strangers. Perhaps I should have kept Gwilym's money instead of handing it over to Stella. I stared out at our lovely garden then my heart did a flip.

Thirza was walking through the gate, Miranda and Alice close behind. What did they want? What did Thirza want? I leapt up quickly and hurried to the hall to find Clara. I grabbed her arm.

'Let's go for a walk, it's lovely and sunny.' Thinking we could leave by the orangery. But Clara just laughed.

'Your mother's arrived, don't you want to see her? She's come to see you.' I stared, disbelieving.

'*You* invited her?' Clara shrugged.

'It seemed the right time, now you're expecting. And, no, I didn't tell her.'

'You never said!'

'It was meant to be a surprise,' said Clara.

A surprise? Oh God! Clara went on.

'Alice arranged it. It'll be fine.'

Alice, I knew it! The interfering cow. No, it won't be fine.

I looked Clara in the eye. 'That woman's trouble.'

'Rubbish,' said Clara, 'she's been a great help. You ought to see your mother, Steph. Now that everything's changing.'

Isn't it just? I didn't know what to say or do. My heart was racing, out of control. Burns strolled down the hall, casually, as the doorbell rang. I gripped Clara's arm, even more tightly.

'Please, Clara, send her away.' But Clara held firm.

'No, Steph, I'm not doing that. It's time we all made peace with the past. And don't try to leave. You're staying here.'

I had to think fast. 'Get Burns to put her in the library.'

'What? Why?'

'We need to talk, before I see… Mama. Please Clara, just for a minute.' Clara looked angry.

'If you insist, but I'm not very happy.' She hurried down the hall after Burns and they had a few words. Then Clara and I decamped to the drawing room. I was pacing the room like a lion, knowing I'd finally run out of lives. So I just said it.

'I'm not Steph, I'm Phoebe Slater.'

Clara was sitting, I was still standing. She didn't say a word.

'I'm Phoebe. Steph died in the fire.'

'But who was the woman they brought up from the river?'

'That was Steph. Gwilym and I had to hide her body. The river was the best place, we thought she'd be safe there. And believe me, Clara, we didn't kill her, the fire saw to that. But I wanted to be Steph.'

'Gwilym,' said Clara.

'Yes, he helped me. But it was my idea.'

'So you're not Steph, you're not entitled to the manor?' Still disbelieving.

'No, that's right.' I was sick to my stomach.

'You and that man planned it all, to steal my home and have it demolished.'

'No,' I said, 'that wasn't my plan. I loved the manor right from the start. Even more than I loved Cross Saddle House and that was a lot. Selling the manor was Gwilym's idea.'

'But you went along with it. I'd have been homeless. You should have told me.' *Yes, I should.*

'It wouldn't have happened, I wouldn't have let it. Remember our plan.' Clara looked grim.

'Oh yes, I remember, our walk by the river and afterwards. But you still let me think you were the heir.'

I shrugged and smiled. 'I love the manor. I wanted a home for me and my child. Have you ever been to Chesterton Court?'

'No,' said Clara, 'but Alice has. She gives bread to the poor.'

Alice, God. I stared at the wall. They were next door.

Clara was frosty. 'So, Alice knows?'

'I think so, yes. She certainly will if you let them in here. Send them away, *please* Clara. At least it will give us more time to talk.'

Clara hesitated. 'Who else knows?'

'Only my ma and she won't say anything. And Seth, my brother, but he's only little. Look Clara, the manor's *your* home and Alice, Miranda, they can't prove anything if Thirza doesn't see me.'

'Why should I care?'

I hated myself. 'Because I'm expecting.'

'That's right, you are, but you're not a Gilchrist. That baby won't be *my* niece or a nephew.' I stared at her.

'But nobody knows that. Nobody will.'

Seconds passed but it felt like hours.

'Fine, alright, I'll do what you ask. I need time to think.'

'What will you say?'

'Never you mind. Get out of the house, go down to the river, go, Steph, now! And go by the orangery.'

I did what she said.

Noting that she'd still called me Steph. Where there's life, there's hope.

19

1912 – Miranda

We're still in the library, waiting. Next door, I can hear their voices.

'It's such a beautiful room,' says Thirza, looking around. I know what she means.

Can I save the manor?

Alice strolls around the room, looking for what? She picks up a picture, a small portrait and shows it to me. Speaking to me softly.

'Is that Steph Gilchrist?' I nod and Alice shows the painting to Thirza.

'Clara's such a good artist.'

Thirza frowns and stares at the painting. Then she turns red. 'No-one can make that woman look good. That's it! I'm going.'

'No, wait, whatever's the matter?' Alice reaches out to Thirza but Thirza pushes her away, roughly and heads for the door. Then she turns round.

'I believed that woman was dead, along with my daughter. And then I discover, thanks to you, that Steph is alive and Clara, my niece has been keeping her from me. And *now* it's clear they're friends with that tart, the whore who stole and killed my husband. He'd still be alive, if it wasn't for her. I thought she was dead!'

'Wait, please,' Alice says calmly, moving towards her and blocking her exit. She holds out the portrait. 'Are you telling me this isn't Steph?'

'No, it's Phoebe Slater – and don't tell me you didn't know.' Alice says nothing.

Then the door opens and Clara walks in. She looks ill.

'Dear Aunt Thirza, it's lovely to meet you. I'm so sorry for keeping you waiting…'

'Steph was always sorry,' snaps Thirza. 'That is, until the next time it happened, whatever *it* was. You and she have that much in common, along with being liars.' She grabs the portrait and shows it to Clara.

'I can't think why you invited me here, given that you're friends with *that* woman. Not to mention, keeping Steph from me.' Clara looks troubled.

'Aunt Thirza I didn't…'

'Don't even bother…' Thirza strides past her and out of the room.

Alice and I look at each other. Alice is smiling.

'Clara, I'm sorry, I've got to go,' Alice says then and she and I leave as fast as we can. Clara doesn't even attempt to stop us.

Nor do we try to talk to Thirza, whose carriage is rolling down Whitborough Walk.

When we reach the churchyard, I stop. 'I'm leaving,' I say, 'and for good this time.' Thinking of the portrait Alice showed Thirza. The woman had looked like the Steph I'd met, but apparently she was called Phoebe Slater. Could it be true that Steph wasn't Steph and that Clara hadn't known? And if so, would it be enough?

'I live here now.' Alice stands firm.

'Do you like it, then?' Wondering what will happen to her, and to the manor.

'It's better than Curdizan that's for sure. But I doubt I'll stay forever, Miranda. I'm bound to get bored.' She winks at me. 'I expect I'll see you again, sometime.'

I agree. On another adventure.

20

Now – Miranda

When I get back, I want to forget how it all went wrong, because I let Steph steal the will. Yet Steph isn't Steph, she's actually Phoebe, and Phoebe doesn't have a claim to the manor. And now Clara knows she's Phoebe, thanks to us. So maybe it will be alright. And maybe it won't.

I can't face looking, I've had enough, at least for now. So instead, I go down to Henry's shop.

To my surprise, the others are there, enjoying a drink and the snacks he's provided. Judy and Henry, Oliver and Cher. I soon join in. It's good to be doing something normal.

'I've posted my first artefact on Insta,' Henry says, proudly, 'and it's already had over 50 likes.' I smile, happily, that's *so* Henry, as if he's run a marathon or something.

'I've given him some tips,' Oliver adds, he's our marketing expert.

I've a tip too, an enormous tip, something I've learnt, but can't share with them. Don't interfere, even to help, it might cause trouble, in unexpected ways. *But at least*, I think, *Alice isn't dead.*

Though of course she is. Now, in the present.

Later on, when I'm primed with wine, I go back to the churchyard and walk through the graves. I clamber carefully onto the railing and look over the wall, my eyes closed. Then I open them quickly. I'm in for a sight. There, below me, stands the manor, solid, substantial, though quite a bit older than when I last saw it, earlier today. All its lights blazing. I stare and stare, I can't believe it. I clamber down, via a tree, walk down the slope and past the parterre and reach the manor.

Read the plaque outside the house, where I saw the For Sale sign.

This library was built to remember the poet Lucienne Hall, who lived here in the 1850s.
And her successor, Steph Gilchrist, who followed in Lucienne Hall's footsteps.
And to all poets everywhere, so they may have a place to work.

Augustin, Frederic, Clara and Sophia.

FEEDBACK

If you have enjoyed reading *Shadows of a Lost Poet*, please leave a review on Amazon. Authors love reviews.

Thank you.

Shadows of a Lost Poet is also available as an ebook.

https://www.amazon.com/Ellie-Stevenson/e/B007UF15I4 (Author page)

https://www.amazon.co.uk/Shadows-Lost-Poet-Time-Book-ebook/dp/B094RCS7KV (UK)

https://www.amazon.com/Shadows-Lost-Poet-Time-Book-ebook/dp/B094RCS7KV (United States)

ACKNOWLEDGEMENTS

Thanks to the Shakespeare Birthplace Trust (SBT) for permission to use the following image: STRST : SBT 1992-98 – a watercolour painting of no. 45, Waterside, Stratford-upon-Avon by William Wells Quatremain (CC-BY-NC-ND Image Courtesy of the Shakespeare Birthplace Trust)

Also for use of the SBT archive in researching the history of the two Avonbanks and life in Edwardian Stratford-upon-Avon, on which the town Issington Halt is based.

Thanks also to my partner Jann Tracy for her insightful blogs on Avonbank and for reading an earlier draft of this book.

Thanks to Bren Littlewood for also providing valuable feedback on an earlier draft.

Thanks to Jane Dixon-Smith for another evocative cover which catches the mood of the novel perfectly.

Thanks are also owed to the singer Paloma Faith whose song, *The Architect*, was part of my inspiration. Music always plays a large part in the initial drafting of my stories and characters.

A special thanks to Mary Nicholls, whose presence and support while I was growing up, *and now*, has made a huge difference to my life. Thank you, Mary.

About *Shadows of a Lost Poet* and the real Issington Halt

While all of my books can be read separately, this is the second book in the Shadows in Time series, featuring Miranda and Alice, who first appeared in *Shadows of the Lost Child.*

You can read an extract from Shadows of the Lost Child after this section.

You can also **join my mailing list** at **elliestevenson.com** to get updates on my books and on writing.

While the characters in *Shadows of a Lost Poet* are all fictional (except for Marie Corelli!), Issington Manor was inspired by a real house in Stratford-upon-Avon called Avonbank. This Avonbank was very close to the site of a former house, also called Avonbank. The former house was used as a school and one of their pupils was a girl called Elizabeth Cleghorn Stevenson (no relation!) who later became Elizabeth Gaskell, the well-known author of Cranford and biographer of Charlotte Brontë.

The first Avonbank (on which the conference centre in the novel is modelled) was demolished by Charles Edward Flower, of the brewing family. (Brewing also features briefly in the novel). Flower then built the second Avonbank and when describing Issington Manor, I've used images and plans of the house as inspiration. Like Issington Manor, the second Avonbank had an amazing conservatory or orangery (where Gwilym and Phoebe have secret meetings in the novel).

Although, to my regret, Avonbank no longer exists, in the summer of 2018 the very warm weather meant that the outline of the foundations of the house became visible through the grass (as happened with some other properties across the country). I took photos of this and you can see them further on in this book.

See also the painting of a small house, formerly the home of local watercolour landscape artist William Wells Quatremain (1857-1930) which was demolished in 1916. I used this image and its approximate location as inspiration for the small house which becomes a memorial garden.

Later on in the novel the river floods. In the book this happens in early 1912. The actual flood on which this part of this novel was based took place in 1901 when the houses on Waterside (Whitborough Walk) were badly flooded and the water went up part of Sheep Street (Bakehouse Lane). Although work subsequently done in the area means that such bad flooding will thankfully never happen again, there is still mild flooding today after a lot of rain.

Foundations of the former Avonbank
showing through the grass (1), 2018

Foundations of the former Avonbank
showing through the grass (2), 2018

No. 45 Waterside, Stratford-upon-Avon

QUESTIONS FOR READING GROUPS

Please note: Spoiler Alert!

When Phoebe meets Jacob she turns her back on her old life. Which do you think is the most problematic – the way she treats Thirza or the way she treats her ma, Sadie?

Who is most important to Jacob – his brother Frederic, his wife Thirza, or his lover Phoebe?

Is Steph in love with Gwilym?

Which home would you prefer – Issington Manor or Cross Saddle House, and why?

Should Thirza have taken Jacob back?

Did Augustin appreciate Lucienne Hall?

What do you think of Alice as a person?

When Clara finds the small painting what should she have done with it?

Do you think Stella was right to leave Dorset and move to Issington Halt?

Would you like to travel back in time like Miranda did?

Should Miranda have interfered?

Which of the characters would you most like to meet and why?

Read an extract from the first book in the *Shadows in Time* Series:

About Shadows of the Lost Child

The Present

Aleph Jones is running away but the house he ends up in turns out to be haunted. Or is it just him? For Aleph has a dark secret that's changed his life.

Cressida Sewell needs Aleph's help. Her daughter, Alice refuses to speak and a team of specialists don't know why. But Cressida has a hidden agenda and Alice knows more than she's letting on. About Aleph.

Guinevere James is not what she seems. Disguised as Aleph's business client, she really wants to solve a murder that happened over a century ago.

And what about the children who vanished? Aleph and Alice can hear them scream.

The Past

Miranda and Thomas live in poverty. Miranda wants to protect her mother but when she seeks help from friends Ben and Tom, they set on a path to even more trouble.

Then Tom meets Alice and the past and the present begin to collide with dangerous consequences...

This is a ghost story, and a mystery. Can you solve it?

Inspired by the legends of York (UK).

Shadows of the Lost Child (novel) – extract

1
Now – Aleph

I've always lived in the shadow of churches. Now, when I see one, I walk the other way.

It was Thursday morning, the beginning of spring. I walked down Narrowboat Lane to the arch, and under the archway onto the street. I saw the house, it was over to the left; it looked quite something. Then I raised my eyes above the windows and saw what was towering high above it. An enormous church. A single word sprang to my lips. Or maybe two.

'Hell,' I said. 'Hell and damnation.'

Not just a church behind the house, but a great big giant, a monster of a thing, all gables and parapets, much more like a cathedral really. My heart sank, for I knew what it meant, another place I'd have to turn down.

'Curdizan Abbey,' said the voice beside me, 'and don't say no to the house just yet. It has some truly amazing features.' I shook my head and looked to the right and there was Gemma, from Cloud House Properties. The word amazing wasn't strictly accurate. I imagined the house had draughty rooms and uneven floors, and doors that didn't quite fit properly. But, what did I think the woman would say? She was an estate agent after all. Gemma Pearce held out her hand.

'Good to meet you, Mr Jones.'

'Good to meet *you*,' I said, smiling, and grasped her hand which was small and neat. She was blonde, beautiful, tall and thin with china doll features and perfect straight hair. I could feel the benefits of the house already.

We moved a bit closer and she jangled her keys, and a flash of the sun caught the edge of the steel. A sharp strip of light fell down from the sky, splitting the steps up ahead in two. There was light and dark and I knew which side of the steps were mine. I raised my head and there was the abbey, all of a shimmer. It almost felt like some kind of welcome.

'It seems to me it's yours already,' said Gemma coyly, as she pushed on the door, which was old and warped. I followed her in.

No, I thought, as we entered the hall, *it's not my house*. But it was, really.

Later that day I was standing inside the estate agent's office. The lovely Gemma had long since gone, leaving me there with somebody different. Exceedingly different. Her eyes were cold and her face disapproving.

'You're self-employed?' she said, frowning. 'We'll have to see your accounts, I'm afraid.'

'But I don't have any accounts,' I said. 'I don't earn enough to be VAT registered.' I could feel the palms of my hands sweating. This wasn't going the way I'd hoped.

'Well, what about your tax returns? We do need to see you can cover the rent.'

The way she was making me feel right now, I doubted I could. I said nothing.

'Do you have any other assets? A house, perhaps, or maybe some savings?' I shook my head. *Nothing*, I thought, *that's what I've got.*

Before, I'd lived in my girlfriend's flat, I hadn't needed any assets, not even things like a washing machine. We'd shared possessions, plates and everything. I thought my life was hers, forever. Now, I needed to rent a place. I knew I could afford it, so what was the problem?

The woman before me was frost dressed up. I knew about that, how people could change, but I still didn't like it, it made me nervous. I knew I'd never win her over.

'I have got savings,' I said stiffly. 'More than enough for the rent, as it happens.' I hated baring my soul like this.

'Well, that's good news,' she said, smiling. The smile went nowhere near her eyes. 'You can pay the rent for the house in advance. The whole six months.'

It was tall and rambling, in the centre of town, three storeys high, and I knew there must be something wrong, for a house this big to be offered this cheap. Well, not that cheap, but cheap enough for me to afford it. Even with all the rent in advance. I guessed it must be a wreck inside.

'How long has it been on the market?' I'd asked Gemma.

'I'm not quite sure,' said Gemma vaguely, twirling her hair around her fingers. 'About three months.'

'So why did the previous tenant leave?'

'I'm not quite sure,' she started to say, but stopped abruptly at the look on my face. 'She died, actually.'

'Ah,' I said.

'Not in the house,' said Gemma, quickly. 'She died in hospital, after a stroke. She was eighty-eight and deaf as a post, the poor old thing. She'd lived in the house all the time she was married.' She glanced ahead.

'The house is a bit neglected, sadly, and I know there isn't a washing machine, but at least that means you can choose your own.'

I laughed out loud, I couldn't help it. The woman was clearly a natural at this, she was already trained in estate agent speak. *I* thought she was very convincing, I guess I wanted to be convinced. The house had something, was in some ways perfect, tall and old and great for an office, as well as a home. I saw myself in my fantasy world, doing it up and making it smart, clients climbing the wide stone steps, pouring happily through the doors. Turning a shell into a home. And then I remembered.

There was no future. Not for the house, and not for me. Even now, I still forgot.

The sun went in and all of a sudden the day seemed cold and the house run down. Gemma and I were standing in the kitchen. I didn't like it. Gemma was right, it was basic.

'There is a fridge-freezer,' she said tersely, sensing my mood but still valiant, gesturing to an upright object, standing squat, in the middle of the room.

'What a strange place to put a fridge-freezer,' I said, indifferent.

'There's plenty of room in here,' said Gemma. 'I expect Mrs Parks thought to make it homely.'

Homely wasn't the word I'd have used. The kitchen was huge, with three old windows facing the back. They had very old glazing and strong iron bars. The glass was cracked and warped in the way that only old glass can be. Ignoring the dirt, I could barely see out. The floor was covered in cheap lino and the air of neglect was incredibly strong, I could almost smell it.

'Why don't we go upstairs,' I said.

2

Then – Miranda

The pub was busy, she hated it busy, she often longed for the quiet nights when nobody came. After Da had just died. But Da had run a successful pub, the people came back, the old regulars *and* the strangers, once they knew it was alright to come. Ma didn't mind, it kept her occupied, a pity hard work wasn't enough. If only her father hadn't died.

'You mustn't say that word, Miranda,' her mother would say. 'I don't like you saying that dreadful word.'

'But he is dead, Ma,' Miranda had said, 'and he's not coming back, now, or ever. He's dead, remember?'

She shuddered to think how cruel she'd been, but at the time she couldn't have cared, she'd wanted to make her mother cry, so they could find comfort, support in each other. Instead of being split by fear and dread, of poverty, loss and not having enough.

It made Miranda feel she'd died too. And that was the worst feeling of all.

Living in Curdizan Low was hard. There were so many pubs, most of them newer or smarter than theirs. Tom once said he'd counted them all, there were over two hundred in the whole city. Miranda snapped back.

'If you've the time to count all the pubs, you're far too idle, you should be in here, helping me out. Hurry up Tom and wash these glasses.' She hadn't seen Thomas again for days.

And now, tonight, he hadn't turned up, and her ma was in another of her moods, and had gone off somewhere, not for the first time. Miranda was on her own in the bar, and people were talking about the weather, so much warmer and wasn't that good? Miranda said nothing, these people were strangers,

361

summer in the Low was as bad as the winter, worse sometimes. There weren't any floods or the freezing nights, or having to manage on poor coal, but the smells that came with summer were worse, the dung and the flies and the local abattoirs. She swatted an imaginary fly away. Then the woman with the coat came in.

She was young and thin and Miranda's height, and wearing a hat, which made her look respectable, almost, but no decent girl would visit a pub on a Saturday night, not on her own, and Miranda knew it. The first time she'd seen her, Miranda had thought she was someone official and had called for her mother to help her out. But it turned out the woman was nobody special, for all she was pretty, and now her mother had vanished again, just like the last time. Miranda glowered.

'I'll have a jug full, love, if you would,' the young woman said, adjusting her hat and her lovely hair, tucking the thick curls under the brim.

She doesn't deserve to have hair like that. She poured out the ale and slopped a little.

'Your mother not in the pub tonight?'

'What's it to you?' Miranda said. She didn't see why she had to be nice. They didn't need people like her in here.

'I'm only asking, love,' said the woman. 'I thought I saw her leave just now, as I walked in. Must have been somebody else I saw.' Miranda's eyes narrowed as she watched the intruder.

'I think she's gone out looking for Thomas.' Miranda wished she hadn't spoken, she shouldn't have told the cow anything, and both of them knew the words were a lie.

'I expect you're right, my love,' said the woman.

I'm not your love, Miranda thought, gritting her teeth and wiping the jug. You're hardly only a few years older than me. She didn't know why she hated Curtis – no, she did, it was what she implied, with her looks and her manner, and the things she suggested, hinted at, even. *Go, why don't you, and don't come back.*

The young woman left.

After she'd gone, Reg came up to the bar to see her. He was kind but dull and both of them knew he was sweet on her ma. He also worked part-time in the pub.

'You don't want to mix with types like her.'

'I wasn't,' said Miranda. 'I was serving her ale, like I always do.' A woman appeared, his sister Cath, she shooed Reg away and stood in his place, her eyes on Miranda.

'He's trying to tell you something, love.' Miranda waited.

'She's young, but a woman with men for friends. If you get my drift.'

Miranda nodded, she did get it. She'd known before they opened their mouths, before they started interfering. What she also got, but didn't say, was that Curtis had implied her mother was too.

3

Now – Aleph

I took to the house, in a strange sort of way, it was tall and thin and elegant somehow, with a road at the front, cobbled and quaint and steps leading up to the strong front door. The rooms were vast, with very high ceilings, and although the window panes were small, and barred at the back, light came in and showed up the dust and all the potential. There was plenty of room for an office upstairs.

The third and top floor I kept for myself, including a room with huge sash windows, which gave me a view looking onto the street. Maybe the street lights would stop me from sleeping. They didn't as it happened. I was often awake.

The street was in a good part of town, although Curdizan High had once been rough. Now it was fresh with refurbished streets and tarted up buildings, apart from mine. There were plenty of tourists wandering around. I lay in my bed that very first evening, looked at the sky through curtainless windows, and heard the shouts of drunken youths. I'd never lived in the centre before, was bemused by the noise, although not that troubled. The things that kept me awake were worse. I mourned the past, and along with the past, I mourned myself, my carefree self, who'd long since died.

I must have drifted off at some point, and was woken up by children's voices. I looked at my watch, it was half past two. *Christ!* I thought, *those kids should be in bed by now.*

I dragged myself up and peered outside, but all I could see were the street lights outside, no tourists, nothing, not even an urban fox or a dog. My house was on an old cobbled road called Old School Lane, a shortcut through from Narrowboat Lane, the main shopping street. Just past my house, at the other end, the Lane curved sharply round to the left and joined a street called Scriveners Road. The kids had obviously gone that way. I swore, loudly, thinking my chance for sleep had gone. I was right, it had.

Later that day, I went to the estate agent's to return the inventory, wondering if I might see Gemma. I walked through the door and as I did, my heart sank, for there at the desk was the woman I'd met the previous time. I read the badge attached to her shirt – Marianne Parks – it made me pause. 'The previous tenant was a Mrs Parks.' She knew what I meant.

'My mother,' she said. 'She died recently. And she was the *owner*. I'll take that.'

'There's not much on it,' I told Ms Parks, talking about the inventory. 'There was too much wrong to put it all down.' Realising then, how tactless that sounded. Marianne Parks didn't bother to reply.

'How are you finding the Old Schoolhouse?' she said, slowly, for once not looking me straight in the eye.

'Is that what it was?' I said, interested. A name like that could be good for business. The woman smiled.

'Thanks for the form, Mr Jones,' she said. 'We'll send you out a copy shortly.' She turned away, I was being dismissed. I headed for the door, thinking; I decided to pay a visit to the library. As yet no clients had found me in Curdizan.

'Have you heard them yet, Mr Jones?' she said. I stopped, short.

'What did you say?' I said sharply, turning around.

'Have you heard the children's voices in the night?'

'Yes,' I said. 'I heard them last night, about half past two. Parents these days are far too lax.'

'And were the children crying or laughing?'

'Neither,' I said. 'They were chattering loudly, in high pitched voices. I was half asleep when they woke me up. Tourists, I guess.'

Marianne Parks gave a slow, small smile, a smile that made

me feel uneasy. But not as much as the words that followed.

'No, Mr Jones, they weren't tourists, or even the kids who live around here. The children you heard were the School Lane ghosts.'

4

Then – Thomas

I should have been helping Miranda in the pub, but instead I went up to Curdizan High, to look for Louise. The High's the part where the abbey is, as well as my school, although nothing about the place is high. I walked past the school and finally came to Pearson's Tenements, that's where she lives, but Louise wasn't there, surprise, surprise. *I* wasn't surprised, the place was a dump, but all the same, I had to look. The tenement building was tall and grim, tiny spaces joined by a stairway and open landings, the black of the open night in between. I thought they were more like rooms than landings, people's possessions scattered about, rooms on the outside. I thought of escape.

I once saw a woman jump from a landing, far too high from the ground to be safe, but almost worse, too low to be dead, and gone in a flash. They patched her up, as best as they could, and she even went back to her room for a bit, but she never walked the same after that and not long after, finally died. I didn't know it at the time, but her name was May, and she was also Louise's ma. I never did learn which room she came from.

It's a maze inside the tenement building, stair after stair to each new landing, the landings themselves being almost homes, with chairs or a table and a dog chained up and even the odd bit of carpet or rug. But the landings were cold, an outside cold and all exposed to kids like me.

I shivered, scared in the black of the stairway, I knew I ought to go back, and soon. Miranda would be wondering where I was. But I'd promised old Pike I'd find Louise.

'He's *Mister* Pike,' my ma would say, but she didn't know

Pike the way I knew him, he didn't deserve to be called *Mister*. He was cold, indifferent and sometimes cruel; he'd said if I didn't find Louise, he'd throw her out of the school for good, and she'd end up lost, like Miranda's ma. I didn't know what he meant by that, but I didn't much like the way he'd said it, and I liked Louise, she wasn't rough like most of the kids, and she lived in a flea pit, storeys high. If I had to live in Pearson's Tenements, in amongst all the privy smells, I'm sure I'd forget to go to school. School would be just a dream or something.

I reached a landing, the fourth or fifth, I didn't know which, so I tossed a huge stone over the edge, and counted until I heard it land. Although I'd looked, I hadn't found her. I'd even tried a few of the doors, but nobody seemed to know her name. A shadow slunk by and I held my breath, you're never alone in a place like this. I turned around, got ready to run, but a hand shot out and grabbed my collar, pulling me back, very sharply. Somebody's hand against my mouth. The somebody spoke.

'Tom, Thomas, you shouldn't be here, I haven't the time to look for you. I wouldn't have come, and won't the next time, it's only because your ma was worried.'

Ma, worried? That was a laugh. I snorted, loudly, and wriggled my collar out of her grasp. It was Miranda from the pub, looking wild as always, her eyes glowing bright in the light from the moon. She tossed her hair and I stared right back.

'How did you know I was here?' I said.

'I know you well enough by now. The sort of place you like to go. Each to their own, that's what I say.'

She looked around as we walked back down and hurried along the shabby street, all shadows and shade and stinking gutters. A rat rushed past and Miranda's nose twitched, as if to say, You see what I mean? I grinned in the dark, I liked rats and I liked Miranda, although not as much as I liked Louise.

'I presume you're coming back with me?' Miranda asked, as we stopped on the corner by Curdizan Church, the church that stood in the shade of the abbey. I nodded, sadly.

'Yes,' I said, torn between my longing for a pie at the end of my shift, and the word I'd given to find Louise. Shame on me, for the hot pie won. We hurried down Scriveners Road to the alley, through the alley to Convent Court and down to the streets called Curdizan Low.

'Don't be dragging your heels,' said Miranda. 'I'm supposed to be serving ale right now, and washing the glasses you didn't do.'

I smiled to myself as we hurried along. Collecting the glasses and washing them after was what I was paid for, and I liked my job at the Keepsake Arms. The money I earned from my job at the pub helped my ma, and it helped Miranda, her da was dead and Mrs Collenge was never around.

Miranda was good in the pub, I thought, cheerful and bright, but not too friendly, sharp enough to keep them drinking, spending their money, not talking to her. I wished again, like I'd wished before, that she was my sister and not just a girl who could boss me around. Neighbours and mates, that's what we were, even though she was all grown up. Miranda Collenge was eighteen.

5

Now – Aleph

Marianne Parks' words shocked me. *I've never believed in ghosts*, I thought, *so why start now?* Or at least, not the ones that weren't in my head. I cycled home in the fading light, forgetting my plan to go to the library, hardly aware of the world around me. Something had shifted inside my head. Starting again was proving to be what I'd guessed all along, another illusion. *You're never allowed to forget*, I thought.

I'd wanted to ask Ms Parks some more but she didn't seem eager to talk fully. The door had opened and someone walked in, another gullible tenant, probably, eager to part with some hard-earned cash. I left them alone.

I cycled away, vaguely troubled, and now with even more questions than answers. I rode with care down Narrowboat Lane, ducking my head when I came to the arch. I was almost home when a woman stepped out in front of the bike. I braked, sharply. The woman shrieked and her shopping and handbag fell to the ground.

Old School Lane was pedestrianised, which was just as well in the present circumstances. I dropped my bike and hurried towards her. The woman was struggling to pick up her parcels, margarine, bread and a bag of potatoes, all in one hand. Her other hand was glued to her ankle. At least she's alive, I thought, detached. My mind froze over.

'Are you alright?' I heard myself say.

'I think I've sprained my ankle,' she said.

When she finally removed her fingers, it was true the ankle seemed slightly puffy, a reddish colour, rather than pale. I picked up her handbag and gathered her food. 'My house is just here,' I told the stranger. 'Please come inside, I'll bandage that up.'

'Oh no, it's okay,' the woman replied, but her voice was faint and the no meant yes. I helped her make her way up the steps. Once inside, I steered her gently into the kitchen, and then to a chair, putting her shopping by her side.

'Would you like tea, or maybe some whisky?' I paused, waiting.

'Whisky, please,' she said smiling, her eyes darting all over the place. 'This is quite some kitchen, much bigger than mine. You've got so much space.'

'It's certainly different,' I said, dryly, passing her a mug with the whisky in it. 'I've just moved in so there aren't any glasses.' I sat down opposite the stranger and smiled.

'Aleph Jones? That's your name?' The woman was reading the estate agent's brochure; I'd put it there beside my tea.

'Yes, that's right. I know it's unusual, everybody says so.'

'A name to go with the house, I'd say. Quite unique.' She took a deep breath and looked behind her, stared at the hall. 'I'd love to have a look at the place; does that sound rude?'

A little bit forward, perhaps, I thought, but I wasn't offended, not in the least. Then she blushed.

'Not now, of course, not with the ankle. Climbing the stairs might be too much.'

'I'd offer to run you home,' I said. 'But I don't have a car.' I stopped abruptly. The woman smiled.

'I don't suppose you need one here, in the centre of town? Isn't this road pedestrianised?'

'Yes,' I said. 'But not round the corner in Scriveners Road. Would you like me to call a taxi?'

'When you're ready,' she said, lightly, and I realised then how lovely she was. Her hair was short and slightly spiky, her dark eyes chocolate, the Bournville kind. She was casually dressed, but quite impressive. I stood up abruptly.

'I'll do it now,' I said and vanished, and before very long the taxi was booked.

The rest of our time together passed quickly. She said she'd come into town to shop, I told her I'd meant to go to the library. I didn't say why.

The taxi turned up before I was ready and I noticed her looking around at the hall. I was suddenly seized by a crazy moment, the sort that defines one's life forever, and I asked this woman, who I'd only just met, to come back again and eat with me. 'Tomorrow?' I said.

'I can't tomorrow,' she said, softly. 'I'm going away for a few days' break. With Alice, my daughter.'

She watched my face as she said the word *daughter*, and it felt to me like some sort of test.

'Well how about a week tomorrow?'

We agreed on that and parted happily; she managed the steps to the street quite well. When I'd finally closed the door on my guest, my mind began to drift in reverse, recalling my chat with Marianne Parks.

'You asked if the children were laughing or crying, the School Lane ghosts. Why did you ask that?'

'It's just a rumour, Mr Jones.'

'Yes, Ms Parks, but what rumour?'

'They say it depends on who you are. The good hear laughter, the bad, crying, or even screaming. It's all rubbish, Mr Jones.' She sniffed loudly.

'My mother lived there most of her life, after she married, and she never heard the ghosts, not once.'

But wasn't your mother deaf? I thought.

Those were the thoughts that engaged my mind as I cycled back to the Old Schoolhouse, and caused me to fail to see Cressida Sewell. As time went on I recalled those words again and again, with good reason. I often heard the children at night, just around midnight and sometimes later. But from that day on, they were always sad.

6

Then – Thomas

Mister Pike was the same as always, bored and boring. I didn't know why he turned up at all, I thought it was kids who were meant to hate school. I did, often. But I also liked the porridge they gave us.

I shifted my bum on the hard wooden seat and played around with a couple of words. The work we did was far too easy, my ma had taught me to read already. I was proud of being able to read and write, most of the lads I knew couldn't count, let alone read. I wanted a better paid job than my da, he worked at the mill, when he was sober. A lot of the time he just didn't turn up.

The mill was everything in our street. We were right at the bottom on Haversham Road, our house backed onto the factory walls, you could the hear the generator's constant hum. Because our house backed onto the factory, it was dark at the back, there weren't any windows. There wasn't much light at the front either, the factory's silos towered above us and blocked off most of the sky and sun. Not far away was the factory chimney, belching out horrible smells all day. I hated our street.

I felt the sting as a huge piece of chalk bounced off my arm and onto the floor and under my chair. I seriously thought about throwing it back.

'Time to quit dreaming and starting working, Islip, unless you'd like to be out on your ear.' Pike was yelling as loud as ever but somehow it never made any difference.

'Plenty of lads would like to be you, sitting in the warm and dry all day. Lads who act a little bit grateful, not as if they can't be bothered.'

Warm? In here? He'd got to be joking. I glanced at my feet, which were bare as usual. Ma said I couldn't wear shoes in summer, or even in spring, the money for shoes just didn't exist. Despite all three of us having a job.

I felt a tiny twinge of guilt. Because I'd been late to the pub last night, I'd be docked some pay and Ma would be short, she was always short. My father drank it all away. She wouldn't be pleased that I'd turned up late and she'd no doubt give me some stick for that. But at least I had a ma to go home to, unlike Louise, whose mother was dead. I tried not to think of Louise anymore. Even more guilt.

It wasn't because Louise was missing, I'd done my best, I'd tried to find her, Louise was a mate, she loved to climb trees and beat me at conkers, and when it was hot we swam in the Blue. Our house and the factory were both by the river, which wasn't as good as you'd think it would be. Not when the days were really warm and the dung had been dumped by the corporation.

No, I felt guilty for something else. I hadn't gone looking for Louise at all, despite what I'd said to Miranda later. Looking for her was what I'd done after, after I'd given up looking for Alice. Alice was totally different to Louise; *she* was a girl, all flowers and hair, and pretty to boot. Strangely enough, that's why I liked her.

I was walking home from school one day, just pottering really, kicking at stones and picking up wood we'd use for the fire, and then in the distance, I saw Alice.

She was right by the gate that led to the church on Scriveners Road, Curdizan Church, and holding something in her hand. It was big and square and flashed in the light. She saw me looking, and put it away in her bag, quickly. *Posh*, I thought, and I couldn't resist walking closer. Her bag was blue and it looked so clean, as if it was new, and her blonde hair shone and wasn't tied back, and she wore shoes, all glossy and smart. None of the kids I knew wore shoes. *Slumming it*, I thought and scowled, jealous, and strangely angry, bitter and resentful. I wanted to live like them, I did, nobody wants to live in a dump. Sorry Ma.

I thought the girl would run away, she was far too smart, and I looked a scruff, with my shirt hanging out and my trousers baggy, and me being the third person to have them, but she didn't run away, she just stood there, staring, so I walked closer.

'I'm called Tom. Who are you?'

The girl didn't answer, just shook her head, so I tried again, a different tack.

'Do you live around here? That's my school, across the graveyard.' I pointed behind us. 'That's the door to the joinery workshop, some of the lads are training in woodwork.'

I thought she'd ask if I was one of the lads in training, but she still didn't speak, so I prattled on.

'There are also some lads who are going to be stonemasons, working on the church.'

I saw her glance across at the church and I laughed out loud and shook my head. 'Not Curdizan Church, the proper church, the abbey up there.' The abbey twinkled in the sun. She still didn't answer. I felt uneasy.

'Cat got your tongue?' I said impatient.

She shook her head, then pointed to herself and clamped her teeth shut. *Then* I got it.

'You're dumb,' I said. 'You can't speak.'

She hesitated slightly, then she nodded.

'Alright,' I said. 'I can write, can you?' She laughed at that and her blue eyes sparkled, as bright as the sky. *Of course she can write, you stupid prat. She's posh, and rich.*

'I don't have anything to write on,' I said. I felt helpless, useless somehow. Her smile widened.

But I do, she said, and although she hadn't opened her mouth, I could hear her voice as clear as a bell. It was light and fine and sounded like summer. And then she brought the thing from her bag.

To be continued…

Want to read more of Shadows of the Lost Child?

Shadows of the Lost Child is available both in print and as an ebook.

Please see Amazon for details.

https://www.amazon.co.uk/Shadows-Lost-Child-Ellie-Stevenson/dp/0957216556 (UK)

https://www.amazon.com/Shadows-Lost-Child-Ellie-Stevenson-ebook/dp/B00NGSSVM2 (United States)

Thanks for reading!

ABOUT THE AUTHOR

Ellie Stevenson is a book coach, and the author of four novels. She works with writers to inspire and motivate them to write their books, then publish and market them. Contact her to discover the difference a book can make to *you*.

'Success! What would I do without you?' Chris Sharpe (coaching client)

She also does reminiscence work so you can share *your* story with future generations.

https://elliestevenson.com/

Ellie is also the author of:

The Floozy in the Park (novel)

Shadows of the Lost Child (Shadows in Time: 1, novel)

Ship of Haunts: the other Titanic story (novel)

Watching Charlotte Brontë Die: and other surreal stories

Writing for Magazines in the UK: how to get paid to write (booklet)

She has also written 70+ articles for magazines and websites on history, careers, travel and the arts.

Ellie is a member of the Society of Authors and the Alliance of Independent Authors.

She is currently working on her next novel, fuelled by inspiration, determination and coffee.

Visit her at:

Website: https://elliestevenson.com

Facebook: https://www.facebook.com/Stevensonauthor

Twitter: https://twitter.com/Stevensonauthor

Instagram:
https://www.instagram.com/elliestevensonauthor

LinkedIn:
https://www.linkedin.com/in/elliestevensonauthor